The Imperial Adventures *of*
A.R. Korn.

SETH ACERNI

authorHOUSE®

AuthorHouse™
1663 Liberty Drive
Bloomington, IN 47403
www.authorhouse.com
Phone: 833-262-8899

Published by AuthorHouse 03/07/2022

ISBN: 978-1-6655-5331-5 (sc)
ISBN: 978-1-6655-5332-2 (hc)
ISBN: 978-1-6655-5337-7 (e)

Library of Congress Control Number: 2022903807

To those whom I have loved, and to those who have loved me; and to my brother, The Colonel's first devoted.

CONTENTS

BOOK 3 A STUDY IN FAIR FOLK

BOOK I

In the Service of A.R. Korn

Being a reprint from the personal journal of Albert McGregor,
Cpt. Late of the 72nd Seaforth Highland Division.

CHAPTER 1

To begin, I am Bound.

I first met the Colonel in the year 1878, myself a young captain of the Second Foot battalion, Seaforth Highland Division, he a colonel of the overall British detachment in India. I, being Scottish and of no great importance, exited my officers' course at the Royal Military College, Sandhurst without any great parade and swiftly found myself en route to India. Sharing my journey and returning to India from one of his many "duties at home" was none other than the famed Colonel Archibald Reginald Korn, who skulked the boards of our shared craft often throughout the nights. Patrolling the deck, hands behind back, slightly bent, puffing out his moustache, he would spend his time giving out many "hurrahs" and "well done, chaps" to the various hands heaving around the ship. The Colonel carried no great reputation as an astute mind for tactics and was generally regarded as being unhinged. It was said that he was given command based solely on his family name and nothing else, and was, therefore, sent home often for various "duties" in order to keep him far from front line command. This was the rumor among the lesser troop anyways, all of whom seemed to mock the man behind closed doors. To his credit, he either ignored this fact, didn't care, or didn't know the reason, for he never seemed to lose his chipper and was always good for a heaping on of "Rule Britannia's" (which often followed long-winded speeches in favor of the Empire). I must say—the man was loyal, if nothing else.

I considered myself more of a gentleman scholar than a soldier, and therefore could only hum a quiet laugh when thinking of the old A-Korn (as so many called him). He neither bothered me nor impacted me daily—all I knew of the man was that of the batty old colonel good for a rousing chorus of "God save the Queen!" I will say instead that I rather liked the man, even from afar, and considered him nothing more than an amusing footnote to later record in my writings. Being that I had greater ambitions of teaching English Literature one day at some university, I merely played the role of soldier in order to advance my family name (as so many good and young British boys do, born not of great families, but families decent enough to secure them positions at Sandhurst), promising myself as I went that I would record all my adventures in order to, at the very least, make some pennies as a novelist after my service was concluded.

"There goes tha old nut again, whas 'es name? Wot? A-Corn? Yes, that's it, tha old nutball's gona get us ull kilt one day."

This, I often overheard to some form or degree. But as I've said, I never was one for the rougher side of soldiering and did not participate, only hummed and laughed to myself. I ignored, mostly, the critiques that seemed to follow the man around, denoting, as I assumed, from the most unfortunate name the man carried (though he never once denounced the name himself, being that he was so damned sincere, as I will continue to mention). Throughout our journey overseas to our various posts, the men aboard the *HMS Hornblower* endured many a speech from the Akorn Colonel, damned determined as he was to see that all aboard were as passionate and devoted to the Empire as he. (The *Hornblower* herself was a dreadful craft, sick with rats and damp at all times. Really a miserable ship—a fact that only added to the troops growing frustration; the Colonel bearing the blame for most of it.)

"NOW HEAR THIS, LADS," the Colonel so often began, "WE ARE IN SERVICE TO SOME GREAT ENDEAVOUR, I SAY. WOT. WEEEEE! WE MEN! OF BRITANNIA! (He never called our home England, or Scotland, or even simply 'Britain') ARE SENT!"

He would go on and on, as they carried out their tasks, trying to smile up at him between jobs, proving to him that they were listening when, in fact, they weren't. And so this is how I entered into my service to the Queen, and was indeed, how I spent the first several months going forward. Listening to the silent mockery and jabs of common soldiers at an overbearing, over-eccentric buffoon of a colonel; one I would come to both love and serve tremendously.

———◆———

My time in India was as short as my time in the Afghan was horrendous. Upon arriving in India, I was quickly sent back to sea with my division, this time heading towards the second Anglo-Afghan war. No sooner had I waved goodbye to the Akorn than was I shaking his hand again back aboard the *Hornblower*. Hardly a day had passed in Kolkata (my original post) before I swayed aboard the damp craft, heading now for Bombay and the greater detachment of arms preparing there for war.

"My good man, McGregor was it? It seems we are to be craftmates yet again! How damned delightful! Might I interest you in a spot of whisky in the officers' cabinet?"

How was I to say no, nervous though I was for the war I now found myself in. He neither mentioned the war nor any aspect of the battles to come during our drink, and instead rattled on about England and Scotland and the many ladies and gentlemen he knew there. I recognize now, of course, that this was of great comfort to me at the time.

"This man, Shirley—that was his name. Or was it Radford? NEVER MIND MY BOY! He was some gentleman! He WAS! WOT! Pickled my goose many a time with the shuttlecock! My GOD! Yes those were some times, those days! RULE BRITANNIA, EH!?" I admit I was poor company and was actually happy to arrive at war.

Waving goodbye again in the most informal way, I departed the man's company once more and was certain I had endured the last of the Akorn Colonel, who I now also believed was insane. What company could that man possibly be in charge of during a war? Never mind, I say. Best to steel the nerves away now and prepare for what cometh next.

I will spare you the gentle brutality that was war in the Afghan, bits and pieces may crop up from time to time, but for now, let me sum it up briefly and say that it was horrid. We seemed to march endlessly through the mountains, encountering varying Indigenous tribal people, all of whom were distrusted and disliked by my men. I did my best to maintain the juxtaposition, soldier and gentleman, but found it harder to do so as time went on. Not long into the thing, my company was ambushed by what seemed to be a hoard of savage beasts. Their throngs poured down the mountain ceaselessly, as if waves of the ocean. It is not my intention however, for this to be a wartime memoir and so allow me to sum it up quickly; I focused my troop into a square and held off as long as we could. Before long, our ammunition went dry and we were relegated to the bayonet and sabre. I imagined my time was up and was aghast to see my lines break and run for the hills. I have already admitted to being no great soldier, and would never suggest being a hero or man of great courage, but I tried in vain to rally my troops back into place, only to watch them scurry for their lives back up the opposite hill. As I turned to accept my fate, a ball struck me left-center below my shoulder blade. She struck the bone cleanly and left me muddled upon the ground. Pitifully I lay, accepting my defeat and my inevitable death when at once I heard the damnedest noise. A gnashing of hooves, from behind my position.

I still hear it in my dreams, if I'm honest. And now that I am separated from that horrid place of battle, sometimes I even laugh to reimagine it. A thrashing and galloping and the wretched cry of a gentleman in battle—

"RuuuuUUUULE BRITANNIA!"

Perhaps you've guessed it, none other than the wild Acorn himself, streaming into battle in his full dress uniform. Plumes of gold and red, his metal helmet shining in the moonlight. Even in my pain, I was shocked with a sort of humor to see him.

He rode like a titan round and round my position, swinging his sword and laughing. I don't, for the life of me, imagine he killed one enemy, but in his wild behavior, and to his great credit, he at least sent them running in confusion.

"BERTIE MY DEAR BOY! QUICKLY! ONTO MY STEED!" He heaved me onto his horse and off we rode after my men, so thankful was I that I even ignored being called Bertie, a nickname I hate, reserved at the time only for my grandmother (it now belongs entirely to the Colonel, damned as I am to allow it). I left many a young Scotsman on that field, but for those I brought home? They were saved by an Acorn. A buffoon, a wild gesture of Britannia, one that hardly even existed for me anymore. And for that reason I became resolute to the man, a barnacle attached to a much greater vessel. He sat with me during months of pained recovery and I listened intently to all his absurd stories. Damaged as I shall be forever, and no longer able to fulfill my duties as a battlefield officer, the man, Colonel A.R. Korn took me on as his aide. Many of my friends and fellow officers told me it was 'a damned shame' and a 'noose around the neck of my career' but sparing the details of war I shall say this: Upon my life, I owe my service to the Colonel. For all the oddities and absurdities that go along with him, I am only too proud to consider myself first and foremost, in the service of Archibald Reginald Korn.

CHAPTER 2

Duties at Home

Now that that unhappy business is concluded, I can put the Afghan behind me as much as possible. Something I much prefer to do, being that it was so damned horrid. In more ways than one the Colonel had saved me, I was so close to cracking. But no more of that. Let me begin where I meant to, with the beginning of my truer service, the one seeing me bound to the Colonel.

Truly, he was only ever 'The Colonel' to me. While others may have jabbed at him with such nicknames revolving around a tree nut, I became quietly adapted to his defense. I never allowed his name to be slandered in my company going forward, and I very much became devoted to him. He was absurd. He IS absurd, even more so now in his old age. But I am very fond of him. His sincerity has become something I lean very heavily upon. Not to mention his devotion to homeland, which as feverous as it may be, has given me a sense of purpose in my own life I otherwise might have missed. Isn't it true that every man needs a brotherhood? Something to fight for, alongside of, etc. For a moment, mine was nearly gone alongside my life in the Afghan; born anew it was in the service of A.R. Korn. But I ramble.

I got along just fine in the months following my wound. I crippled along behind the Colonel, arm in sling, learning his habits and oddities. Very often something would come across his desk which demanded his immediate attention. And while I never did learn why or how the Colonel was out on the front that day I needed saving, I came to realize that his job was, in fact, mostly about keeping an unhinged colonel 'busy'. Nevertheless, he would sweep to task with absolute brutality when it came, shouting "BERTIE TO ARMS! THE QUEEN HAS REQUESTED

OUR SERVICE!" before becoming desperately distracted before another moment had passed. Leaving me, most times, to do the job myself. His scotch (A good Scotsman, he is) or his many social demands always seemed to distract him, but I was bound, by honor and by my life; and so I made it my duty to faithfully remain his servant, and still do.

I've been told I can be stuffy at times. Mostly by the Colonel. In my defense I have not yet met the man who can rival his energy and social attributes— but still others in my life have quietly confirmed this idea as well. I make no apologies, however. I am a gentleman. I thrive in a very secure sense of order and duty. I keep my literature as orderly as a librarian and my duties the same. Here is where the great Colonel and I are different. While he may go about a task with gusto at first, he very quickly falls off the wagon, as they say. But as I've said, it's all the same to me; I go about his work as any good aide might, careful to keep the Colonel out of trouble as I do.

In one particular instance I can recall, the Colonel was asked to reassign a group of once wounded men into new divisions. Shaking the hand of his superior he promised a speedy and appropriate response for the men in question. However, no sooner had he set the stack of names upon his desk than was he off to the officer's club for a promised "nip of the King's with a burly chap from Sussex!"

I assigned the men to their new regiments myself; I don't think the Colonel ever thought about it again in his life. But please, don't make any assumptions regarding this. I was very happy to do it, and laugh about it even now as I type these letters on my machine. I am very fond of the man, have I mentioned that? He is as sincere in an unknowing way as can be explained, which I suppose is the very definition of the word sincere, is it not? I don't think the Colonel ever felt a pang of negativity in his life. Maybe he's ignorant, maybe he is crazy? But everything he does is on impulse and straight from his heart, which I both love and admire him for. Which is why I could only shake my head and assign those names myself. And was also why I was only too happy to hear that we were leaving for England again soon—as the Colonel had "DUTIES AT HOME MY DEAR BOY," which were in desperate need of his seeing to. Meaning more probably, my own seeing to. What in heaven's name did the Acorn ever do before the help of his stalwart aide? I shudder to think.

CHAPTER 3

Return to the *Hornblower*

"Double quick march now, Bertie, my boy!" said the Colonel as I bumbled on behind him, a teetering stack of hat boxes doing their best impression of the Pisa Tower in my arms. "We must board our craft, AT ONCE! I SAY!"

"Yes but MUST you carry along so many hats, Colonel?" I struggled to get out. The man stopped short and, turning, raised his swagger stick high into the air. (The man was always in full dress; Thick military coat, medals, some various form of hat, monocle of course, and while walking, a swagger stick.) "I should say, chap! Why yes, of course! One never knows what mood one may find himself in! Does the day denote an officer's cap? A gentleman's top hat? Are we in battle? Why, then the pith of course!" (meaning his safari helmet, as the regulars called it). "I must insist, various forms of hat, A MUST! Wouldn't you agree Bertie, my dear boy?" he said as he sailed down the dock, full of activity. "Yes, I would, I suppose," I grumbled, mostly to myself.

The dock was a flurry of local laborers and hired hands of the East India Company. Stacks and boxes of exotic fruits, tobaccos, teas and rums. We had returned from the Afghan to India again, this time via a convoy over land (which was an adventure all its own) in order to board another ship heading home from Bombay.

The Colonel strolled down the planks, observing and making comments on all the happenings. "Look sharp there, Chappie!" he squawked and patted some Sepoy on the bottom with his stick. The poor bugger jumped and darted out of his way, dropping several green bananas into the water as he did. "My apologies," I said as I struggled on down the way.

"Colonel, I must beg your pardon, but you still haven't said the reason for our departing and it's just that I—"

"WE HAVE DUTIES AT HOME LADDIE! As I've said! Now, do be a good sport and find our craft, for the life of me I don't seem to see it— AH HAH! There she is, Bertie my dear boy! There she is! Dock five! Just as promised!" The Colonel trotted on again swinging his stick and adding a lively step to his jaunt, towards an all too familiar ship; one that now sails through my dreams, haunting me.

"WHAT LUCK DEAR BOY! IT'S THE HORNBLOWER AGAIN! DAMNED GOOD SIGHT, ISN'T SHE?" I am quite certain that Archibald Reginald Korn is the only man alive who could ever look upon such a wreck of a ship as the *Hornblower* with admiration, but there you have it, the man loved his Empire and everything that went along with it. "Yes sir, what luck we have," was all I could muster.

The Colonel quickly went aboard and most probably found his way to the officers' cabinet (which was more of a shanty than a club) for a drop or two of scotch, while I saw to his many boxes and effects. Upon seeing the task quite finished, and after tipping the poor Company men who'd had to heave one very oblong and oversized trunk into the Colonel's room, I went in search of my charge. I found the old bugger already stuck into a bottle of something deep brownish red with a naval officer of some degree. "Ah yes, Bertie! Here he is, Caldwell, was it Caldwell? YES CALDWELL! Here is the man I spoke of! MY VALET! BERTIE McGREGOR! COME BERTIE, SOME RUM! THIS CHAP—now where did you say you found it?"

"*Captain* Albert McGregor sir, pleased to meet you," I said as I shook the man's hand, careful to emphasize my proper first name.

"Won't you have a drink, Bert my dear boy!" the Colonel said ignoring the small talk I made with the naval officer, one Lieutenant Caldwell heading home to be married. "You've got your hands full with this one!" said Caldwell. "Quick to a drink he is!" He was laughing—I, was not.

"Not tonight Colonel, I have some paperwork to fill out and it's just that I am quite tired, my wound see…" I said, leaning towards Caldwell.

"NONSENSE!" said the Colonel. But I insisted. "Very well, boy, very well. All the same! Go and find a rack, you weary soldier of Britannia! GOD SAVE THE QUEEN!"

I left the Colonel at that and laughed as I strolled the deck thinking of poor Caldwell. I wonder if he knew just what he was getting into. Poor sod.

———◆———

The journey went on as one might imagine, the Colonel stomped around the deck by day, cheering on the weary hands, rubbing palms with officers by night. Very soon, everyone aboard knew the Colonel, just as he knew them (though I had to remind him of names very often). And soon, the common men whispered about acorns while the officers darted out of rooms, as if under attack.

"Now where has everyone gone?" he said to me one evening that I had agreed to join him in the officer's cabinet. "Perhaps they're tired, Colonel. No one fancies a drink tonight." I offered. "BAH! Soldiers always fancy drinks! And fine women! EH WOT!" he howled, digging into my ribs with an elbow. "Yes I suppose you're right, Colonel." We drank alone that night. And while the Colonel never seemed to get fit, I myself became woozy after one or two drinks.

Now hear this, because it is what it jolly well is—we shared a room aboard the *Hornblower*. I made a small bunk among the Colonel's many hats and trinkets which exploded from his trunk the moment he opened it, while the Colonel lounged happily upon a spacious bunk below mine (The sea life being what it is, racks are often layered on top of one another to conserve room. Thank the Lord I never joined the Navy). Regardless, I lay very near to the ceiling as the room seemed to spin round and round. The Colonel chattered on happily below. Several times, I rolled over in anguish to stare down at him angrily. His hands were bent behind his head and his eyes looked straight up at the bottom of my bunk, he smiled from ear to ear, the devil.

"And that, my dear boy, is how I came to know the young vicar's daughter! I SAY WOT!" He howled into laughter. I never caught the full story. "But it's just that I've always said!" he continued, kicking the bottom of my bunk, raising it a bit and lurching my nose mere centimeters from the ceiling. "Are you with us, Bertie?!"

"….urg. Yes, Colonel." Lord in Heaven, how I longed to sleep.

"But it's just that I've always said, my boy! That all a man needs is a

10

damned good war! And a few decent men on either his right or left flanks! EH BARTY?"

"Bertie." I said.

"BARTY?" he replied.

"BARTY!" I shouted and closed my eyes.

"WHAT'S THAT BOY? BERTIE?"

"No—confound you old man! Barty! Bert- ALBERT. CHRIST! And anyways, much to your point! We've had our war, Colonel! Let us find some different pursuits. Something which both enthralls us as much as provides for us a sense of duty!"

No reply from below. Perhaps he had fallen asleep—

"DAMN WELL SAID, MY BOY! IT REMINDS ME OF...."

But I never caught the rest. We landed in England several days later.

CHAPTER 4

Lively in Liverpool

We arrived in the port town of Liverpool, where most ships of heavy burden from Britain wind up. None onboard were prestigious enough for the craft to sail up the Thames, directly into London, though the Colonel made sure I knew how preposterous this was. "We ought to sail RIGHT on to London. This sideshow mockery of Liverpool is ghastly! Never mind, chap, never mind! Find me with the true soldiers of Britannia! That's what I always say, isn't it!"

True, it was what he always said. Even if it typically followed some comment about the 'gentlemanly behaviors' of the upper crust. The Colonel was indeed a soldier's officer, even if they viewed him as a nut. I saw to the man's trunk and gathered my few belongings (mostly books) into my own tiny haversack. The Colonel of course, made sure I'd left out his finest dress uniform and was arranging the plumes in his cap when I found him again.

"Ah! Capital, Bertie. Are we ready to disembark then? No time for a nip of the King's, I'm afraid. We've business to attend to after all! These damned duties are EXHAUSTING! For the Queen, of course, of course..." he mumbled and arranged medals on his lapel. "Colonel..." I began to say. "Hmmm?" he lazily returned, adjusting his monocle strap. "Colonel, it's just that I was wondering what exactly—"

"GOOD SCOT!" he shouted. "IS THAT THE TIME?!"

"Half three, indeed, is what I have. Are we meant to be some—"

"MY GOD MAN! TO ARMS! QUICK STEP, MARCH!" and off he flew from our room. I quickly followed in his wake as fast as my wound would allow. No sooner had we reached the deck then had the man shouted from behind—

"Don't forget the hats Bertie, my dear boy!"

"Yeeees, Colonel," was all I could manage.

I left the deck of the *Hornblower* with an armful of packages, looking for the Colonel. I can't be certain, but I believe the moment Archibald Reginald Korn's foot stepped from the gangplank and onto the dock, the deckhands erupted into applause and cheering.

…They're lucky the Colonel didn't hear, he'd have misread the situation and led them in a chorus of *God Save the Queen*.

Home Again.

I found England as I had left her, running amuck with the delicious sorts of commonplace one grows fond of when among the truer peoples of England. Shopkeepers rubbed their hands on aprons and children ducked between hansoms and outdated hackneys. Men milled about on the docks and a growing sense of home grew as we made our way into the city, heading through Kirkby and St. Helens. The Colonel was all a-glow, he strolled with the familiar ease I had come to admire. He did not swagger, as his stick suggested—no. His pace was as absolute and intentional as the man himself was sincere.

"Ahhhhh—LIVERPOOL. My good man! Have you ever spied a more telling hive of English indecency!"

He smirked and shouted over his shoulder as we walked, having turned down a cab ourselves. (The Colonel's idea, for as he put it, 'I need to inspect the stock, haven't I!') It was truly a horrendously English place to be, something I now believe all those living here loved her for.

To the outsider's eye, Liverpool was the ugly stepsister to London. Both ugly, true. But an ugly seaworthy additive floated about here— something brought in with the vast hordes of sailors and merchants who swarmed about. But as with London, it was her ugliness that pleased the senses. Some sort of loveliness in the familiarity of disdain lingering in the nostrils. Call it nostalgia, call it insanity, call it whatever you like! Liverpool was the gateway to England! She may be ugly and she may be dirty, but she reminds us immediately when we disembark—you are home. And that's why we love her—

But I ramble. The Colonel was speaking...

"And it'll be just round that bend there man, just there! Now be a good lad and see to our things! They should be coming along just presently!" was all that I caught from the man, dreaming of this dreary land as I had been. (It *is* my home after all, and I had been missing from it for some time.)

"I'm sorry Colonel, what's all that now?" The man stopped and placed the crooks of his wrists on his waist. He wasn't staring at me with disappointment however, he was squinting and flitting his eyes around the corner at which he had stopped.

"eeee-yes," he whispered.

I cocked my head and sort of raised an unsure eyebrow at the old nut. A gesture I was already far too used to employing at such a moment (I was so young at the time, I'm afraid—as our relationship went on, had I been as comfortable with him as I am now, I would have had something very cheeky to say to him just then).

Regardless, he continued to stare with squinted eyes until I interrupted him again.

"Colonel."

"ee-yes. Yeees," he murmured.

"COLONEL."

"Yes! Yes, Bertie! To the South! Quick march! On with you, boy!"

"But what on Earth for!"

"Haven't you been listening to a word I've been saying, chap! Too busy eyeing the ladies of the town, eh?" He smirked and jabbed with that, by now famous elbow.

"Hardly the case! I am merely wondering what it is we are doing! As I have been, since India! Thank you very much!"

The Colonel never seemed to bat an eye at my outbursts, as if reason was not a thing to be considered by him. Reason is everything to me, I'm afraid to admit. (Which could perhaps explain the course of my own life *and* his...)

"Right, then. Remind me Bertie, what it is you are in service of?" There was no malice here, this was no snide remark, as I've said the Colonel didn't acknowledge my outbursts, ever. Nor did he respond to them with any sort of anger himself, the devil.

"Oh, no. Not this again, would you just—"

"Bertie?" He cocked his head. "Remind me."

I rolled my eyes, and recited the by now, age-old creed, the man had invented and made me memorize.

"I am in service to the Queen, and with her the Empire of Britannia and all its holdings." I rattled off like a schoolchild being forced to recite his Latin verbs.

"Capital. And as such?" he went on with an annoying amount of blasé as he continued to look around the square.

"I am duty-bound to see to their success, by pain of death, or mockery in the streets."

"Very good, man! And then, to your charge! As I've said, whilst you gandered the local fare, you are to see to our lodging at the White Swan and await my return in one and one-half hours. It is just there—as I've said." He finished bluntly with a jab of his swagger stick.

Up until this point I had not known the man to exhibit such composure and frankness. I know now, that it is a quality that rears its head only when he has the chance to mock me. He is much like a father, or perhaps more so like an uncle with whom you are forced to spend time (but are secretly very fond of). Our relationship was blooming, and yet, I was in a fit.

"One and one-half hours—but what on Earth for! Colonel! Are you ever going to tell me exactly what it is we are doing here! As one has only ever been told—attending to *business!* I assure you, this is not the Army way, and I might add—"

But the man was laughing and strolling off, waving a hand as he did, leaving me a quarter-block from the White Swan Hotel, which, as the Colonel had said, was right around the corner.

I swear I heard the whistling of *A Soldier and a Sailor* as he marched away, but I couldn't be sure.

CHAPTER 5

The White Swan

As I arrived at the door of the White Swan, laden with several of the Colonel's effects, I was taken by the very ancient bones of the building. Covered in the vines of English Ivy and made entirely of brick—it was as if she were a complete secret, one designed only for the oddest of all transients. Tucked in as a row house she was a total mystery. I would have passed right by without a second glance had the Colonel not pointed her out; her only whisper of existence being a wooden sign made to look like a swan, painted white, creaking in the breeze above the entrance.

Door of red, plainly cut, with one very detailed lion head chiseled into its dead center. I will admit, I was happy to find her (and would always be so in the coming days when I myself would be considered among those wild transients she housed). She was a true English gem, a fitting place for one Archibald Reginald Korn to frequent.

I don't know why, but I knocked before entering. There was no answer of course, and so after the briefest moment of slight panic, I pushed the door open and found myself in quite possibly the warmest place in England. The reception area was one large square room; the concierge desk being built into the wall facing a very small but quaint common area. A staircase wound round the outside of the structure and up a considerable distance I could not make out. One small black sofa faced an enormous fireplace, absolutely roaring, giving the only light outside of the candles and chandeliers hanging on the different levels. It seemed every available inch of space was given over to book shelving, and therefore, I—was in love.

I admit at this moment that I am stalling. It is important to relate the parameters of the White Swan and necessary for any record that I do so, as in the coming days and years myself and the Colonel seemed to always land back in her comfy space. Almost as if constantly trapped in her orbit, she being the sun of course, and we—simply... meteors, or perhaps a moon even?

I am stalling.

The truth is, I'm dancing around how to explain the better—nay, best part of the Swan. I have never had to put it into words before, and I'm not quite sure how to go about it just yet. I suppose the greatest taste of a thing is the truth, and although I try to doll it up in my own imagination, the truth of what happened next is, unfortunately, exceptionally bland—though not to me of course. And though it passed right on by very inconsequentially, it had a profound impact on me—and still does. THEREFORE, here it is.

The lady of the hotel came, just then, through the parlor—and in a word, she was stunning.

"Hello," she proclaimed.

And I—said nothing.

"Are ya after something?" she said, and I woke up.

"Ah, yes. Well, yes, that is—I am sorry. It's just that I believe I'm looking for a room, is all. Well, two rooms actually, I think."

She continued with whatever task I had interrupted and paid me a very professional amount of her time as she did. I may have been a faltering, blubbering mess of a schoolboy, but she was not. She was, if anything, the schoolgirl in this scenario, blind by choice to my absurdities. I loved her for it.

"It's a room you're after, is it? We don't get many come-ins." She laughed. "Have ya got a reservation?"

"I don't, I'm afraid—It's rather a long story but my associate sent me along—well, here specifically, to secure a room for the night—" She seemed to smile.

"You wouldn't be in the service of AR Korn, would ya now?" And now I know she was smiling. How on Earth?

"I...well yes, yes I am. He is my Colonel and I'm his...his valet." I said with a sigh and a swallow. It's a wonder what a man admits when his tongue is so swollen.

17

"Then ya do have a reservation. Colonel Korn has a standing room here—I'm afraid it is just the one though."

"Ah," said I, thinking of course of the *Hornblower* and how similar my lodgings here may be.

After some working behind the desk, she showed me up three flights of stairs to room number 3B. I unloaded the Colonel's things after having been given the spare key, as apparently the Colonel keeps the main key on his person at all times. By this point I am not surprised by anything, though my list of questions grows ever on. How the Colonel is connected with this place and just what he does here is an utter mystery to me. I'm no closer to discovering what his 'duties at home' are and to say that I am frustrated by the blatant lack of clarity would be an understatement. But here we are, and here I always seemed to be with the Colonel. My service to the man being a constant tempest of uncertainty mixed in with rapid orders and objectives right up to the moment of transparency (if it ever comes at all).

But I'm smitten. And it seems my frustrations may serve some purpose to me at this time. I make plans to question the young lady at the desk and set off to do just that.

The Swan exists more like a museum than a hotel it seems. I brush past several house plants and globes, paintings and sculptures on my way back to the parlor. Not to mention one very friendly orange cat with tiny, white feet. "My word," is all I can manage.

"Hello again—"

"Hello."

"I'm afraid, I uhh. I didn't quite catch your name. My name is, um. Captain Albert McGregor. I wonder if I might ask you a few questions?" As I blubbered, the girl sat behind her desk reading a copy of Shakespeare's *Much Ado About Nothing*.

"Much Ado About Nothing? One of my favorites." I coughed.

"Oh? I'm afraid I'm having a bit of a rough go at it, I can't quite keep up with who the bad men are and who the good ones are." Delightful, I thought. "I'm Abigail Stuart by the way."

"Oh, well the trick with Shakespeare is quite simple really, no one is really good until someone else is obviously bad." I seem to have made her laugh. (I apologize for becoming sidetracked.)

"And what was your question, Captain?"

"Right, well. It's just that I was wondering how on Earth it is you know the Colonel? He must be here quite often." I tried not to let on how little I knew of my own reasons for being in the White Swan. Abigail looked up from her book.

"The Colonel and my grandfather, Hector, were quite close as boys. My grandfather was a bit of an adventurer in his youth—he and your man were always in and out of here. I'm afraid I don't remember much from when my grandfather was around, but the house passed to me when he died. I just sort of picked up where he left off. I suppose we have that in common, don't we?" she explained.

"And what's that?"

"Well we both seem to be in the service of AR Korn, don't we?" I must have failed to seem competent at this moment, she went on with a confused smile—

"You do serve with the Colonel, don't you?"

"Well, yes, I do, it's just that I—"

But just then the door flew open with a bang and there stood none other than the devil, himself.

"AH BERTIE MY DEAR BOY! You've met our sweet Abigail. Capital! And how are you my dear, charmed, charmed." He swept in and kissed the girl's hand. "Have you seen to our lodgings, Bertie? Quite the digs here, AYE WOT? Fit for a soldier!" The man flew about as if he were at home, sweeping into the common area and rummaging through doors and cabinets.

"Colonel, I—" I stammered.

"ABIGAIL, DARLING, WHERE IS THE GOOD SCOTCH—AH! HERE IT IS!" He poured himself a dram. "Ergh. Damn good stuff, I say. And have you been getting along all right, dear boy?" he shouted from around some corner.

"Yes, I... I have sir, I've just been talking with Abigail sir—Hang on, where have you been?"

"There's a letter here for you, Colonel," Abigail quietly announced.

"EXCELLENT! That'll be from the Queen's man, I presume!"

"A letter? Hang on—from the Queen?!" I shouted but neither seemed to pay me any mind.

"Yes, sir. He brought it here himself this morning, told me you'd be coming 'round. Some tea, Colonel?" She went on, ignoring me further in the best of ways.

"NO TEA—THANKS!" shouted again from around some corner, seeming to be farther off even than before.

"I'VE BEEN WITH THE MAN FROM SUSSEX, ABBY! Told me the letter would tell more!" His voice trailed off as he made more and more noise shuffling through things further inside. "I'm afraid this one seems to be quite the pickle. HAD THE MAN IN UTTER HYSTERICS, IT DID. Couldn't go on any further though, told me the letter would explain more! They always do…" His voice grew fainter. I grew ever more frustrated.

"JUST WAIT A MINUTE!" I shouted now, to my embarrassment, stalling the whole room.

"What's that now, Bertie?" The Colonel's head shot round the corner as if he had been there the whole time, scaring me halfway to death.

"Just what Is the meaning of all this Colonel? A letter from the Queen's man? This business in Sussex? What on earth is going on? Just WHAT is our business here! These duties at home! Which you have still FAILED to tell me anything about!" I admit I was a bit stuffy, as the Colonel would say, but to my credit I was completely in the dark in this moment.

"My dear boy, ee-yes, duties at home! Why on Earth do you think the Queen's Military sends me home so often? A HOLIDAY?! With a war on? Bah-HAH!" He smiled. I did not.

"Colonel, would you please tell me JUST what's going on?" Abigail laughed and my head spun.

"My dear boy. I have been to see the man from Sussex, who has informed me that my assignment will arrive via the post of the Queen's own man, as it always does. YOU have seen to our lodgings and have done a capital job as such. Young Abby here has held the fort and now you are to assist me in my duties! Remind me Bertie, what it is you are in service of…"

"Oh no—No! Not this time! Not before I've had some real answers, Colonel. What exactly is all this nonsense! Just what is it we're doing here in England!"

This was the moment for me, I think. The moment I realized Colonel Archibald Reginald Korn was not assigned home duties simply to keep an unhinged old officer busy, that we were not here to 'holiday' as the man put it, and as I had assumed, but that we were in fact here for a real duty; one that carried enough weight for the Queen's own hand. One that would be relative to all our adventures to come—one that was always, and before all others, in the service of AR Korn.

"We're here to serve the Queen of course! AND GOD SAVE HER!" was the answer that I received.

———— ◆ ————

I sat rubbing my temples, swirling the whisky Abigail had poured for me (I turned down the tea). "And tell me again, Colonel, what exactly our duties here are?"

"As I've said, dear boy, we are to service the Queen on any special assignment she may need! So far the facts are obscure! Something is afoot up north, that much we know! The letter will tell more I imagine…" the Colonel rambled again over his second or third glass of scotch.

"Well can we not read the bloody thing then?!" I stammered through my pounding temples. Just then my old wound began to throb. I never quite got over it, it always seems to come back in moments of stress. Oftentimes I use it as an excuse with the Colonel, but every so often as well, the excuse is warranted. This was such a moment.

I rubbed my shoulder now as the Colonel went on. "Ah yes, the letter. My dear girl, might we see it. I think, perhaps, it is in fact time, as young Bertie has pointed out…"

Abigail ran to fetch the letter, I rubbed my head and looked over at the Colonel. He met my gaze with a boyish smile of his own, made comical over his great moustache. I heaved a sigh and rolled my eyes.

"Here it is, Colonel." Abigail returned and handed the man his letter.

"Capital, capital. Errmm. Let's see, he-ar!" He affixed his monocle and made quite the show of cutting open the letter. "Must be careful with the seal—and—we've got it! Now, now, let's see here…errmm yes." With one eye shut and the other squeezing the monocle, the Colonel began murmuring as he read.

"Well?" I said. "What does it say?!"

"e-yes. Yes. Ermm." He continued to murmur.

"Confound you, old man, what does it say?!" I began to lose my patience again, Abigail giggled at my agony (I loved her for it).

"Ah-Hah!" shouted the Colonel as he slapped down the letter. "Bertie, my boy! We are off to the Tin!" I was speechless.

"The Tin? What on earth are you talking about? What does the letter say?!'"

"The Tin Lizzy is a pub in Merseyside." Abigail told me.

"Not just a pub my dear! THE best little ramshackle in Liverpool! Yes, my dear boy, we're off to meet an associate there!"

"Oh, but WHY Colonel?! It's late. And if it's true that we do have some mission, I'd like to know what it is and be done with it. I don't have the energy for a drink just now, and it's just—" I said, through a weary-eyed face.

"WHY? WHY because the letter instructs us to do so, of course! (And why wouldn't it?) We'll know more in a moment! OFF WE GO LAD, OFF WE GO! Abigail! We shall return post-haste, and I think, with more information in tow! AH-hah! OFF WE GO BERTIE!"

The man was up and moving, and I staggered after him, as was my charge.

"NOW BERTIE!" the man shouted as we made for the door. "REMIND ME, WHAT IT IS YOU ARE IN SERVICE OF??"

"I am in service to the Queen, and with her…" I said under my breath as I followed. And as we pushed through the door, I turned round to see Abigail smile at me—both with pity and with joy. I have no idea where or why we are going, but that smile will see me there. To the Tin Lizzy I suppose! Whatever she may be…

CHAPTER 6

The Tin Lizzy

Liverpool had gone dark on us. The city, like her sister to the East, maintained her liveliness however, being that she, like London, is a working man's town—she never does sleep. I, however, desperately wanted to do just that myself, having had a glass of the Colonel's scotch on an empty stomach. (The Colonel never seems to stop for nourishment, something I have learned is a result of his forgetfulness brought on by his absentmindedness encouraged, I now realize, by his works at home.) My head was fuzzy. My shoulder ached. And the Colonel kept such a quick pace—for the life of me I never would discover where he got his energy. At this point in our relationship, the man had to be well into his 50s and yet he moved with the tenacity of a man half his age. Meanwhile, I lumbered on as if I were wearing his skin and not my own youthful duds. You must think me soft. But I have never claimed to be the soldier my uniform may denote.

I am a gentleman. I long for books, and large cups of tea. And perhaps if not such a bother—one or two biscuits to marry it with. I might very well have been out of the Queen's military by now had I not been saved by an acorn! But here I was! In Liverpool of all places, well into the night, chasing after the very nut who saved me! MY, HOW HE MOVED!

"Quick now, Bertie—there's a lad!" he'd say to me from time to time.

The city belched and lurched around us as we strolled. Hammers fell on metal in dark alleyways and factories roared into their second or third shifts. Men and ladies ambled about as if no one had any real need of direction—save for the Colonel.

23

"And why couldn't we get a taxi this time, Colonel?" I said as I walked. He did not answer me. We marched on.

After some time, he stopped short, puffed out his moustache and said, "It's better we walk this time, old boy..." Squinting his eyes, he became quite serious; it threw me off. "It would serve us now, I think, to talk a moment in private. See here boy—Taxi men can have the largest of mouths, second only to their ears...ee-yess." He said and squinted his eyes, darting them around the street corners. We marched on.

"Excellent, I'd love a chat, Colonel." I began, with an air of rudeness, I'm afraid. "Why are we going to a bar? What could the Queen of all people possibly have for us to do at a bar in Liverpool. And really Colonel, to be frank, I'd just like to know more. If I could sir, and please, take no offense—but it's just that I really am quite confused. I admit—I did not imagine these duties at home to be so, well..."

"SO DAMNED DUTIFUL, AYE?" he shouted.

"Well, yes! And the whole business at the White Swan? Who is Hector Stuart? And what of his granddaughter, is she part of all this? Are you truly in correspondence with the Queen?" I unloaded on the man.

"A beauty, no?"

"Who's that? The Queen?"

"HEAVENS, no! God save her, but no! ABIGAIL, MAN!" he said with a sneer, the devil.

"Ah, yes. Well, yes, she is a fine-looking young lady—but Colonel!"

"Yesss, yes. To your questions, man." And thus, he began:

"What we do, Bertie, is of utmost importance to the Empire. We serve the Queen, yes. But not directly. HEAVENS, NO. The Queen cannot be seen to acknowledge such things as we find ourselves about. It is a vast Empire, my boy—and God save it! But with such vast things comes a world of small and yet crucially buoyant oddities and challenges one cannot tackle head-on! Certain things, shall we say, that the ruler of such an Empire cannot directly acknowledge, yet must see to entirely! This is where we come in, dear boy. We serve the Queen, yes, but we do not serve her directly, always in the back channels. In such a way, the problems that arise may be solved without the slightest bit of acknowledgment from the crown! These things the Queen cannot be seen to acknowledge—that is what we do, my boy."

He clasped his hand on my shoulder and with that, gave a rousing 'Haa-rump' puffing out his moustache in a wild gesture of air. We were finally getting somewhere.

"So? Alright. Very good. All of that, yes. So this business at home is truly—"

"From the Queen, dear boy, yes." He seemed to read my mind.

"Right. And so, he sends for you via this man from Sussex? And off you go?"

"Off *we* go, Bertie. You're in it now, old chap!" That smiling sneer I was becoming too familiar with.

"Well—okay. So Hector Stuart? And Abigail? What's their role in all this? And what sort of things do you do for the Queen? Are they quite dangerous?" Just then, I imagined the man in full plumed uniform charging into battle in the Afghan. I swallowed hard. "Which raises the question, Colonel—what were you doing in the Afghan when you found me that day..."

But the Colonel had stopped. I seemed to have lost the old bugger again. He was staring proudly, hands on hips, across the street. He seemed like a very old father admiring some grand accomplishment a son might have achieved. The way a man stares as if in shock and deep, deep veneration for someone he loves.

The Colonel, however, was not admiring a son. Nor a loved one of any kind. To be fair however, I suppose that would depend upon your definition of a 'loved one' and whether you believe someone can love some*thing* as truly. I turned to see what the Colonel was after—it was the Tin Lizzy. There was the slightest hint of a tear forming in the man's eye. I rolled my own.

"Ahhh. There she is, Bertie. The Tin. Many a weary English boy has found his way here, he has! AHHHH, for the days! Isn't she something, lad?!"

I'm not sure we were looking at the same place. The Tin Lizzy was built into a row, seemed to be at least several stories high, and I swear, sat on a tilt. From inside I could hear the dull roar of men at drink—bottles broke, chairs and tables scrapped the floor. My heavens it was a mess, a true English pub. Perfect for an Acorn, anyways.

"Oh, Colonel. This old thing?"

"BERTIE, PLEASE," he quipped as I chuckled.

"What of my questions, old man?" I asked.

"I'm afraid they'll have to wait for now, my boy. We best crack on! Our man from Sussex said our contact would be inside, but for how long, no one can say!" He squinted his eyes and looked from left to right.

"Oh, stop that, you old fool." I was growing far too comfortable with the nutter already. "How will we know who our man is? It seems like the place is alive with them tonight, Colonel."

"How? Oh goodness, man. I've known him for some time…" More squinting.

"Known him—how?"

The Colonel scoffed. "Hah. His name is Barnaby Barnsworth—CAN YOU IMAGINE! What a horrid name! I'm sure he takes quite the cracking for that one, aye Bertie?" The Colonel was laughing and digging with his elbow. I squinted my own eyes this time and could do nothing but shake my head at the man. "Yes. I'm sure he does, Colonel KORN, sir." He never knew, bless him.

"I'm not sure how, Bertie, but old Barnaby always seems to be involved one way or another. Confound the man, he is a wealth of knowledge on the locals from toe to tip! What a WASTE! I've always said—could have been damned useful in the service, no? No matter, no matter. Apparently, he's the man to see tonight, has a head full of information! But we must be careful, dear boy…" More squinting. All I could do was sigh heavily at this point. He went on.

"Old Barnaby is NOT well-liked."

"How am I not surprised by that?"

"Too right, old boy, too right. Now. Let's talk strategy. We must keep a clear head in there, chap. We cannot allow ourselves to become sidetracked with the indecencies one finds in the pub. Damned as we would LOVE to enjoy a nip, we must plow on! Old Barnaby is a slippery fellow, hopefully by now, he's half-winded—What's that now, Bertie?"

I'd been interjecting as he went on with protests about getting sidetracked and who was more likely to fall prey to such 'indecencies,' as he put it. He largely ignored me, as was his way.

"Now, as I was saying. Old Barnaby will have the information, but we must be careful. He'll dodge anything he can. Lord knows, the man owes money to half the Empire! Including me, now that I think of it. Half a crown, if I remember correctly! Don't let me forget Bertie, I'd like to mention that to—"

"Colonel, shouldn't we worry about the information he may or may not have first?" I said, very plainly.

"Yes, yes. Quite right. Always on the ball there, boy. GOOD OF ME TO SAVE YOU, AYE?!" He laughed heartily at his own joke and ribbed me again. "As I was saying, yes. If he realizes we're after information without reward, or if he fears we're after a debt, which technically we are—ahh yes, yes. I'm joking—but if he thinks we're here to collect on him, he'll dart Bertie. I've seen it before!"

I wondered how many times the Colonel had questioned this poor sod for information. I wondered about so many things, but if I could brag a moment it was quickly becoming a skill of mine to let things slip on by as it were. I was learning the true oddities of the Colonel. One had to simply 'bear the job' as they say. Take it as it comes, if you will! And for all my questions just then, standing across the street plotting as we were, to my own great credit I did my utmost to simply go along with the flow of the mission at hand! And I believe I was doing just fine at it, thank you! I thought of Abigail.

"Right then, old boy. Shall we have a drink?"

"I thought we weren't supposed to get distracted, Colonel?"

"Oh, I was—oh, just forget it. Off we go, lad." Off we went indeed.

<hr />

We crossed the street and pushed our way into the pub. No sooner had the door cracked open than had the sound escaped like a cannonade. It was one of those moments in life you can recall easily—as if, the second you drum it up in your mind, you're brought crashing back to it. For me, it was the true beginning of my service to the Colonel. Before then it had all been just talk and imagined leisure pursuits (which, though we often made time for, were always a side note to the duties at large). This was the moment for me, there was no turning back, not that I would have.

The bar erupted with the shouts and cheers of the many men and several ladies inside. We were not at all out of place in uniform it seemed. Sailors with their stripes and caps. Soldiers with their tall dark bitters.

Some swayed and sung. Some held others up *while* they sung. Some played darts or table games. All drank heavily. The floor was damp with beer and boot prints. A fire roared in the hearth as one group of men tossed bits of rubbish into it. The place was hot. Thick with the heavy air of men doing what they do best. I admit, one of my loves in life is witnessing a bar in all her glory. Mind you, I don't care to stay long, but still, who can ignore the feeling of fraternity that permeates a pub? The place begged a man to stay a while. Forget. Sing a little! I immediately worried about the Colonel.

His eyes seemed to light up as he strolled further inside, eyeing the chaps at their work. He slapped a few shoulders and heaved on several "Hurrahs!" with the boys at play. He laughed and gazed in boyish amusement. I loved him for it—it was not my game at all, but it was his; being among the true men of England. He was in his element to be certain, and I enjoyed indulging with him at it, if only for a moment.

"Bertie!" he shouted as we shouldered through the throngs, "Bertie, my boy! Men after mine own heart!" I gently pushed the man deeper into the pub.

"Do you see your man, Barnaby?" I shouted back while a very large man in Naval uniform and cap stood at a piano hammering away in the corner. Several men surrounded him singing and swishing their glasses back and forth far above their heads. Bitters sloshed at my feet. The Colonel swayed and hummed—I began to sense his distraction. As we passed the singers, the Colonel launched himself up against one adding in a rousing *"BUT BEFORE WE PART—LET'S TAKE A DROP OF BRANDY, OH!"* to a chorus of cheers and slaps from the soldiers. I was losing him, confound it. Somehow a drink materialized in the Acorn's hand. He swished it along with the men around him. I swear to you, I only looked away a moment! We bumbled along. The Colonel finished the drink and found another. Where was this efficiency when paperwork crossed his desk? I cannot imagine!

"Colonel!" I shouted. "Colonel, do you see your man?" He seemed to search the place while his foot kept up a rigorous tapping. He swayed and hummed. "Ah-hah! There he is, Bertie, there he is! Just there! In the corner!" He pointed and poked at my old wound. "Let's see what the old codfish knows, shall we?!" He laughed and shouted, keeping up the pace of his foot tapping. We made our way to the corner where a very dirty looking fellow was drowning in a tankard of ale. His head was faced down at the table he occupied, alone, I might add. He seemed, even from a distance, to be in no shape at all for the dishing on of information pertinent to a Queen. I frowned as I pushed the Colonel along. "What's the plan?" I shouted as quietly as I could into the Colonel's ear. He ignored me and went straight to the barkeep instead.

"Colonel—what? Where are you going?!" I followed like a lost child.

"We cannot approach without a drink, Bertie, don't be silly! We must seem disarmed!" Distractions and indecencies, it seemed, were winning. The Colonel stuck three fingers up at the barman and shouted, "Three of your tallest bitters, we're soldiers at drink, after all!" He laughed. I sighed for none to hear.

After gathering our weapons, the Colonel bumbled towards who, I could still only assume, was one Barnaby Barnsworth. As we approached, the man still did not lift his head, only swayed a bit to the shouting and singing. If one thing kept me from losing my hope in success, it was that no one would hear any of our business tonight. (If only *we* could hear it ourselves, first!)

"Fancy a pint, Barnaby you old sod!" The Colonel thrust a beer towards the half-conscious man, spilling it as he did. "Careful there, Barnaby! All hands on deck!" He laughed some more. The man looked up and squinted. Curse the expression—I was dead tired of it by now.

"Aaaye?" said the weary man.

"Capital! And how are you, fellow, how is the wife? Is she still with you, I say, Wot!" the Colonel went on, as if the two had seen each other only a few hours ago.

"Who—arrr ya. Wah?" Barnaby gasped. I stuck my hand out sheepishly as the two of us joined him at his table.

"Captain Albert McGregor, sir. And how are you tonight?" I spoke softly as he weakly shook my hand with several damp fingers. "Juuuust, fii-knee." He wobbled and blinked.

"Ha-hey. HEY. Colonel Korn!" he spittled out. "I havn' seen yees since—well, since yees was here last! Do I owe yees any money, Colonel!" He wobbled and shook as he eyed up my charge. He was a pathetic man, sure. But charming nonetheless it seemed, in his own simple way.

"Half a crown!" the Colonel shouted. I darted an angry look at him and quickly tried to rectify the situation. Even in his confused state, Barnaby seemed uncomfortable with the talk of money.

"He's joking, sir! We're just here to talk, is all!" I shouted and tried to reassure the man.

"Who—who ess this, Colonel?" Barnaby said, ignoring me but jabbing a thumb my way. One day I would love to be taken seriously by literally anyone myself and the Colonel do business with, sadly that will hardly ever be the case, as this journal will tell. But I digress—

"Why, Bertie McGregor of course! You know! My valet!" the Colonel laughed and shouted back.

"Ahhh, yes!" Barnaby said, and laughed as well (he did *not* know me, of course).

A whole career in military service and this is my prize, the joke of two old English drunkards. I suppose my life is the true prize, but it's hard to admit in such a moment. REGARDLESS, the Colonel went on.

"Barnaby, my dear man. We've just returned from the front! Tell us, how has our great empire been doing?" I'm not sure if it was his plan at all, but I gaped at the Colonel. Did he just impose some tactic?

"Ahh-ll shot to shite, you know." Barnaby wobbled and answered. The Colonel now switched to tapping his hand on the table, swaying merrily and humming along to the soldier's tunes.

"Is that so, old man?" he announced with the sort of cavalier I had come to expect.

"Bah—Corse it is, Colonel! You know us wee folk, always mixed up in the baggins of it all, innit so!" I had no idea at all what the man meant. The Colonel's drink shrank, as did Barnaby's.

"I see, e-yes. E-yes." The Colonel almost seemed bored of the man!

"And tell me, Barnaby, what has them so shook up now? Couldn't be that blasted Ghoul in Brighton again could it, now?" He gave me a sly look, the Colonel. What's your game now, old man?

Barnaby spat a horrible wad onto the floor at that. I was appalled. It nearly hit me.

"Tha Ghoul was FER REAL Colonel. I seen it meself, I did! Run amuck on those poor people for near a month, dinnit?"

"Oh, yes. Yes. I'm sure it did, Barnaby my old boy. And surely it wasn't possibly some wee thieves scaring the townsfolk before running off with their things!" I continued to eye the Colonel, not saying much. Forming the relationship between these two as I went.

"Ah—piss off," Barnaby said, his face drooping back towards the floor with a sway.

"Barnaby, old boy, your drink's gone dead. Ah! So's mine! Back in a spot, lads! God save the Queen!" To my shock the Colonel left me alone with Barnaby.

"Good, ah. Good drink, aye?" I attempted to make small talk. Barnaby grunted in return. I tapped my hands on the table, desperate for the Colonel to return. I looked around and saw him roaring with laughter at the bar, arm around a sailor denoting the rank of ensign. He gets too dangerously close to the lesser ranks, that man. No wonder they bash him with insults regarding nuts, curse him! Leaving me here! Blasted Akorn Colonel!

"Wells, yoo believe me doncha boy?" Barnaby shouted.

"What's that now? Believe what?" I said.

"The GHOUL, BOY! In Brighton!"

"I'm afraid I don't know that one, sorry."

"AH! Damned thing. Real, says I. But nothing like tha Fairy in Uig." Barnaby rambled on, I smiled and nodded, pretending to listen, trying to catch the Colonel's eye. I had nearly stood to go and find the man when Barnaby grabbed my wrist.

"This one's real, boy. Got the people all torn up there, he has. They say—He's got ONE EYE. Why—it's troo!" He raised a finger and squinted an eyeball shut as he did.

"Yes, I'm sure—A one-eyed fairy, in Uig. Where's that, the highlands?" I tried so hard to change the direction of his thoughts.

"Aye. The highlands, boy. Stay away from there just now, if yee know what's sound fer a fellar..."

"Right, then. Ah Colonel, there you are!" The man had returned, laughing.

"Bertie, ah! That man there, just there—the Navy man! Says he once drank with Bishop! The BISHOP, I say!" I yanked him into his seat where he plopped down with two fresh drinks.

"Mr. Barnsworth was just regaling me with fairy tales from the highlands. Don't you have a few questions for the man," I sort of bounced my eyes in his direction, desperate for the Colonel to take the hint so we could get whatever information this man could possibly have before leaving.

"Fairy tales? From the highlands? How interesting! Do tell, Barny old boy!" My mouth must have noticeably dropped in shock, the Colonel of course, being the only one in England who could have missed it.

"Colonel!" I whispered. "Ask-Him-About-The-Letter," I said between my teeth. He waved a hand at me and turned the other way.

"Fairy tales- BAH! Just the one fairy's tales allll, shite. Just one fairy, Colonel! Hell. He's real, damn ya. Terrorizing the fine folk, he is. They say he's only got one eye, one eye that'll freeze the hell out ya bones! Stealin' all the grain and crop with his band of fairy thieves—he is! Strikes as the sun sets, always on the highroad! Leaves em blind with fear, ee-does!" The man stumbled and fell through his story.

"Oh my, my. How terrible!" The Colonel egged him on. And I gave in. Better to let the man play whatever silly games he might—the bar has totally taken over. Distraction has won again, and for all my efforts, I can't for the life of me set the Colonel straight to task. And things got worse.

"OI! Barnsworth! Tha's right you old drunk! You owe me MONEY," said a very large man in braces over my shoulder. I shrunk lower in my seat, my eyes as wide as saucers.

"Now—hold on just a moment, boys!" The Colonel addressed the large man and the SEVERAL friends I now noticed around him. "This gentleman may owe YOU money, and fair is fair, I say. BUT. He owes me half a Crown! And I found him first!" Barnaby looked like a toad. I felt like a toad. The large man squeezed his fist shut and visibly ground his teeth. A very large vein formed on his head.

"Look here, old man. Either he pays ME. Or you pay FOR EM." Barnaby smiled and shrugged. The Colonel lifted his eyebrows and his chin. "Oh, very well…"

"RUN BERTIE, RUN!"

The Colonel shouted and splashed his beer at the would-be debt-collector. The beer hit me entirely and either knocked me backwards or scared me backwards. Either way I found myself looking at the ceiling in a pile of large, angry men. The squirm was on. Chairs screeched; arms flung all around. I saw stars. I saw sweaty forearms. I saw the Colonel bend over and heave me up. Barnaby was rolling and squealing in an effort to kick an assailant's arm from the toes of his boots.

"Run, boy!" The Colonel pushed and launched me around the table. Hot on my heels, we circled round and round. Half-way around the table fully, now back the other way, dodging the original large man who had his arms spread wide to catch us. "RUUUUULE-BRITANNIA!" the Colonel shouted, damn him! We made our break around the heavier, slower man, but we misjudged his reach. He clocked my behind with a boot the size of a boat and flung me into the piano. I smiled at the piano player who eyed me in shock.

"Excuse me, fellow. But that man there," I pointed at the large man, "just told ME—that the Navy is nothing but Jollocks and Cuckolds."

"Ee-Wot? I'll show him a Jollocks!"

The fight was on.

"Run, Colonel!"

And so we did, as the bar crashed on around us.

The Colonel squeezed one eye shut and pinched his monocle in the other. His hair was ruffled, and he wrinkled his moustache back and forth. I limped behind him, matching the pace. My collar was disheveled, and my left arm sleeve hung loosely from a tear.

"Well, that was a success," I said as we marched back towards the Swan.

"Yes, I say, indeed! Well done inciting the Navy to war, old man! Very clever! Very clever, indeed!" The man seemed to smile; I do believe he meant it!

"Hang on, Colonel, you can't seriously believe me honest. That—that was a disaster! Lord knows what ever happened to poor Barnsworth, but my God, Colonel, why didn't you ask him about the letter? How will we ever find him again? I can't imagine we'll find him floating about the Tin Lizzy any time soon! We've got nothing! We're no closer to discovering what the Queen's aim is, and my uniform is wrecked on top of it! Not to mention, your hat! Where has it gone?!"

"Don't be silly, Bertie old boy! We've gotten everything we needed and more!" I stopped. So did the Colonel.

"Best to keep up the march now I'm afraid, Bertie—least until we find ourselves safe back in the Swan…" He squinted around the street again.

"Heavens, Colonel." I shrugged. "What could you have possibly taken from that man? He said nothing. Nothing at all. Not unless you're concerned with a fairy terrorizing the highlands, of course!"

"Why, that's precisely what we're concerned with, Bertie!"

"You can't be serious."

"Of course I am! Why do you think I left you with the man? To talk about the weather?!" He was laughing. "Noo. No. Come now, boy. I knew he'd let slip what was on his mind—he always does! Just as long as you seem disarmed, see?" He touched the tip of his finger to his nose.

"What on Earth are you talking about?" I said.

"Oh, well the letter was quite clear—trouble up north."

"And!?"

"And it suggested we discover exactly what the people are troubled with, of course!" He smiled as if we hadn't just been beaten in a pub; as if the answer was obvious.

"Fairies," I said, exhausted.

"So it would seem, yes."

"You're telling me—that I am to believe the Queen sent us to a pub in Liverpool, because of a fairy problem in Scotland?"

"Yes. Well no, not quite." I must have seemed to ask a question with my facial expression, the man went on.

"The Queen herself never mentioned the Tin, Bertie—there you have it! Not exactly! She couldn't possibly have cause in such a place, HEAVEN'S MAN. Noooo, no. But my man from Sussex did suggest we discover what the people knew before taking further action ourselves, boy!" I considered this.

"…And you knew Barnaby would know…" I was putting the mad puzzle together, as upset as I was.

"Yes of course, he always does! As I've said! And now we know! Grain supplies for the war effort are suffering, man! These attacks come at evening—something about the highroad, we'll have to look into that further, I'm afraid. Ee-yee, yes. No, it's all adding up now, chap! And! Of course, we know the cause of it as well! A one-eyed fairy in Scotland, it seems! At least, that's what the people believe…hrmm. Hrmm. A tricky one, indeed."

"And what do you believe, Colonel?" I asked. He winked.

"I believe we have business in Scotland, old boy!"

"Might we rest a bit first, sir?" I sighed and rolled my eyes.

"Yes. I think—perhaps a nip or two of the King's before we head north. To the Swan now, lad! Quick march!"

We kept up the walk. I thought of fairies and grain shipments and the war ongoing in the Afghan. Perhaps it wasn't too late to request an order back to the front.

CHAPTER 7

The Swan Again

I found myself back in the warm light of the Swan. In fact, the very place itself seemed warmer after the night's activity. I sat in a comfy armchair picking at some exposed stuffing. The Colonel also sat in an armchair—however he was slumped much further than I while he twirled a scotch and fidgeted with the chubby orange cat, perched now in his lap. His legs were draped up and over one of the arms while his head bobbled above the other. He sat rather like a banana, one with a moustache. Or closer, perhaps, to a schoolboy. He giggled and regaled the staff at hand—one beautiful and radiant Abigail Stuart.

"And then, Abby! THEN—BERTIE INCITED THE NAVY!" He roared with laughter, showing no signs of discomfort. I admit, I was smiling myself this time. I could only shake my head and roll my eyes however, as my tongue seemed to have swollen to an unspeakable size.

I made my way through a glass of the Colonel's private stock of scotch as well. (He had, of course, rummaged off in search of it immediately upon return) I was beginning to feel quite warm indeed. We laughed on, the three of us, while the Colonel did his best impression of Mr. Barnsworth.

"EEEYYY-ayyyye. WHO'S THAT KERNAL-A GHOST?! WOOooOOO!" He made faces and threw his hands around. Abigail laughed, I laughed. And for the sake of the man's reputation I will add, although he seemed to mock Barnsworth, somehow the Colonel managed to remain sincere. I believe the Colonel would have done the very same impression had Barnsworth been present, and I would even go so far as to add—I believe Barnsworth would have been laughing as well; it was a *very* good impression.

"You must know the man, then? Barnsworth?" I said to Abigail as she moved around the room seemingly at work.

She began with a small laugh. "Only through stories, I'm afraid." The Colonel kicked his feet happily and dipped his head down and up, he made cooing sounds at the happy cat.

"Yes, young Abigail has practically grown up with the man! SHE HAS! Thankfully, however, it has only ever been through the stories of myself and the late Hector, GOD REST HIM!" He blabbered and laughed. "Abigail, love! Another scotch please, that's a girl! Bertie—Bertie, your glass!" He was so gentle with the girl. "Sit. Sit with us, my dear!" She obliged the old nut, thankfully.

I was beginning to feel the effects of the drink. Though my tolerance had greatly improved since entering the service of the Colonel, I was still no match for him.

"When did Hector pass, Colonel?" I asked.

"Ohhhh, my my. Hrmm," the Colonel said, stroking the chubby little cat. "How long has it been, my dear?" he asked Abigail. "Round the time we got this little fellow, aye?" He looked at the cat. I could sense sadness around the room—it made me sorry to have asked, and yet, I felt I must. He seemed, at that moment especially, to be of great importance to the both of them.

Abigail nodded at the Colonel and he added, "Yes, the wee Master Robert of Fishington here must be somewhere near abouts seven? Is that right, my girl?"

"Robert of who?" I stammered.

"The cat, man. Fishy-Bob as he is known in some circles." I merely shook my head and smiled. The names associated with this company are astounding. Sometimes I wonder if my name is really something fantastically absurd as well and that I'm just blind to it—as so many around myself seem to be with theirs. No matter.

"Fishy must be close to seven, we lost Grandfather nearly six years ago," Abigail said. She seemed quite strong to me just then.

"Was he in on all this, Colonel?" I asked. I was curious and the drink had broken down my cordial senses. The Colonel seemed to choke on his whisky a moment.

"Was he—MY DEAR BOY! He was the very ROCK OF THE EMPIRE!" His head bobbed up and down as he answered. "Hector and myself had many an adventure in the name of our King! That being the one before our dear present, QUEEN, of course! And God save her! Yes, my boy—one could say soundly, it were Hector who drug ME along!" Abigail smiled. I couldn't imagine such a truth.

"The Colonel and my grandfather were always in and out of this place, Captain," she said to me. CAPTAIN. My heart melted. "This place is packed with their adventures. Busts and old maps of ancient Egypt and the like. I grew up sort of keeping on after my grandfather. Keeping the place tidy, you know. I spent hours going through his things. When he wasn't out on one of his adventures, as he put it, we'd be here, having adventures of our own."

In the coming days, I will always be on Abigail to keep her own journal where she can recount such stories as these herself—she never has. But I've heard many of them, and since some will appear here in my own journal from time to time, I won't rattle on about them just now. However, I will say that, at this moment, and in so many to come, I was filled with a warm sense of childhood—one I never had myself, as many don't. But to imagine Abigail and this man Hector, here at the Swan, having their own adventures, is how I would explain the feeling the Swan gave me going forward, each time I crossed her threshold. Yes, the Swan was quickly becoming for me, what it clearly already was for the Colonel. An abbey. A safe house. Where an adventurous old nut and his companion (whoever that happened to be) might find some peace. Our conversations swirled on with stories of Hector and the Colonel—Abigail and her Grandfather. For now, I will keep them to myself. Some memories are better left inside one's head, I think, far away from ink and paper. But, enough of that for now.

Before long, my head was full and very warm. The fire roared on, the chubby orange cat, Fishy-Bob, as he was unfortunately called, had found his way onto my lap. The Colonel and Abigail had laughed and said that he must like me. I felt very much at home. I had so many questions, but—the Swan was a warm place. It demanded a man such as myself, dictated by order, to relax and unwind, and let things be for a moment. I obliged. And drifted off to sleep in my armchair.

I awoke sometime in the night to find the lights dim, the only glow coming from the dying embers in the hearth. It seemed I had fallen asleep sometime during the warm conversations the evening prior. Everyone else had made their way to bed, leaving me, no doubt, sleeping soundly. Whether they didn't want to disturb me, or Fishy-Bob, I never discovered. But when I awoke, not even he was to be found.

No matter, I was happy to be heading to the third floor and to the bed I knew awaited me there. I half expected to be woken early by the Colonel, bags already packed, yelling something like—"BERTIE QUICK MARCH TO THE HIGHLANDS NOW BOY!"—but the world was still dark, and therefore I suspected I had at least several more hours with which I might find some precious and sound sleep—in a bed for once. With that happy promise bouncing around in my heart I arrived at the door to room 3B, turning the key already sticking out of the keyhole, I pushed my way into the room.

"Ah, there you are, Bertie," said an all too familiar voice.

"COLONEL!" I said, very shocked. "What on earth are you doing awake?" The man lay in his bed, arms bent cradling his head. He lay, in full uniform of course, above the covers, looking my way.

"I've been thinking, Bertie, about this fairy—and how we might go about tackling it." He wrinkled his moustache; I did my best to ignore him as I made my way into the room.

"Oh, can't it wait until morning, Colonel? It's still early and I—" He plowed on. I was exhausted.

"It's just that I've always said, my boy! What the people believe is as good as truth!"

I ignored him and got ready for bed. "Well, truth or not, the people can surely wait. Hang on—where's my bed, Colonel?" I hadn't noticed earlier; I hadn't noticed until this moment—there was only one bed in the room.

"Just the one, old chap," the Colonel said, as if an afterthought, "afraid we'll have to shack up together for the night—I say, wot! Like the scouting days of old!"

"Nonsense!" I shouted. "I'll simply find another room!"

"Afraid this is the only one, dear boy. Aside from Abigail's—and we certainly don't take you for that sort of fellow, now do we?!" he laughed with a spit, arms still bent behind him.

I said nothing. I merely stared, squint-eyed, mouth half agape.

"What sort of hotel only has one room, Colonel!"

"What? The Swan? Hardly a hotel man, come now," he laughed.

"It's literally CALLED the White Swan Hotel!"

"No it isn't," he replied.

"Yes it is!"

The Colonel sat up on one elbow. "Bertie, this fine establishment is known as THE White Swan only. Heavens man, a hotel! What, and let any ramshackle old bugger roll in here off the streets? Nooo, no! My heavens, we'd have the likes of old Barnsworth knocking on our door—No, this is a HOME, Bertie, a home!"

"Oh, move over you old cod fish!" I gave up and shuffled towards the bed. I jabbed and poked at him to roll over, done with arguing and wanting only sleep—even if it meant sharing a bed with the Colonel. He laughed and whooped and jabbed back, much like a child. Heaven help me.

"Move over, Colonel—heavens. Don't cross this line. Why are you in uniform? Never mind, never mind—better this way. I am going to sleep, Colonel. If you want to stay up until the sun joins you, just fine. But I will have some sleep now, thanks. This day—this NIGHT. Heavens. Move—move, old man!"

The Colonel merely laughed into a wheeze, adding all sorts of quips like, "Would you just—" and "Would you—BERTIE," all while laughing and coughing and jabbing back with his elbow. I imagine if these adventures he spoke of in the name of the Queen were true, and I AM starting to think they are, then they must have been completed in the most ludicrous and sideshow fashion one could possibly picture.

I settled in and doused the light. Adjusting my shoulders to make the Colonel know I meant business about sleeping, we settled into a calm quiet. He finally seemed to relax. My eyes closed.

"Bertie," he said.

"What." I replied.

"Do you know, just now, it's occurred to me we never found out where in Scotland this fairy is."

"Yes, we did." I said shortly.

"We did?" He asked.

"Yes Colonel, we did. Barnsworth said it's in Uig."

"Ahhh—yes, that's right, that's right he did say that! Why, Uig? My goodness boy, that's all the way up on the Isle of Skye, that is! I didn't know they dealt in grain that far north." I tried to close my eyes again.

"Neither did I."

"I wonder, this fairy, what sort of use would he have for grain supplies? And the one eye—that certainly is strange, isn't it chap?" The Colonel blabbered on as if we hadn't just wrestled into bed, HEAVENS.

"Colonel. You can't actually believe there's a fairy, can you? Surely It's just some thief making a mockery of the locals."

"Well, Bertie—as I've said, what the people believe is always the truth."

"Colonel, a fairy? Really?"

"Yes, my boy, they do say it's a fairy. Strange, indeed." He mistook me, bless him. I gave up.

"We'll figure it out when we get there."

"Capital, laddie. Capital. We'll find a way north in the morning." I fell asleep, unsure if the Colonel ever did.

CHAPTER 8

North! But not before...

Several hours later, the grey morning sun shone through a small slit window tucked in beside a large bookshelf. A sheer curtain blew in the breeze; the Colonel was nowhere to be found. His side of the bed, however, was somehow meticulously made. Which either suggests he managed it without disturbing me (probable, but unlikely) OR he never got under the covers to begin with and therefore spent the entire night thinking (the more likely of the two).

I stretched and fumbled over to the bookshelf, leafing through several old books with no agenda. If I closed my eyes (and perhaps my ears too) and imagined, then I might be retired from the soldiering life—sitting in my own study or office, grading papers or reading for pleasure. Far from some outlandish adventure with a nut and a catfish!

Oh, for a draught of *that* vintage!

I grabbed for a copy of Keats, some collected works, and imagined for a moment that I might kick my feet up in bed and read a few lines. This was not to be the case however, as very quickly thereafter my bliss was run aground by the various hands and paws that heaved around the White Swan—be it a hotel or a home—she is filled with creatures, regardless—all of whom descended upon me in rapid order, starting of course, with the smallest.

It went like this:

I grabbed for a copy of Keats, some collected works. I relaxed back into bed and opened the index to find a particular poem.

"'Ode to Nightingale,' fantastic. Ah—page 84. Lovely." I thumbed through the pages. The door creaked slightly open causing my eyes to flit in that direction.

"Just the wind, then." I sighed in relief before being startled by an orange blur which landed with a soft thump and materialized into the form of one chubby cat, licking at a paw.

"Ah. Fishy-Bob! And how are you this morning, chap." He meowed, but generally disregarded me. Perfect.

I read on. I believe I even started to hum a little. This was to be short lived.

"Good morning, Captain McGregor, I've brought tea!" said a lovely voice.

Abigail came strolling in carrying a tray. I nearly lost my balance lying flat upon my back.

"Abigail! Fantastic—good morning! I'm so sorry, I'm not decent!" The cat startled and leapt towards my head. It shrieked. I shrieked. I fell out of bed.

"BERTIE MY LAD!" came a thundering at the door. The man walks like an elephant.

"Good morning, Colonel." I said from the floor on the opposite side of the bed.

"Where are you, boy?"

Abigail began to laugh.

"Down here, sir." I said with a heavy sigh.

"My word man, you're not in the field anymore! Sleep in the bed some time, why don't you?" I could kill the old man.

"Yes, sir. Fine." I said and struggled up. Fishy-Bob was already back on the bed, totally unharmed it seemed, licking a paw. All three stared at me as if *I* were the silly one. Abigail, with her tray and sweet smile. The Colonel, with one eye squinting through a monocle. Fishy-Bob, chubby and grooming. It seems this was to be my lot, like it or not. My company. Those who, I supposed in that moment—would be with whom I would sink, or swim. My, what wild times I have lived to see.

"Well." I said. "Let's get on with it then, Colonel."

They all three laughed and cheered in their own ways and moved towards me in a rush. Sweeping me up and out towards the door. Abigail said "Lovely!" The Colonel let out a 'Hurrah' and a rousing "GOOD

MAN, BERTIE, THERE'S A LAD!" and Fishy-Bob meowed, of course. Oh, how I loved them all for it.

"Some tea first, I think! Abigail?" The Colonel shouted as we fumbled out of the room.

———— ◆ ————

The Colonel and I sat in our armchairs again. The fire rumbled and cracked in its weak morning state. We made small talk and chirped over maps and ideas. Abigail rustled around at the command of the Colonel. She gathered note pads and ink pens. Hats of various degrees. Two haversacks and one medium sized suitcase.

"Right then," I said, "it'll be the 2 o'clock train to London before turning round and making the 6 o'clock train to Edinburgh. Are you quite sure this will be the fastest route? Why not head north first through Wigan? Seems a dreadful waste to head so far south before heading right back towards the North." The Colonel merely scoffed.

"Yes of course, my boy. Everyone knows the layovers from the Southwest are a nightmare! Direct route to London before a direct route to Edinburgh? You cannot possibly do better!"

I was not convinced but was learning not to argue reason. Not to mention, the idea of sitting on a platform in rainy Wigan with an Acorn for God knows how long was not something I was not eager to try on. I accepted his ideas.

"Right then. Well, if you're sure. That's the battle plan then, isn't it?"

"Too right, my boy. Too right." We both reached for and sipped on our tea. Content enough between the both of us.

The plan was quite simple, simpler even than I'd have thought it would be. The Colonel even seemed a bit on the reserved side. He agreed to sit and plan out the attack, as he called it. I had thought we'd be running round from platform to platform screaming like baboons to make the right train at the right moment. But here we had it; We were to stroll to the Liverpool station, take the afternoon trip down to London before turning right round on the Northbound trip to Edinburgh. Although I still believed the trip south to be a bit wasteful, the only real tight spot was the short time between trains from Liverpool to London and London to Edinburgh. But with some aggressive management, I believed that I could manage that task with only a bit of fuss. I was actually content. The Colonel sat with one leg crossed over the other, bouncing it happily to a tune he was humming.

"Abigail, my dear. Are you quite certain you can get along without us?" He gave me a wink.

"Of course I can, Colonel. Who is it that always takes care of the place when you're off wandering around? Not to mention our wee Fishy-Bob of course!" I admired her cheek.

He bounced his foot happily and waved her off, "ee-yes. Yes." He murmured with a deep smile. The man was content. He always seemed happiest when things were "afoot". Something I have grown only so fond of regarding the man as time has gone on.

Abigail materialized again and sat next to us in the common area. Here we all sat, some ramshackle form of a military company. Even Fishy-Bob seemed on edge, ready for intense action, even as the scene dully rolled on.

"Right then," I half-murmured and began to rise.

"BERTIE!" The Colonel declared.

"What?!" I shouted back, quite shocked at the outburst.

"A CATASTROPHE!"

"A what?! What on earth is the matter?"

"My hat!" he shouted again with even less information somehow.

"Which one?!" I shouted back, the scene now an uproar. Fishy-Bob meowing and scattering off.

"I lost it at the Tin last night!"

"Goodness, Colonel. Well how many more have you got? Surely you can stand to lose just one hat—" He cut me off. "You don't understand, dear boy! That hat is EVERYTHING!"

"That silly old officer's cap? You've got TWO more, right here! Pick one you old buffoon!" I grabbed at one of them and tossed it at him (I was becoming quite comfortable with the old nut).

"I don't want THAT hat, Bertie. I want MY hat!" He crossed his arms like a child.

"Are you seriously—"

"It had the letter inside Bertie! The one from the QUEEN'S man!"

"It had the let—with the Queen's signature, no less." I sighed. I knew what this meant.

"THE QUEEN CAN NOT BE SEEN TO BE INVOLVED!" He

was upset, the poor old nut. Although he never lost his boyish charm to me, I laugh to imagine it—the sincere old dog was as loyal as they come.

"Surely no one would find an old letter stuffed in an old cap lost in a bar scrap!" I tried to convince the man.

"ANYONE COULD FIND IT, MY BOY! THE ENEMY EVEN!"

"Have we got many enemies?" I practically whispered.

"No, no. Heavens, no. This will not do. Off we go lad, off we go! We must find the cap before we leave! That's that!" He was already standing to move.

"Oh, come now, Colonel, we'll miss our train! We'll never find it! No one will ever find it!"

"BERTIE! WHAT IS IT WE ARE IN SERVICE OF!"

"Oh, for heaven's sake! Forget it! I'm going, I'm going!" I slapped my knees and pushed myself to a standing position. Best not to argue, of course, even as annoyed as I was.

"Good man, GOOD. ABIGAIL! OUR THINGS, LOVE! FOR THE QUEEN!" She rolled her eyes and stood along with us. So much for my steady plans! So much for a civil stroll to the station! How could I ever have let myself dream as such! Looks like I'll be chasing the old nut around again. How I wish this sweet creature Abigail were coming. Her ability to simply go along with the man and his oddities is the stuff of dreams. I admire it to no end! And could stand to learn a thing or two from her.

Nevertheless, we were moving again.

"RUUUUUULE—BRITANNIA!" The Colonel swung his swagger stick which had materialized in his hand as if on command of action. I bumped along after the Colonel, stopping to pick up the one or more odd effects dropping from his person. I tried to catch Abigail's eyes.

"Abigail I wonder if I might—" was all I could manage before the Colonel cut into me with some sort of deranged order.

"Calm down—WOULD you just!" I stammered. Things fell from their spots on shelves. Fishy-Bob twirled around my legs. Abigail's tray was weaved in and around the Acorn and myself.

"CALM?! At a moment like this!? HEAVENS BOY, NO! To ARMS!" The man continued his rapid assault around the room, aiming for the door.

"Colonel! WOULD YOU JUST STOP. STOP. STOPPP." The room seemed to freeze. The Colonel froze half-bent over—he eyed me with a worried face and a squeezed monocle. Abigail and Fishy-Bob seemed to have frozen in absurd positions as well—they mocked me. I plucked up my courage.

"Abigail—Miss Abigail. Abby. No. Noo." The Colonel's face now twisted into a smirk I shall never forget.

"Out with it, lad!" he shouted.

"It's just that I wondered if I might write to you—oh well! For, well you know. To keep you well aware of our movements…you see I just—"

The Colonel smirked. The cat even seemed to smirk. I must have blushed. And to my great amazement, Abigail calmly walked up to me and pushed an envelope into my clumsy hands. It had my name written on it…

"Please keep me well informed, Captain."

Was all she said…was all she needed to say. My head spun round and round and my cheeks became increasingly warm. Before I knew it, I was outside the White Swan on the streets of Liverpool, absentmindedly listening to the Colonel go on and on about his hat. I chipped in with many "Yes sir's" and even a few "Hurrahs". Quite out of character for me, I admit. But my eyes and mind were fixed upon my name, written on my letter.

CHAPTER 9

...The Tin again

We made a brisk pace towards the Tin Lizzy Pub, retracing our steps from the previous night. I admit, in my mind, it would have been a long time until I made this trip again—if ever. But here we were, doing it for the sake of a hat no less.

"Colonel—really. Do we absolutely need the letter? It seems we have enough to go on already—the Queen wants us to solve this mystery up north, we've discovered some detail from the common man—I mean, what else do we need?"

"The hat Bertie—we need the hat," he smugly responded. He seemed a tad on the crankier side this morning—I wondered if his lack of sleep was to blame.

"I see," I said, learning as I was not to question his ways. Anyways—it really shouldn't have been too much of a bother. Poke around the pub, inquire about the hat, find that it is, in fact, gone forever, and hopefully convince the Colonel to depart in time for the Southbound train to London.

We continued through the winding streets of Liverpool. I would miss her once we left, this is certainly true. Though I am neither from Liverpool, nor have I ever spent some lengthy amount of time within her—she has always felt like a sort of devilish home to me. I imagine many Englanders feel similar, she is like the worn-out welcome mat we have come to recognize as being truly home. Those of us who have been prone to wander away, that is. I ramble.

"Colonel, we must be quick about this business if we are to make our train to London…" I casually reminded the old fellow.

"Yes, yes. The train. Bertie my boy, that letter MUST be found! In all the years I have found myself duty-bound to the Queen's own hand I have never once betrayed her trust in our secrecy! It simply must be found—Ah hah! There she is again, old sport!" That same familiar tear welled in the corner of his eye.

"OH, COME ON!" I shrugged and pulled him towards the door.

The Tin Lizzy was an entirely different place when the sun was shining. The door pushed lazily in and revealed (to my shock) a clean and tidy place. One old man sat at the bar drinking a pint, clad in cap and jacket; he neither acknowledged our entrance nor our presence. A bar man worked a rag into a glass behind the pub.

"Aya—Yoo two again. avn' ye tore up the old Tin enuff fer a few days? Nearly 'ad this place knocked down, ya did." The Colonel smiled at the barkeep. I'm sure he was smitten with his accent. The Colonel LOVED all English accents, for all their differences and oddities—as he loved the Empire for the same reason.

"Ahhhh yes. Terribly sorry about all that, chap. Nasty business, nasty business." He dropped his eyes and shook his head, making a clicking noise with his mouth. I knew the Colonel well enough to know that this was a form of flattery—he most probably felt not one drop of remorse for what happened last night. As he probably would have said something like 'What else do Englishmen do in a pub?' if he were being honest. However, he had business with the man, and needed him on his side. I wasn't about to allow it however and so I stepped in.

"We are sorry, fellow, truly. And we have indeed returned for the very reason of addressing our indecencies to you and this fine place—and, I admit—to inquire about one lost possession of my dear associate here." He stopped rubbing his glass and stared as if insulted.

"Wahht?"

The Colonel edged past me and gave his own try—to my dismay.

"What he means, dear man, is that I seem to have lost my hat in all the excitement last night. Being that I AM an officer in the Queen's Army— well, let's just say, it would be quite the ribbing from my superiors if I were to show up to formation absent my denoting feature, eh wot?!" He poked at the man across the bar with a sly grin.

"avn't seen no 'ats round here—What'd it look lyke?" he rubbed his glass again.

"Well, you see. It sort of has a flat top, there. And it's adorned with a sort of—" the Colonel moved his hands and squinted as he began to describe his hat in fine detail. I turned my head as he spoke, ever so slightly towards the back of the place—sitting there at the piano I found the hat, at the exact same moment the barman did.

"Yoo mean tha' hat?" he said. The Colonel squinted towards the piano.

"Colonel don't—" was all I could manage.

"THE VERY ONE!" exclaimed the Colonel. His excitement was for the hat, for sure enough it *was* his. My reservation, however, was for whose head it now sat upon—a man the Colonel either couldn't see or couldn't remember. Or perhaps both…

Sitting near the piano was one very large man in braces. In the light of the morning, his forearms bulged as if they had spent a lifetime hurling anchors and nets over the sides of boats. His great big black beard disguised his face, but not his eyes—one of which bulged and throbbed in our direction. Clamped between his teeth, a seaman's pipe. Atop his head? One cap, officer's regulation, His Majesty's Army.

"Lookin 'fer this hat, then are yee?" He snarled from his seated position. I gulped; I admit it.

The Colonel rose from where he had been perched at the bar, extended one hand straight in front of himself and approached the man with the sort of ease one might picture in a formal dinner setting.

"I say, dear man. Yes! Yeeees! We are! I might thank you for finding it for me—well! The Queen herself might even!" He squinted and laughed as he got closer, me on his heels begging retreat. The veins in the large man's head pulsed and bulged like his one black eye. His fist squeezed shut tighter and tighter as it sat on the table—I believe some nuts were smashed in its vise.

"DAMN IT, OLD MAN," he shouted and slammed his fists on the table. The Colonel stopped abruptly, concern on his face. More of a concern for the man's lack of decency, however; in fact, I'd say the Colonel was more disgusted with the man than afraid of him just then.

"I say, old boy. What is the meaning of this outburst! I only mean to thank you for finding my HAT!" I rapidly found the Colonel's ear and attempted to whisper advice—he shrugged me off.

"No—no, Bertie. And let me say another thing, young man!" He still addressed the largest man in the place, who by now seemed ready to explode.

"SIT. DOWN. SIR." The man said between clenched teeth.

"Ah-hah! There's a good lad, and so we shall!" He pulled up a seat before I could stop him—I must have seemed like the toadiest of all toads. I sat. The Colonel began.

"Now then—" He patted the man's balled up fist. "To begin, I say THANKS. For finding my hat—and do wonder if you might now hand it over?" He smiled. I shrugged. The Colonel clearly doesn't remember this man as the chief assailant from last night, but I do wonder if his nonchalance is working.

"The HAT. IS MINE." He again said between clamped teeth.

"Now, now, dear man! Clearly—as I am dressed in full military uniform—sans hat! It must belong to me! Would you not say that stands to reason? Ee-yes. I will have it now, and forgive your indecency, I say!" The Acorn said smartly.

"YOU OWE ME MONEY. The hat—is mine. Until I get wots owed—OLD MAN." His eyes bulged ever so slightly more as he spat out the last of his words.

"Ohhh yes. ee-yes. Now I do recall." Said the Colonel through squinted eyes. "You were the lad who ambushed my company last night! I say— we have YET to retrieve old Barnsworth! I wonder what has become of HIM! And another thing!" My shock was beyond measure. The Colonel continued.

"LISTEN HERE NOW, OLD MAN—" the large man in braces began himself and I, stuck between the two. They traded verbal blows back and forth in a slightly growing uproar. To my credit, I attempted to calm the storm. Both rose—fists were shaken, the Colonel to his OWN credit did not back down.

"Now wait—WAIT. Goodness." I interjected. The barman shouted from his bar. The drunk there turned and rambled something incoherent. The table shook and bounced, chairs screeched. The large man grabbed the Colonel from over my head—I found myself pinched in his armpit. From behind, the Colonel grabbed *my* leg, of all things. I struggled out of the hold and put myself between the two forces, fearful I may be crushed.

"NOW WAIT JUST A BLOODY WELL MOMENT!" I shouted and pushed the two apart at an arm's length. "SURELY. Surely. We can find a suitable agreement here! Now—you. YES, YOU, COLONEL. Sit. And you—sir, very…large man—if you would sit also. Thank you. Now," I said as I patted my own hair back into place. "Now." The two looked on like angry schoolchildren…

"Now…It seems we are at a disagreement as to who owns the hat, currently. I will say—the hat does originally belong to my associate here— AS I'VE SAID—originally. Now, I cannot possibly speak to the reason as to why old Barnsworth may have owed you money but from what I *have* seen, it would not be ridiculous to imagine your debt on him is well-placed or even fair. That being said—we may have come between you last night as you attempted to collect on it. And we do apologize (the Colonel snorted over crossed arms). However, I am certain you will find the bugger again, and when you do, I can promise we will not stop your attempts to collect your debt again. And so, my dear man, let us pay your bar tab in thanks, collect our hat—and be done with it."

"Well said Bertie!" the Colonel slapped his knee and smiled.

"No deal," the large man said.

"Now there, man. My terms were fair. Come now!" I said, bolder than I had been before.

"There is no guarantee I will ever see that RAT again. Took me four months lookin round all the pubs in town to find him last night! And just like a RAT! Now you've scared him off again. I'll take the money I'm owed, now, If the hat's so important to yee! Or I'll be keepin it meself." He crossed his arms and looked away, the Colonel mimicked him.

"Keep it," I said.

"BERTIE NOoo.." The Colonel stammered, ruining my bluff.

"Ah-hah. Like I thought. You want the hat—I'll have the debt. One hundred pounds, today."

"One hundred pounds! It's an outrage!" the Colonel shouted.

"Surely you can't expect us to carry that sort of money!" I said, fully committed now to the idea of getting Colonel Korn's hat back.

"Like I said, lads. You want the hat—you pay the debt. Otherwise, it stays atop mee head. I sorta like the way it looks anywees." He shrugged back into a comfortable position, confident in his blackmail.

"A duel." The Colonel spat. "What? No!" I said. "A duel!" He said again.

"You want to duel…for this hat?" the large man said.

"A duel of sorts, yes. I'll tell you this, fellow—if you can outdrink me, the hat is yours." I couldn't believe my ears.

"You want to have a drinking duel? Against me?" he thumped his iron chest.

"That's right, laddy. And if I win—the hat."

"And if I win?"

"The debt shall be paid." He puffed out his moustache.

"DEAL. BARMAN!" He shouted and turned to the bar.

I pulled the Colonel aside and whispered furiously. "Colonel, are you INSANE? Look at the size of that man! My God—you'll never win! We don't have the money! Surely Colonel, this hat is NOT WORTH IT!" He batted me off. "Hush, hush. The Queen's signature MUST be preserved, boy—we won't need to pay anything; we shall leave this place with hat in hand!"

The barman approached with a tray of whisky and other dark drinks in small glasses. "Colonel, he looks like he could drink FOR DAYS! We have a train to catch in less than two hours! We'll never make it in time!"

"Agreed, my boy. Seemingly, the man *has been* here for days—do not doubt the Queen's man now, Bertie me lad! It'll just take an hour—a quick jiff and we'll be off for the station! I'll sleep the way there and we'll be none the less damaged, save for the fact the Queen's decency will have been preserved!" He waved his hands again with a wink.

"Ready, old man?" A shot was slid across to our side of the table.

"Rule. Britannia." Bottoms up.

I will say I was nervous at first—as if some great battle were about to commence. However, it didn't take long for me to sink into a state of near boredom and sure annoyance, my head resting on my hand. The two men drank a shot of liquor every couple of minutes, and as time went on both became more and more docile. Before long, they talked like friends through mumbles. Soon after, and to my utter annoyance, they even began to hum and sing the same songs!

"And it—it goes like—HMMM, mmm MMM. Mm. MMMMMM!" The Colonel romanced and waved a finger like a conductor. The large man, now with crossed eyes, wobbled and waved and added in hums of agreement.

"For goodness sake…" I rolled my eyes.

"Barty! Bert! Ah 'nother round—There's ah lad…" The circus continued. I was as sober as the vicar on Easter Sunday. Here I sat, two complete drunkards swirling around me. One in 3/4ths of a full English Military Uniform, the other dressed as a seaman save for one very out of place military cap. The both of them drinking and laughing and spilling drinks as if they had been friends for an eternity.

"AND IF! And ifff…." The Colonel began and raised his finger high in the air. The large man's eyes sort of followed it up towards the ceiling, crossed and blurry.

"WEEEeee. WE few. MEN OF ENGLAND," he was now standing, "SHALL GO ON TIL THE END! WE. WE SHALL HAVE…" He rolled his head. Anticipation built.

"VICTORY!" He shouted and laughed. The large man did the same, his own head flailing about, until he stopped. Smacked his lips a few times. Smirked. Laughed. And fell over backwards.

"Dear God. You've done it." I said.

"Done what?" stammered the Colonel as he grabbed for my shoulder—unaware as of yet that he had toppled the great man.

"Oh yes…look at that." He said. "Grab my hat Bert. Let's be off, what is the time?"

"Heavens—we've got half an hour. Quickly, quickly, sir!" I grabbed the hat and heaved the Colonel's arm over my shoulder.

"Wait wait wait wait wait…" He stammered. "The letter. Is the letter in the cap?"

"Right, right." I said and began to examine the cap. I checked under the folds and in between the stitching. Nothing.

"Nothing, Colonel. NOTHING. BE damned! Where did you put it!" He muttered and started patting his own pockets as if that would help. I nearly broke the hat apart looking for it, the time now beginning to weigh on me. The idea of sitting in the rain at a Wigan train station crushing…

"Ah-hah! Why? Why—here it is, Bertie—it's been in me pocketbook… all this time. Hm mm mm mm."

I crumpled the hat in my hands. Stepped over the sleeping giant and heaved the Colonel towards the door.

"Confound you, old man, hurry up!" was all I could manage.

CHAPTER 10

Wigan in the Rain

You might have guessed it—

We missed the train to London.

Furthermore, you may have also guessed the weather in Wigan.

Rain.

Ah! But we did get lucky! As the Colonel put it—for there was a train to Wigan available when the woman at the ticket box had told us we'd missed our train south.

"There you have it, lad! Just what you wanted in the first place, wasn't it?" was something along the lines of what the Colonel had shouted. The train ride to Wigan was short—and now, as I've said (and as I had feared) we were sitting quite alone on a Wigan train platform—in the rain, waiting for our connecting trip to Edinburgh.

We shared a bench on the platform, but my back was turned towards the Colonel with my rain jacket pulled high above my eyes. My wound throbbed and panged in the cold, dreary air. The Colonel hummed along and kicked his feet on the bench. Just then, the scratching of wood on potassium chlorite, ignition, and the sounds of puffing.

"Are you really smoking your pipe right now?" I asked, annoyed.

"Yes?" the Colonel replied simply as if he's been caught in some act; a puff of smoke emitting from his cheeks as he did.

"You do realize it's raining." I continued bluntly.

"Sure, it always rains in England! It's just like I've always said, my boy! We English pots grow best in the shade of a cloud!" He laughed and I turned back to my side of the bench grumbling as I felt I was warranted.

"Oh psh—Bertie my boy! What's gotten you so low down! Here we are, gathering our wits—the Queen's letter in hand, mind you—on our way to complete our duties to the crown!" he said with an annoying amount of joviality.

"The Queen's letter was always in hand, Colonel! Had you checked your bloody pocket book…"

"Yes, well, you never suggested I look there!"

"You cannot be insisting this is my fault!" My arms crossed, slumping further into the bench.

"Perhaps I assumed this was your ploy to avoid London after all!" He crossed his own arms and harrumphed into a similar stooped stature.

"Anyways, I'd have thought a letter from one Miss Abigail Stuart would have cheered a man up," he said, candidly.

"Ah! The letter!" I had completely forgotten. Suddenly, sitting in Wigan was miles behind my concern. I fumbled through my layers looking for the letter. The Colonel turned from his slumped state and eye-balled me from the side of his face. "Yes. ee-yes. Have you got it?" he practically whispered. "Shuh-SUSH. Shush." I stammered as I fought with a few buttons, turning away from the nut further yet.

At last, the letter. My name written in a swirly cursive on the front of the envelope—

-Captain Albert MacGregor-

I fumbled to open it carefully as the Colonel craned his neck to see. I turned yet further and gave him a devilish look. I still have the letter, it read very simply…

> *Captain,*
>   *Do please take care of the Colonel up north. We both know how easily the man can be distracted. I wanted to write to ask you a favor—it's just that I worry about the Colonel these days, adventuring alone as it were. I wonder if I might ask you to keep me informed of your travels with him. Please, won't you keep that between us? I don't want to upset the Colonel. I was so happy to see you come through our door in*

> *his service—in return, I promise I will do my best to help you*
> *however I may from here.*
>
> *Do write often, won't you Captain? I was just getting*
> *used to your being around when you both set off. I await*
> *your return.*
>
> *Best—and with fondness,*
> *Abigail.*
> *(And Fishy-Bob!)*

I could feel the Colonel straining to get a look at the letter. But my head spun. That last part? That last part. THAT LAST PART.

"WELL," the Colonel shouted.

"Well, what?" I said, startled.

"Well, what does it say! Out with it, boy!"

"Oh just…nothing, you know."

"PLEASE. A letter from a woman got a Queen's soldier so befuddled hardly says NOTHING, EY!" he ribbed and laughed at my expense.

"Nothing—just." I said, turning red and laughing. "Oh, it—it just tells me to keep the girl informed! You know? That's all. Should we need any help and the like!" The Colonel puffed on his pipe and considered my answer with a sly—nay, indeed, a devilish, grin.

"Hmmm. Hm. Always on the top, that girl—very smart of her. Wouldn't you say, chap!" A punch at my guts with one hand, the other clutching and ripping on his pipe.

"Yes. Hah—YES! You old baboon. Ah! That must be our train I hear! Shall we?" I said and hurriedly changed the subject, gathering our belongings and rising.

"Oh yes, yes. Sure, SURE. Bertie, do be a good lad and grab my personals. I shall make for the bar car! See if this beast has a decent drink for a weary man-at-arms!" He fumbled up and patted his belly, stretching a bit.

"Yes, Colonel." I said. I could have made an offhand comment about his surely having had enough to drink of late—but I was content, and let it slide.

We boarded. Now to Edinburgh.

BOOK II

The Highlands

CHAPTER 11

The Ancient Capital

We settled into our train compartment; too short of a journey to warrant a sleeper car—not that I fancied sharing a small room to sleep in with the Colonel again. He had been quite occupied running amuck up and down the train for the first hour or so of our journey. I had enjoyed several blessed moments of peace and quiet before he returned. I fumbled over the letter several more times, convinced myself I was looking much too far into the words, and resolved to simply respond when convenient, and to keep it short. Something like, "Dearest Abby…" No. "Dear Abigail…" Wrong. "Abigail—" Simply. Curse it all.

"You know Bertie," the Colonel began from his lounged position. Stretched out on his side of the car, one foot crooked over the other, bouncing slightly. He gripped his knee with both palms as his foot tapped on and on in the air—I might have been annoyed, had I not been feeling quite light upon my own seat just then.

"I've been thinking…"

"Hm? Is that right?" I said over my books and papers. I attempted to look busy with anything but the letter, sitting over top of the open page of my book.

"Yes, ee-yes. It's just that I've been thinking we ought to spend the night in Edinburgh—rest up a bit, you know. Sample the local fare a tad! Couldn't hurt…" I slapped my papers down and looked up.

"Sample the local fare—haven't we done quite enough of that already?" I said.

The Colonel snorted out a breathy laugh—as if my point was ludicrous and held no ground. As if the light of recent events could possibly have been imagined by me! Or worse—I'm sure, in his mind, I over-exaggerate recent events!

"Come now, lad. You couldn't possibly be over-exaggerating recent misdoings, could you now?" He laughed. I frowned.

"No Colonel, I don't believe I am. At any rate—we won't arrive in Edinburgh until this evening, hardly enough time to secure proper lodging for the night. No—no, I say it best we simply plow on to the North! Find a train with a sleeper car…" I gulped at the last bit, but it was the soundest idea—I do believe that, even still!

"Nonsense, boy! We'll stay with old Fergus Dillwyn!" as if I were to know the name.

"Oh—silly me. Of course! Fergus Dillwayne, how could I have forgotten old Fergus!"

"Dill—WIN. My boy, WIN." The old man said matter-of-factly.

"WHO IS FERGUS DILLWYN?" I nearly shouted.

The Colonel turned towards me still crossing his legs and said, as if to scold a child, "Fergus—is my BEST friend, Bertie. And he would CERTAINLY welcome us into his home. Of that I have NO DOUBT!"

"But must we stop, Colonel? Shouldn't we hurry to the highlands to complete our task?!" I said, with great effort to remain neutral, careful not to reveal my true fears—that we might pop in on this old Fergus character simply for a round of whisky and a few songs!

"I believe stopping in the capital would suit our interests, Bertie. Not to mention old Fergus may be a wealth of knowledge on the subject of fairies! One never knows what—"

"A wealth of knowledge on fairies— no. No, I refuse to hear that for reasoning, Colonel, tell me now if your aim is to simply pop in on an old friend! I mean it Colonel— say it!" I interjected.

He paused his toe tapping and pursed his lips. His eyes rolled and looked in every direction but mine. He bobbed his head, as if thinking.

"Colonel," I said. Nothing from the man. He began to hum.

"Colonel. Say it!"

"Say what?" he chirped.

"That you don't want to stop in Edinburgh just to drink with this old Fergus chap!"

"Really a fantastic marvel this thing, isn't it? You know when I was a boy— hardly a locomotive track to be found! Now this bloody GWR lad has got us covered all the way round the Midlands and up to the Humber!" He was stalling.

"You mean the GNR." I rolled my eyes and gave up.

"What's that lad?" he said, as if confused.

"Yorkshire, sir. It was the GNR that connected the rail lines all the way North to the Humber— not the GWR." I said frankly.

"Hardly! It was the Midlands man who won the battle of the gauges and brought us to the North! Come now, lad." (His pride in the midlands was sincere, but misplaced next to my knowledge, I am quite well read after all.)

"Isambard Brunel—LATE of the Great Western Railway favored the WIDER gauge for the rail line! And he lost— when Parliament concluded Stephenson's smaller gauge line was more efficient! Anyways! It's not relevant! The Great Northern Line or, GNR as it is commonly called, was already well in place by the time any sort of connection to the Midlands was to be made! Having been laid long before and in Stephenson's smaller gauge! That's why the man favored it in the first place! He worked on the GNR as a young man before moving to work in the midlands! But as I've said— your point is moot. Mixed gauge won in the end. You could hardly attribute any THING to any ONE person! Thank you very much!" The Colonel looked at me, mouth quite agape.

"At any rate! Quite the marvel, wouldn't you agree!" He puffed out his moustache and looked away, that foot bouncing on again.

"Don't think I don't know what you're doing, old man." I swerved back to the matter at hand, not entirely sure if I'd gotten the facts straight, but sure enough that I'd put the Colonel's attempts to distract me to bed.

"Hm- what's that?" he said.

"Trying to distract me— it won't work. This Fergus I'm sure is a lovely man (I'm not sure exactly what I did imagine at that moment, but it wasn't that) but what I'm not certain of is if stopping in for a visit is well worth our time!" I am the Colonel's Aide, mind you. It is my job to keep him working, after all.

"Bertie— we haven't got the foggiest idea what we're up against! You've said it yourself! We don't have a plan! Well I agree! Wouldn't it serve us to pop in on old Fergie and see what the man knows? He has made his fortune in grain trade after all! Not to mention the man is quite fashionable with literature! He may know all about fairies and how to tackle them!" The Colonel went on complaining like a long-winded school boy trying to get out of a rap on the knuckles.

"Hang on—he's done what? Made his fortune how?" I asked.

"In the grain trade, yes. But he may know all about fairies! And I for one—" I cut him off.

"Oh would you forget the fairies, Colonel! Grain trade! That's the ticket, isn't it! Perhaps this Fergus could be of help to us!" The Colonel stopped and puffed a few times.

"Yes. Well. Yes, his connection in the grain trade— that's it. That's what I thought. Yes. That is the reason, young Bertie!"

"If it's true— why? He must have receipts! Bills of sale! Correspondence with growers! Anything that can tell us where exactly the grain is gone missing…" I was thinking mostly out loud.

"AND HOW!" The Colonel said, excitedly.

"Yes—and how. How indeed. I wonder…"

"Fairies." The Colonel said proudly.

"Fairies?" I said with one brow up.

"Well— I, I, I should say! Fairy! Just the one! So they say!" He nodded his head, proud. I laughed, all I could do.

"Yes, Colonel. Just the one— that is what the people seem to be saying." I said, meaning Barnsworth, not at all convinced of the notion. But— that matter will be solved at a later time. My mind was working on what this man Fergus could in fact offer us. Perhaps, with his help, we might indeed pinpoint where this product had gone missing. At this point, any lead would have suited me. I had been in the dark for too long.

"So then! Edinburgh for the night, lad?"

"I think it best, sir. Yes."

"CAPITAL! GOD SAVE THE QUEEN!"

———◦———

As our train whistled through Berwick the Colonel seemed to fuss and rustle with the revelry of an Oxford University boy. He hummed tunes better spent on the pipes and waved his hand at passersby from his window. Many Hurrahs and Huzzahs were issued.

"Huzzah! I say— Huzzah there, man!" He shouted and waved at some poor sod fishing below our bridge on the Tweed. The sun crested oddly in the sky warning we would not arrive in Edinburgh with much more than a few hours of light.

"Ahhh… Berwick-upon-Tweed!" The Colonel began with a laugh as his head came back in from the window. "Quite the little town she is— but bigger than her boot size suggests, wouldn't you say Bertie? I was listening to the Colonel but gazing dreamily as we chuffed through the ancient town, her ruins showing off her place in the deep history of Scotland. I am a Scotsman myself, after all, and I hadn't been home in some time…

"ee-Yes…" The Colonel romanced without an answer from me. "…She has always been the gateway to our home, hasn't she Bertie?" He seemed to read my mind.

"Yes, Colonel. Berwick certainly has that mark for my kin." I mused.

"Yes- yes. The Clan McGregor! So much PAIN in our home, eh Bertie? Deep history…deep history indeed…" His voice trailed as if in some deep fantastical way, denoting thought.

"You're Scottish, Colonel?" I asked. (I hadn't known the answer just then.)

"My dear boy, YES! I am a MacDonald on my mother's side!" He nearly shouted. "MacDonald of Glencoe to be precise— My grandfather, God rest him, would ALWAYS renounce the Campbell name until the day he died himself! That nasty business of murder and mockery of hospitality! Pah-tooh!" He made spitting sounds. I pitched in a few laughs.

"Yes, that massacre was a nasty piece of work. But— it couldn't be worse than the abolishment of my clan's good name with the hanging of our thirteen leaders in Edinburgh!" I egged him on.

"Ohhh…yes. Very good Bertie, VERY good." He admired my knowledge of clan history with a wink— I encouraged it, though in truth it was only ever purely educational to me. I, like the Colonel, am a good Briton alone these days. But I took the chance to quip with the Colonel— He loved everything about his empire of course, as one must know by now, and I loved to encourage it, even then.

"And your Tartans?" He asked with a sly eye.

"McGregor red and black— of course! My mother has claimed them since she was a girl— I wore them all through Sandhurst. And once, we had an American attaché visit- they called it '*Buffalo Plaid*' can you imagine?" This got the Colonel's attention.

"BUFFALO. PLAID! MY GOOD MAN!" He shouted and wheezed into a coughing fit. I shook my head and chuckled as he punched at my knees. I take great comfort in these moments— The Colonel is rarely one for educational debate, but if it involved The British Empire in any way? Well. I was only too happy to play along.

"Those Yanks, Eh? DAMN SPIRITED!" He laughed more and I did believe him sincere. Our train rolled and steamed on through town. I have made this trip twice before; once when leaving *for* and again when returning *from* my schooling. It always feels like any track beyond Berwick is moving uphill...as if the whole world is sloped below the Scottish Highlands... At any rate, they are to me.

"Our history as Scots is bleak, I'm afraid." The Colonel said, finally choking away his fits of laughter. "But I will say, I am damn glad the Crown saw fit to allow highland dress again! Damn decent part of our Empire this land— wouldn't you agree there laddy?" He smiled as if suddenly lost in a song.

"Yes— Yes, I would, Colonel." I said with a sigh as we wound on and on.

"And where is it you're from then, Bertie?" Just then I imagined what my mother would have said of the ability of men to pass great lengths of time and danger together without ever truly getting to know one another.

"Near to Inverness, sir." I said.

"Ah— Not far from our target then, eh?"

"Quite, sir. Although I never have seen the Isle of Skye. Uig is an even bigger mystery, I'm afraid. Hang on— Where are YOU from, Colonel?"

"Ah- here and there. The Empire of course!" He said with a wave.

"You're from- *The Empire.*" I asked with a visible eye-roll.

"Indeed, indeed." My questions are always an afterthought it seems— he went on. "At any rate, I will say we can expect much better hospitality from old Fergie than we might have received in our own storied histories! The man is a TRUE Scotsman Bertie— His mother was a Duncan I believe...or perhaps...perhaps a Campbell now that I think of it.... No matter, no matter! He will receive us with an open door and a warm hearth, I can tell you that! And the WHISKY BERTIE! AH THE WHISKY SHALL—" I cut him off.

"The whisky shall be second to our questions of grain trade, right Colonel?" He eyed me with large bulbous eyes, damp with concern.

"QUITE!" He said with a puff of moustache.

"At any rate—" I began by mocking him. "At any rate— I wonder if we might head straight to this man Fergus and inquire about lodging. Where does he live?"

"He lives on Lawnmarket— Lawnmarket and James to be precise. House numbered four and twelve." The old man rattled off.

"Right. Amazing your ability to remember and forget."

"What's that now?" He shot back.

"Amazing your ability to remember every nook and cranny where one might find a drop of scotch, yet completely forget a letter WITH THE QUEEN'S NAME ON IT, NO LESS! Tucked into your pocket book!" I did not relent.

"YES, WELL. YOU NEVER SUGGESTED I LOOK THERE!"

"Oh well! Heaven forbid your valet forget what is or is NOT in your pocket book!" I must have been lacking sleep more than I'd have guessed.

"CORRECT." He crossed his arms and looked away. I had to laugh. I really had to laugh.

"What— What's that?" he began to laugh as well. "What's that now, boy? What *is* so funny!" He laughed heartily with me now. The Colonel has a way of catching a laugh, you see. I imagine he'd have laughed at the funeral of a very dear loved one if someone had started it first.

"Nothing— oh confound you, old man. Nothing." I waved him off, his crossed arms began to slack open again.

"Colonel—" I said. "Let's make this one pack, shall we?" I was feeling quite jovial.

"And what's that lad?" He eyed me through chirps of calming laughter.

"Let us affix ourselves to this one promise— That we shall not resign ourselves to the same fates of our ancestors, no. Let us be some of the first Scotsman to find victory in OUR highlands."

"Yes…." He whispered, allowing me the chance to finish, building anticipation. He was very excited already.

"Let us find this thief, or fairy." I went on.

"Fairy, I think!" He chipped in.

"And let us sort them out— For the Queen." I put out my arm, he clasped it.

"For the Queen, laddy."

We Shook our pact.

"RULE BRITANNIA!"

He shouted. I loved him for it. A whistle and a lurch of the train; we would not be far off from the ancient capital now.

———

Not long after, our train rumbled into Edinburgh. The Colonel had been in excellent spirits since our tiff on highland history and subsequent pact for the Queen. We arrived at the North Bridge Station, as we had made our way North on the line from Berwick. North Bridge Station, more commonly called 'Waverly', sat on the proposed spot of a canal born from the narrowing of some 'noxious lake'. The result being a lovely exit from a stuffy train cart up into the glorious views of Princes Street. Somehow, no matter the time of day, a bagpiper might be heard welcoming travelers into the city; happily, our arrival was none so different. Myself and the Colonel fanned out on the street— happy to stretch our legs and be truly home. Edinburgh for me, is actually home, my favorite place to be. I have always had envies to teach here, live here, revel in her spirit. She is ancient, you can feel it in the air. As if all the gases hovering the city were the breath of Scotland—exhaled in the way a tortured and hard cut peoples would be. Edinburgh *is* Scotland; her castle being the gem. Loaming over Princes' street and the gardens off her slope- she truly exemplified the dream of perpetuity as in pleasured ground. Hello again, old friend- I whispered to the castle. Breathing in the evening air, I was lost in the beauty of a fortunately sunny evening in town.

"AHHHH! AULD REEKY!" The Colonel shouted with hands on hips, tearing me from my dreamy state. "SMELL HER SWEET STINK" He went on. (I wished he wouldn't) "You know, Bertie— They call her that for the way she smells! You can smell her eh? DAMNED GOOD, YES!" I rolled my eyes and sighed heavily, I never thought this rumor was true. He continued to flit about the street however- upsetting women and children and shaking the hands of total strangers.

"HALLO! HALLO THERE! THREE CHEERS FOR SCOTLAND! HIP HIP!" Several men in business attire darted away- too gentlemanly to insult a man in uniform, too aghast to participate. I chased after the man.

"Colonel!" I shouted, my back to the castle and gardens now. "Colonel, please!" We went on like this for several minutes at least.

"Come now, Bertie! Let us walk! My stick please, good man— there she is!" I produced his swagger stick, which he tucked beneath his arm, now smartly moving as if inspecting a battalion of men. He nodded and strolled, judging the fine Scotsmen of Edinburgh— But judging them well. I gave in and merely followed as any good aide might- sure that he knew where he was going. As if a hound, I was certain the man had a nose for fine Scotch, and therefore could find his way on to Fergus' just fine; even IF he didn't remember the address of the place (and he did).

"Ah— yes. Yes. There she is. There she is, Bertie! Quite the castle, isn't she my boy!" He waved and pointed to the towering structure. "You know; I was once locked in her dungeon for THREE days! Why— It's true! Myself and the current Laird of Haltoun! Oh he would HATE to be reminded, he would! GOOD MAN, THAT!" I struggled to keep his pace, as was my usual debacle. I was carrying our things, mind you- and he was in *true* Acorn form! We made our way down Princes, weaving next to the left and around St. Johns Chapel. He moved like a pecking bird- hands behind back. I did my best to enjoy the many street shops and windows we passed, spotting a bookshop I'd have loved to revisit. But this was not to occur, not with the Colonel, no. We never made time for any pursuit I may have enjoyed! Perhaps a bit of tea and a quiet sit? No. Up Lothian Road we went next! Heading towards the Castle and Old Town. Soon it was Kings Stable towards Grassmarket- we climbed and climbed as the street rose ever higher to the castle. I admit I was becoming quite winded; my wound you see!

"Colonel— Heavens, it seems we're taking the long way round. We could have taken the mound straight on to Lawnmarket!" I begged.

"Nonsense, Bertie! And miss the good people of Auld Reeky? No man...nooo!" He kept up the pace, missing the good people of town I thought. At once he stopped and bent over an old woman's street stand.

He inhaled with a great harrumph and complimented the woman on something "Damn good!" —was all I heard.

Finally, we marched on Lawnmarket, the castle ahead of us. St. Giles Cathedral loomed on our left up ahead; what I would have given to have stopped for a moment, even if only to hear the evening homely. Several men of arms ambled about across the street, clad in kilts, they must have been members of the detachment of soldiers who keep the castle. The Colonel shouted and waved- they stared back as if some grown adult like child had stolen a 'Colonel's' uniform to play soldier with. Only after seeing me did they sort of snap a half winded salute in return, eyes all amused. I swear I heard them mutter something about an Acorn once we were decently out of ear shot- but perhaps I imagined it…

"Here it is Bertie! Here it IS!" The Colonel pointed with his stick and extended his stride— he sort of glided towards a close, or court actually. James Court to be precise. "James Court—House number four and twelve!"

"Four Hundred and Twelve. James Court— right." I muttered as we approached the door. A wooden door, ancient like the city it seemed. Crescent top, and a large knocker right in the center. The Colonel knocked and then stood waiting like a child on Christmas— He eyed me with a ridiculous smile, mouth agape, his eyebrows bounced up and down once or twice.

"Oh for heaven's sake, man. Keep yourself together." I said. Honestly, for the life of me, I will never understand the Colonel's adolescent tendencies, though as I write this I admit—they do make me smile. For Christ's sake even his legs seemed to bounce— Like…like a dog perhaps. Yes, I think so. More like a dog waiting for his master than a child on Christmas. In fact? In fact— It's more like this: Like a puppy dog on Christmas morning who is SITTING next to his master (also a child) waiting to open a package that is surely ANOTHER puppy. That is how I would describe the Colonel after having knocked on Fergus Dillwyn's doorway.

The door creaked open. Heaven help me.

CHAPTER 12

In the Company of one 'Fergus Dillwyn'

As you might have noticed- at times, I allow a moment to float by before addressing it. Sometimes in journaling I find it best to advance a length in time before returning to better address how a particular moment might have unfolded. In such a way, the passing of time on page seems to be as violent as it might have been had you experienced it yourself. At least—it seems that way to me. And so—

I sat listening to the Colonel and Fergus banter on like wild chipmunks— my head in my palm, swirling the rock in my whisky-placed by the one bulging eyed bald abomination that is Fergus Dillwyn. I might try and describe the banter, but I would fail. Fits of wheezing. Coughing. The slapping of so many shoulders and knees, bellies and bulges. And the laughing, oh for the gods IN HEAVEN. The laughing. Somewhere between the wild commotion of war in the Afghan—or perhaps the ongoing battles that might be raging against the Boers- and a train derailment. That is the laughter and the banter I am now succumbed to. Which very nearly started the precise moment in which that blasted crescent-topped ancient wooden door creaked open! Could I go BACK in time, I'd have broken both the Colonel's arms and forbade him to knock at all! HOWEVER- I cannot GO BACK in time. Only can I merely allow it to jump lengths on page to better explain my current condition.

And so here we sat! At Fergus' kitchen no less! It seemed to me he had a whole house in which we might have conversed— no! In the kitchen is where I was dragged. And while on the topic let me describe in fine detail the man's living space! Oh for that is a BOOK all unto itself!

Upon seeing the man's confused face beyond the door, one eye bulging as if the other permanently squeezed a monocle, I was pulled through a narrow foyer that was utterly LINED with trinkets and oddities. The man lives in a museum- no. The man lives in a scientific laboratory— no. The man lives in a space that is both a museum AND a laboratory. Foreign plants and species galore in tanks and cages, pots and PANS, Lord help me! Everywhere! It's no wonder I was pushed into the kitchen for a whisky- the man's living quarters are so CHOKED with THINGS! Books yes, which I can admire! But strewn all about in packages and piles. Some of which had empty tea glasses affixed on top! I cannot imagine living in such a space! Oh and the LAUGHTER. It will not CEASE.

"Archie?" The man had said! And then the laughter and the slapping and the clapping and the dragging throughout the house—

I am in Fergus Dillwyn's kitchen. As best as I can tell from perhaps, what may be a window, the sun has nearly set. We've been here almost an hour— I have gotten perhaps two words in, both of which were to deny being a 'valet' and to mutter my full name. Both ignored, of course, of course. The two are going back and forth mentioning things I have never heard of, never seen, or never experienced- mostly because I was most certainly not alive when they occurred, but to them? It is the happiest of reunions and I must say, not a word has been spoken of our actual reason for arrival. Though many times Fergus has said something along the lines of— "And what brings you here, Archie?" before hurling in wildly different directions for some joke or rebuttal to a joke stated by the Colonel.

Fergus Dillwyn has no idea why we are here. The Colonel has had at least THREE whiskys. The sun is going down, and we are no nearer to solving the case of some fairy in the highlands then we would be if we were actually acknowledging the fact that fairies may be real and hunting them because of it!

I digress. And so I sat— head in my palm and listening. Given in to the Colonel as I have done so many times, and will do again. And now this journal is up to speed. We have arrived in the company of one Fergus Dillwyn and we, or shall I say 'I'- are none the better for it!

"And wasn't it SO!" Cheered Fergus to the end of one of the many stories started by the Colonel. "I say, Archie— How damn delightful it is you are here!" Round and round we go. I finish my whisky and pour myself another.

"Fergie, I say old sport. You never looked better!" ROUND AND ROUND. Shall I describe Fergus now? I think it best to. Fergus was NOT a military man. The many times since that I have run into the old sod he has always been in fine suit- The sort with a tail and bow tie. White cummerbund, etc. He is balding and combs his wiry hair to one side- his eye bulges, as I've mentioned, and his belly festoons his belt line. Fergus Dillwyn IS in fact in the grain trade, as he is in many other things, though it would be quite inaccurate to state that he has ANY knowledge of the pursuit. He is both unconcerned and unbothered with being around military men, as some others may be— And in point of fact, is quite content with his place in society as a wild eccentric, born into money. (And quite a large sum at that) No, Fergus Dillwyn was not much on the topic of business, for most of his business was run by "My man at the bank" as he put it, and therefore would be of short use to me in my attempts to solve the Queen's case, placed into the lap of my charge, at any rate!

"Ah- yes! YES!" The Colonel went on as I fizzled and burned beside them. I imagined a thick cloud of smoke emitting from my ears just then- perhaps a grinding sound from my teeth… The only thing keeping me sane was that the sun would indeed set soon; though who could be sure from inside this dungeon- A fact which would keep us from advancing North for the time being anyways. That and the certainty that a train with a sleeper cart- which at this point I shudder to imagine, would most probably NOT be heading North at this late of an hour regardless. No, it seemed I was resigned to this fate for the night. And so it went- and I allowed it! I hardly interjected! To my GREAT credit- I allowed the Colonel his fun…for the time being anyways, as I was indeed- trapped.

"Her name was Eliza- If I recall. And she fancied ME! Oh! Yes, you damned monkey!" I'm not even sure who said it- did it matter? They laughed on into the evening. I sipped on my third whisky, or was it my fourth? What number did that put these two boys at then? I wondered. How long could they go on for until they got too woozy and needed sleep? Even the Colonel needs sleep at some point, correct? I honestly didn't know the answer. I wonder what-

"And it's just business with the Queen we're after again, Fergie. Yes, yes. You know- yessss! All hush, hush of course, of course! Well God save her, I say indeed! Ye—Yes, indeed!" The Colonel. My ears perked up.

"Something about a Fairy stealing grain up North." I interjected, my head rising- eyes widening.

"What's that now Alfred?" Fergus said, his eye bulging, a look of concern. The very look I now attribute to the man entirely. With his one eye, he always seemed concerned. As if ever on guard for something— As if constantly wondering what's going on…no matter! I went on, careful to seize a moment I believed had finally arrived.

"Al— Bertie, actually. It's just the grain trade sir, it suffers up North— The reason we find ourselves, uh, at present…sir." I was careful not to bombard the duo with too much reality- their eyes a slight tint of glossy.

"Yes— Yes of Course!" Fergus replied. Even to me, he seemed quite warm. This is how my mother described men who were at drink. Warm. The man was very warm. Face flushed, silly grin. Innocent, of course. Docile. Totally disarmed. I do appreciate both these baboons for their sincere nature— however, I have a mission to think of!

"In fact, the Colonel here was just telling me of your connection in the grain trade. Weren't you Colonel? He said you may have some knowledge on the shipment disruptions up North? Being that we are in service of the Queen— I wonder…"

"I did— YES!" The Colonel caught up, distracting Fergus for a brief moment. I was quick to move on, my hook and anchor slipping.

"I wonder if you might know anything about it? Have your shipments been delayed of late? Where exactly do they arrive from?" Careful, Albert. Careful now lad.

"Oh yes— well. My man at the bank may have mentioned something of a minor disruption— I, I, I do wonder. What was it you always said about him, Archie?" Fergus blinked and turned towards the Colonel.

"Who's that?" The Colonel said, stumply.

"Why— the, the, the BANK MAN! Of course!"

"Oh— right! Right. Damn decent man, I've always said!"

"Damn decent." Fergie agreed and trailed off. I could explode— though tact now, careful tact.

"He hasn't said anything about shipments from the highlands has he?

Specifically, say— From the town of Uig?" I winced, perhaps I'd gone too far. Fergie seemed very concerned, his brain working on it. I wondered if he knew who I was at all. The Colonel, however, interjected exactly as I'd feared he might.

"Ask him about the Fairies, Bertie my boy!" He said with a smile. I audibly sighed.

"Oh, Fairies!" Fergus shouted, quite on board with that notion.

"No—Colonel I wonder if perhaps that bit might…I just wonder if perhaps we ought to start with the facts! Mr. Dillwyn may be of some sort of help in the business of delayed shipments!" I stammered.

"Nonsense! Old Fergie is a treasure trove on the topic of science!" Science, he said.

"Oh my, yes. Now fairies— that IS interesting. And what about fairies was it then, Archie? I hadn't heard…" He leaned into the Colonel like two old salts would at telling tales of imagined fish caught at great peril and magnitude.

"Well. I say, old boy! It's the fairies that are delaying the shipments of your grain, I think! So say the people! Well…in fact, I think it's just the one Fairy. Wasn't it Bertie? Something about a fairy with- with one eye!" The Colonel stoked the fairy tale idea. I seemed to have lost all chance of decent investigation— the conversation being totally derailed then.

"A one-eyed Fairy, my my. That is something, isn't it?" Fergie stroked his chin. I didn't believe it was. I sighed. Supposing I'd give up again and let the night play out- throw it in so to speak until morning, when I might get the Colonel on a proper train heading North…

"Now—Fairies are quite tricky things." Fergus began, the Colonel seeming to settle in for some great scientific lecture.

"Prone to tricks and mischief, they are. But, at times? Also quite kind and helpful—I say, if only one trade proper company for a moment! Yes— Yes! There are all sorts of fairies— and what sort of fairy would ya be after then, Archie?" He said as if the conversation were completely sane. The Colonel eyed me with concern and puffed out his moustache.

"Well, I'd say. I'm not entirely sure— Just the one-eyed sort I suppose. That's all we know of the bugger isn't it Bertie?" He said, quite seriously.

"Mmhm." I managed.

"And just how many types are there, Ferg old boy?" The Colonel genuinely asked. I could tell old Fergus was quite happy to tell...

"Well— many. Many! You've got Ashrays, you know wee folk who live in water. And ya've got them Brownies. Happy lot them, so they say. Like a warm home to visit, wear little green and brown tunics. Fearful of cats, god knows, those ones!" He wiggled his hands and made squinting faces. "And uhhh- well. Let's see, you've got Pixies and Gnomes and the Fachan. Say- The Fachan appears as a small man, so they say! One of everything! One hand...one leg...Why— And one eye! Loves to play tricks on Shepard types! Perhaps your fairy is one of them! Grain trade...shepherds...One Eye. I say hmm..." He trailed off but the Colonel was hooked.

"I say! The Fachan! That must be our type! Wouldn't you say, Bertie lad? And how will we know one when we see him, Fergie?"

"No— Colonel, I don't think..." But I was cut off.

"Well. The Fachan wear little red hats, I think. I, I, I, I mean, that is if I'm remembering correctly!" The Colonel hummed agreement and egged him on.

"Come now!" I said.

"Yes— yes. In fact! Here, here! Come along to my sitting room. Yes. Actually— I think I have a few things..." Fergie said as he rose and shuffled out of the kitchen, trailing off. The Colonel rose immediately and started to follow— I grabbed his elbow and drug him back into his seat.

"Colonel for goodness' sake!" I whispered. "This is nonsense! Surely you can't believe fairies— I mean for goodness sake, shouldn't we be asking about missing grain and the names of men who ship it who we might question?" I believe, even now, that I was speaking reason. The Colonel didn't take my advice however.

"Nonsense, lad. Let's see what old Fergie has got to say! My word— haven't I always said that what the people believe has got to be true? This may well be a source of—" I cut him off. I shot back something about fairy tales. He whispered a retort asking me who I was in service of. I denied him that. We argued on. We whispered on and on in hushed and aggressive tones. I pulled at his uniform, he poked at my shoulder. We tussled like small children.

"Coming, Archie?" Fergie's head popped back into the kitchen, we froze mid scramble.

"Course old boy!" The Colonel said and moved to join him immediately. I sighed. Ground my teeth. Waved my hands around in a completely silent fit of wild rage- and followed.

Fergie chatted on ahead, his voice muffled in the other room. I finally caught up with the two standing in what might have been a library were it not for the many tanks of reptile-like creatures and boards of preserved beetles and butterflies. More sighing.

"Here it is— Just here!" He picked up a glass case. Inside were carefully preserved bits of what looked like trash to me. Perhaps a twig. A leaf or two, it seemed. And a very old penny-farthing.

"Now, Fairies can be quite the little mischiefs— as I've said. One. Must. Be. CAREFUL!" he said as he pried open the glass case, "NOT. To offend. Here we are, see here. Now— I have in my collection several pieces I think you'll find very handy to your concerns. Fairies— as the legends go, are quite private. Seldom do they cross over from the 'OtherWorld' and when they do, often they are offended- this leads to their mischief I'm afraid, they are private little buggers after all! See, when fairies are blamed for a crop failure, or perhaps missing crops in your cases. It is USUALLY because one was offended in some way or another…" He trailed off and presented the penny farthing.

"Of course…" The Colonel half whispered, fascinated by the old coin. I rolled my eyes at him.

"It's just an old farthing." I said.

"Not quite, I'm afraid Alfred," he stated and went on. "This penny represents an offense to a fairy— My Uncle Duncan took it from a fairy garden…"

"Ah, yes, UNCLE Duncan. That's where I got the name, Bertie!" The Colonel shouted. I looked at him angrily, quite annoyed by now.

"What's that, Archie? Oh yes, it's my UNCLE Duncan. Yes, no— Yes, I am a Campbell on my mother's side. Yes— Yes. I do apologize for that nasty murder business!" They both laughed as the Colonel interjected with comments on our clan history debate from earlier.

"THE COIN PLEASE." I shouted and brought them back.

"YES! The Coin! Yah, yah— you see! It was taken from a fairy garden. This offended the wee folk and is why my Uncle Duncan was cursed— Damn drunk he was. Never could hold a job! Not after he pocketed this coin, see? There are rules, you know, with the wee folk- and to violate them is the problem. Yes, yes. I wonder if these people up North, what did you say? Uig? Where in the Queen's name is Uig? The highlands? Well. I say. I wonder if they might have offended the wee folk!" Of course Fergus spoke quite matter-of-factly. And the Colonel hung on every word.

"I say— Fergus. That is some Coin. And how is it you don't become cursed yourself for having it?" The Colonel asked.

"Well, that's part of the rules, see! With the fairy folk!" He said, perplexed almost.

"Right. And what are these rules then." I hated to ask.

"Well first things first— they hate to be called fairies. Fair Folk they say is best. And second, you never take nothing from a fairies' garden! Big mistake. Uncle Duncan learned that. And if ya do! Best have a witch wash it in milk…or was it brandy? No matter, see, my coin was made safe…" He nodded as if convincing me more than himself. "Right, anyways— Thirdly, they hate seeing ya in green. Their colour, so they say." He went on as if reciting the Magna Carta.

"Do they?" The Colonel said, amazed.

"And worst of all Archie—" Fergus went on, hinting at crescendo. "Ya, never! NEVER! Lie to a fairy! They know! And they'll hate ya for it! Curse ya even! Really— In fact. Really best just to avoid them all together, I'm afraid old boy." He finished and made a brushing motion with his hands, as if dusting off some dirt.

"Well. There you have it, Bertie." The Acorn announced. I pursed my lips and looked at him sideways.

"Fascinating little buggers, fairies. Fair folk, that is!" He said with a wink. "Love games— Oh they LOVE games! All sorts— cricket, darts, memory games. Can't ever say no to a game! Fascinating bit of history and science, I say." I wondered if he was finished, the Colonel clasped his back.

"Well, old boy. You have done your Queen a great service, I say. Perhaps we may yet use these rules to our benefit! We do thank you, don't we Bertie!" They laughed.

"Was that all you were after then, Alfred?" He said to me with a bulging eyed look of great concern. I sighed. And took the Colonel's hint.

"Yes, sir. I thank you, indeed. Now, I'm sorry to say that I am quite tired, Mr. Dillwyn. I might inquire about lodging sir?" I hoped at least I might excuse myself, having endured such things as I had.

"Nonsense, Bertie! Hardly late evening! I for one thought we might take a stroll to see the judge! What do you say, Fergie, old boy!" The Colonel clasped us both around the shoulders and pushed us towards the door. Fergie shot up a finger and asked—

"I do hope you mean the Jolly Judge?" They both laughed and laughed and somehow, against my great wishes, my feet moved towards the door.

CHAPTER 13

The Jolly Judge

"Really Colonel— Must we go out? I feel like we haven't hardly stopped since we've arrived in Britain! That was, what? Four days ago?" The three of us, quite the troupe, marched outside of Fergus' door and onto the street. The evening was just settling in— Honestly I felt as if I had emerged from a long winter's rest in some sort of den...or perhaps cave...I certainly wasn't prepared to be entertained by another of the Colonel's many socialites here in Edinburgh. This judge? I can only imagine what he might be like surveying my current group, as is. One Acorn smartly dressed in uniform. A mad scientist sort dressed like an Opera Conductor— And me. Again, as I have done before, I wonder if perhaps I am just as mad as my company and too blind to see it. A slight chill goes up my spin, I do not attribute it to the darkness brought on by evening.

The street lamps had come on— Several Hansoms slowly drug their way up the cobbled street. It was a delightful scene, and a warm night as well. At least there was that. Suddenly I recalled the day of the week— Friday I believe. Perhaps it isn't so bad to be out after all, I thought. A gentleman tipped his hat at me as I strolled, slightly behind the Colonel and the Ferg. (My new name for him) I tipped my own back, a renewed sense of joy suddenly inside me. I did feel much lighter- I hadn't realized how stifling old Fergs house had been on my spirit. Yes. Yes, indeed! Edinburgh! What a lovely little town to be outside on a warm Friday evening! Why? I may even enjoy this Judge, fellow. A man of the law, he must be something for decent conversation! Having achieved such a noble position, himself...

"I say, Colonel!" I started with an actual chipper. "And where does this Judge friend of yours live? Does he sit here in the Capital?" The two old timers giggled like little girls.

"Oh he sits in the Capital, indeed young Bertie!" the Colonel said over his shoulder.

"Doesn't do much BUT sit!" laughed Fergie. I frowned.

"And what is his name?" I asked.

"His name? Oh-hoh! Why, the Jolly Judge of course!" Fergus said with a wink. They stopped suddenly at the entrance to a small close— I never learned its name. At the end of this close sat a tiny building built into the row, sitting inside a small square of sorts. A creaky wooden sign swayed in the breeze, illuminated by a lamp. It read: 'The Jolly Judge. Pub and Justness'. I couldn't say a thing. The two men stood and stared, a tear forming in the corners of their eyes.

"Look at her, Archie!"

"Ah, yes! The Judge!"

"Oh for God's sake! Honestly! A pub! Another pub! Here I thought we were meant to meet someone official! Pity me for daring to imagine such a thing! And you two! WEEPING! For a PUB!" The Colonel shot me a brief and unpleasant look before turning back to his image of pure beauty.

"Oh— Move aside you old dramatics! I'm going in for a tall pint, maybe two! Stay and gawk all you want!"

I pushed past the two rather violently— suddenly damned determined to have a good time myself this night. They might have the stamina for constant banter and whiskys, fine! And good on them to boot, says I! But this night I shall not reserve myself to the station of valet! Should these two baboons care to frolic about at one of their old main-stays, then I shall do the same!

I pushed through the door. Several steps further inside the place a small bar ran the length of the dodgy and dimly lit room, on and towards the left. Going further and to the right was a darker portion of the bar reserved for a small amount of sitting; this space seemed to bulge on and away from the bar itself making the entirety of the 'Jolly Judge' out to be the rough shape of a chubby letter "L". One patron sat at the bar, clad in cap, smoking and reading a Newspaper. In the back- a large man in a knit cap sat on a stool tossing darts against the wall. Not what I would call the Ritz— but I will NOT let that bother me this night, thought I!

"Barman!" I shouted. "A Pint of your darkest beer, please!" I moved towards the tender— he did as I asked. I leaned and sipped on my beer as my company ambled through the doorway in fits of closed laughter. My face must have been one of deep annoyance, perhaps even anger— for when I asked the man reading his paper what the news was he scoffed and ruffled his pages before turning away. No matter, says I! No matter!

"These two with, yoos?" The barman asked. "I should say— They are not!" I answered, feeling quite devilish for a moment, as if for a brief shooting passage of time I, for the first and only time, viewed the Colonel as one might who had never met the man. As I did so long ago onboard the *Hornblower*...

"Ah-hah! Bertie! Saved us a spot on the log I see, Capital!" The Colonel slapped my hand and ruined my story. The barman gave me a concerned look and hurried away to fill the orders thrust at him from the bulging face of Fergus Dillwyn. Two of his finest whiskys. You might have guessed.

"I won't allow it, Colonel. Not tonight. I won't." I said flatly.

"Allow what, my boy?" He said almost in jest. I poked my finger in his direction.

"I will not allow you to carry on and tear down this bar, myself picking up the pieces in your wake! Not tonight! You are ON your own! In fact—In fact!" I was half whispering and jabbing with my finger. The Colonel giggled and waved his hand at me offering many different counter arguments to my points. Fergus meanwhile, conversed with the paper man on the business of some scandal in town.

"Consider me OFF duty, tonight! I— I mean it! I mean it!" He grabbed my finger, I jerked it free. He poked my chest! I poked his! He laughed! I fumed!

"Come— Come now, Bertie! Won't you, COME NOW LAD!" He laughed and laughed, quite stuck in the whisky already. I stammered on; he wrapped his arm around my shoulder and tousled my hair. I had had QUITE ENOUGH, thank you very much! I pushed him off and raised my hands- Fergus now laughing and trying to poke at me as well. CHILDREN! I SAY, CHILDREN!

"Nope— No. Definitely NOT!" I patted my hair down and raised a finger again. "You two BUFFOONS have your laughs! And I— I say, I! Will be over in THAT corner! Minding my own business! THANK YOU VERY MUCH!" I pointed towards the darker side of the judge. "Barman! You may refresh my pint— OVER THERE!" I pointed again and almost stormed away, that itching feeling a man gets after rolling around in the grass, covering my body. Several more people pushed into the Judge, the Colonel whooped and promised to "pop over for a visit". I hoped he wouldn't.

I arrived in my dark corner of the Jolly Judge and leaned on one of the high top tables there in the corner, absolutely fuming. Tapping my fingers, I watched as the Colonel welcomed the many new faces arriving in the judge. Huzzahs. Hurrahs. God save the Queens. Et cetera. With every new guest the place grew louder, the walls, I'm sorry to say— did not grow with the company and the place became quite small. I thought very seriously about slipping away to pen Abigail a letter.

"Dear, sweet, charming Abigail. I do NOT regret saying that I am leaving the service of one A.R. Korn POST HASTE. —And do readily suggest you run as far and as fast from him as you possibly can..."

No. I won't do that. He is my charge after all, and after all— he is most sincere. The Devil. I do love him, for all his burden and brashness. I will say however the idea of slipping out to write Abigail did sound charming just then, something neater about the Colonel and I having arrived in Edinburgh. Perhaps compare her to the beauty of the town. Was it too forward to suggest something so bold? I hadn't decided when I was interrupted yet again.

"Will ya's sit fuming all day or will ya toss some darts there, laddy?"

I snapped my head towards the figure in the corner. He was sitting on a high top stool launching the occasional metal dart towards the wall. I hadn't paid him much mind— with his massive beard and person, he set off his own shadow, almost melting into the very structure of the Jolly Judge. I'd not have noticed him whatsoever had it not been for the occasional *twap* and *chunk* of his dart flying and finding home.

"I'm sorry?" I half shouted as the place was getting quite rowdy. A quick glance towards the bar and I noticed the Colonel waving a finger high above the crowd leading them in a chorus of some thing or another. "I don't play." I continued with a shake of my head, hoping he'd let it go. I say, it's not that I'm against being social, it's just that I'm not very sociable! Being around the Colonel takes all the social skills I have. I find myself so exhausted at the end of the day, when anyone strange wants to parlay I almost always quietly search for a way to end it! He didn't allow me that, this large and shadowy man.

"Don't play like ya's won't? Or don't play like ya's don't know how?" I believe I observed some sticks in his beard, possibly some moss... doesn't writing a letter sound lovely right now? I could almost certainly slip out...

"WELL, BOY." He was shouting. The angry giant was shouting.

"I— I. Well! Both, I'm afraid. At any rate—" He cut me off.

"I'll teach ya, come on! The name's Bongo! Bongo Ryan!" His accent pronounced the 'go' portion of his name the way one might describe the sound a stick makes when beat against a stone wall. Which is most certainly the sound his giant palms made when they slapped both sides of my shoulders, squeezed and lifted me into position next to his table.

"Oh my— Yes! Yes! Here we are! Thank you!" I coughed and landed with a soft thud. "Thank you. I'm Albert, thanks. *Captain* McGregor, I should say. Thanks for that." I nervously said and patted his arm. "It's just that I'm to keep an eye on my Colonel over there— Yes. Yes, the one waving drinks around and singing. That's him, yes. I'm to keep him out of...trouble, you see. So. Not to offend my good man— my very large, and good man. Yes. But I just can't be distracted, see—"

"Nonsense, laddy, the old Acorn will drink here all night. Might as well learn tah toss some darts while ya's wait, no?"

"You know the Colonel?" I sighed and shook my head.

"Everyone in Edinburgh knows the Acorn, boy!" He laughed with his great big belly. It wound up like the engine of a tramp steamer. He nearly knocked me over when he slapped my shoulder again. I stood rubbing it.

"Yes. Well. Sure, then you know. I suppose. Sure— So, darts. Yes. Cracking." I said and snapped my fingers, swaying a bit. "You just sort of, give 'em a heave I suppose, then?" I asked, not at all convinced that there was any sort of skill or merit in the trappings of a pub game.

"Bah!" He shouted. "If yer so sure, let's try it your way then! Give 'em a heave! See that ring there, ya that's the one— The one on the wall in front of yer face, yes. First to three in the bullseye— Hang on. Ya do know what a bullseye is dontcha? Ohhh- course. Course. Sandhurt Academy, Eyy?

84

Archery, suuuure! Sure! The Champion of your year, you say? Myyy, my. How fascinating!" We bantered back and forth. I didn't care for his tone but I will say I admired his ease at making new acquaintances.

"Yes, Archery. And I don't want to cause concern, Bongo, but I was quite top in my class there! A game of patience, that is. One I am well suited for! Darts, I assume, is no different!" I was getting warm with my pint but I didn't want him to smash me like a bug when my old dead eye habits caught up with me in a game of darts in Edinburgh. Most soldiers played— though the rules and the board seemed to change depending on where one found themselves. I never cared for the pursuit. I so infrequently found myself among the drinking population, you see, but I was confident my archery skill would translate. And why not play with the giant! As he himself had pointed out- we might be there for some time.

"Say? That's alright. Well in that case since you've admitted your skill— why. Let's not make a bet? A gentleman's game of course... Say? Loser buys the next round?" It seemed harmless. His toothy grin, charming enough.

"Sure. I'll have another pint." I played my confidence, the only card I had. He smirked and sort of raised both arms towards the board, inviting me to begin.

I squared up, wobbled a bit and grabbed my dart. Pinched it between my fore-finger and thumb and squeezed one eye shut. I tried to imagine my hand as the bowstring I was used to- the dart, of course being the arrow. When I was confident I had my target, all that was left was strength of pull. I eased back my hand, careful to judge the distance to target. No wind factor inside— I was ready. I tossed. Confident I was about to check off one bullseye, I opened both eyes again and saw my dart pathetically low on the board. Bongo roared with laughter slapping his belly, winding itself up again.

"THE CHAMPION ARCHER OF SANDHURST!" He bellowed and slapped my shoulder. Careful to wound my pride, but also careful it seemed, not over step. A happy giant, he. Hm.

"I say. Beginners error!" I squeezed my eye shut again and tossed. Miss. I repeated the charade once more and found myself out of darts, out of luck, and all out of sorts. Not one bullseye for the champion archer of Sandhurst. My military college days were far behind it seemed. Woe to me!

Bongo Ryan laughed and laughed however and it was contagious. I found myself laughing in short bits along with him.

"Well!" I said. "Let's see if you can do any better!" I poked at his large gut and mused to myself at the ease of fraternity inside a pub. It seemed my drink had gone empty, and I will admit- old stuffy McGregor was beginning to have a decent time. (Decent, I say.)

"Stand back, wee man!" He said and stood. The earth seemed to shake and I made a great deal of commotion so as to throw him off. He pushed me aside, grabbed three darts in rapid motion and seemed to toss them one after the next until— He had it.

Thunk.

Thunk.

Thunk.

Three Bullseyes. Without the slightest bit of effort. My mouth hung open like a cow gate. "How on earth did you do that?" I stammered shortly. He laughed and creaked back onto his stool gripping his knees as he did. "Get me another drink, wee man- and I'll tell yah's all I know." He smiled and laughed and I followed his orders.

I made my way to the bar with our empty vessels. By now the place was a complete commotion, I had to push my way through the throng. Somewhere between halfway and the door I bumped into the Colonel doing his best impression of Shakespeare. Quoting some ghastly war poem, it seemed.

"Sound! Sound the Clarion! Fill the Fife! ONE CROWDED HOUR OF GLORIOUS LIFE— Ah! Bertie, there's a lad! Grab a spot for me!" He cheered as I shrugged past. "Don't stop on my behalf, you old nut!" The crowd around him erupted in laughter and he bellowed on something about 'an age without name' never skipping a beat. Bless him. I was having a good time. Fergus I found next leaning onto the bar, squinting and sweating. He dabbed at his head with a neckerchief and debated a man thoroughly on something I'm sure was less than scientific. His companion, I think, was asleep. In either case, my two old charges were safe it seemed. I got another round and headed back to the dart board, surprised with myself at how excitable I was. Very out of character; would make a damn decent letter for a lovely girl—

"Two pints her' on!" The barman shouted, bringing my mind back. I tramped through the chaos and found Bongo Ryan where I'd left him. I pushed his pint towards him, he nodded.

"How did you do that?" I asked and slumped onto a bar stool myself.

"Not a problem when ya's know the secret!" He alluded to his skill as being something mystic. I imagine he thought this would wound— it did. But I can laugh about it. I may have been a champion Archer at Sandhurst, but I hadn't thought of that in years, and never truly was one for stiff competition. I don't mind losing at darts in an Edinburgh pub to who must surely be the darts master.

"Well! What's the secret then, man! Out with it!" I shouted over the noise. Turning my head, I saw the Colonel riding the crowd like a man on safari, directing the pulsating room as if at war. I shook my head and turned back to Bongo.

"I've been around the board for some time laddy— served with the Black Watch as a wee man, I did! When they was still the 42nd 'course. We'd play in billet or what have you. You know, you know. Sometimes a board would even appear out in bivouac! I can recall one instance in particular in which we had the bloody Earl of Halifax chucking darts!" He laughed, and I enjoyed to allow his story to unfold. He took a long pull on his drink and continued. "Isle tell ya tho! I figured it oot quick how tah win! It's all about the EYES, laddy!" He squinted one shut and jabbed at me with a giant thumb.

"The eyes?" I said.

"You did it! Yah did! That's why I let ya's go first! What's the first thing yah did with that dart in yer hand there!" He shouted over the roar the Colonel incited at the bar. I'd lost sight of him, but I knew he was most certainly the cause. I considered the man's question.

"Well. I pinched it properly I think, and then I shut one eye—"

"YOU SHUT ONE EYE, YAH DID!" He pointed with a giant thumb again.

"Why— hah. Why yes, of course! To better my aim!" He began shaking his head.

"Tha most commons of mistakes, young master McGregor..." He touched his finger to his nose. "People think it gives them better aim— BAH! The board is too close! Seven paces, on! Yah need the proper depth perception! And THA' IS ONLY DONE WITH BOTH EYES WIDE

OPEN!" He laughed and laughed. I joined in, though in truth, was hoping his answer would be in fact, more mystical. A tiny let down.

"It can't be that simple." I egged him on, though I was genuinely interested.

"Try it! Try it, laddy!" He shoved three more darts my way and I got up to participate.

I grabbed a dart and almost instinctively squeezed one eye shut. He bopped me on the back of the head with a deep voiced 'bah!'. I shook him off, opened both eyes and began my wind up.

"AH! Bertie! There you are!" The Colonel shot into my ear. "Playing at sport! Capital! And how are you, Bongo! INDEED!" Just like the Colonel to interrupt right as I was getting serious.

"Not now, Colonel." I said as I steadied my throwing arm. "I'm just showing old Bongo here the proper way 'round darts." I do have a layer of competition, after all. Bongo laughed, but I didn't look, I was too focused. I let my dart fly, both eyes wide open this time— and I watched her sail with a delicate 'Plunk' into the dead center of the board. Bullseye.

"I'll be damned." I whispered.

"RULEEEEE BRITANNIA!" The Colonel shouted.

"THAT'S IT, WEE MAN! JUS LIKE ALD BONGO TAUT YA!"

Just like old Bongo taught me. I tossed a few more darts. Paid up with the barman, shook the largest hand in Scotland, collected my two old charges and found myself sitting in Fergus Dillwyn's house again. I thought to pen Abigail. Which I did.

I left out any sign of frustration and told her we were on our way North first thing in the morning. Told her we both missed her, being careful to bring up the Colonel just then- and that we were alright. Closer to solving our mystery up North? I was confident in my letter, but in truth, I wondered what we would find up there. I could not imagine.

CHAPTER 14

North of the Five Sisters

I stood with the Colonel that next morning in Fergus' sitting room, if you might call it that. The Colonel was fresh from his morning routine and wore one of Fergus' old robes. He had a towel around his neck and he pointed and slapped at a map between the both of us.

"Nonsense, nonsense!" He shouted, turning down my idea that we leave early and head directly North towards Skye. "We'll take the route past Sterling! North then, around Loch Lomond- It's the only way Bertie! The ferry to the Isle leaves from Kylerhea, only!" He slapped at the maps provided to us from old Fergus.

"And just how do you know that! Surely there is a crossing onto the Isle of Skye, here! At Kyle of Lochalsh! Judging from that symbol for ferry crossing— JUST THERE! I'd say that there is!" I slapped a bit further North of him on the map.

"I know because I know, dear boy! Grand-mama always said— the best and ONLY way onto the Isle of Skye is via the ferry at Kylerhea!" He was insistent.

"Oh— sure! Sure! Let's just make travel plans based on the word of your grandmother, shall we! I imagine the ferry at Kylerhea will be much like your train from Wigan! And I don't fancy sitting in the rain with you anymore! Thank you very much!" He waved his hands at me and shook his head as if to offer a rebuttal, but it never came— Fergus popped his head round the corner of the kitchen just then.

"Eggy then, Archie?" He asked, squeezing his eye shut.

"Good man, YES!" He returned and strolled off towards his friend. I merely shook my head and began rolling up the maps. Smiling as I did, I found myself in a much better mood this morning to the mishaps and creatures that make up Fergus Dillwyn's place of residence. In fact, I found both the old fools quite charming indeed, as I truly was in much better moods. The sun was coming in from the cramped windows, which I could fully make out now were, in fact, windows, and Fergus had made tea and poached eggs. So. What could a man really be upset with? Regardless of which route we did end up taking North, the Colonel was set on going today, and so that was a start. I worried about his route to Kylerhea, not that it wouldn't work— just that Kylerhea was much more off the beaten path then Kyle of Lochalsh seemed to be. I could already see myself on a one horse ferry to the Isle of Skye, leaving Kylerhea in the rain, with a man babbling on about his grand-mama and the 'joyous Scottish weather!' I shuddered a tad.

However we manage it, from his path or mine, the one truth was just that- there was only one way onto the Isle of Skye and that was by ferry. Train first to…Sterling I suppose, as the Colonel demands. And then a train to perhaps Shiel Bridge? The nearest train station- and then I imagine some sort of horse drawn cart towards one of the Kyles and the crossing overs to Skye. My my. It will be an uncomfortable sojourn; of that I am certain.

"Bertie! Your Eggs!" Shouted the Colonel. I sighed and went to join them.

———— ◦•◦ ————

I never care to leave dear old Edinburgh. The last time I did my mother had made the trip South with me to see me off before my post in India began. There was no talk of war then, no worries other than that of distance and time. That isn't to say my mother wasn't in a fit, she was; but it didn't carry the weight of an ominous fear of no return. I went to war once, as this journal has told— and now that I am once again leaving the Capital, though for different reasons and directions, still I can't help but wonder how it would have felt to leave here, knowing I was bound for combat and perhaps great danger. The sadness my mother showed when I left in peace makes me worry of how painful it would have been to leave in war. That sadness, the idea of it, makes me quite melancholy. As our train steamed away from the platform Fergus waved a handkerchief in grand fashion; trotting along in his chubby style. I think of my mother. I think of that day I actually *was* leaving for war, so many miles from my home- and I am then damn grateful for the Acorn sitting beside me, now waving his own handkerchief at Fergus, dabbing his eyes between flutters. His companionship on that journey back to sea? Back aboard *The Hornblower?* Well. My mother would have been comforted to know I was in good company on my way to war. Though it may have seemed annoying at the time, I do believe the Colonel provided a familiar sense of distraction— And then? I never really endured that sensation of going to war at all, did I? No.

I watch the Colonel and old Fergie's pitiful goodbye— like a mother and child's might be before war. And I am happy to be in such a way. It's funny the way family defines itself throughout life; It's funny who we find ourselves bound to. But I ramble— I turned to the man, and patted his leg.

"There, there, old Boy. We will see Fergus again soon. I'm sure of it." I may roll my eyes— but it is the least I owe to this man now; I know that to be true.

The Colonel merely blew his nose in great trumpeting fashion. I asked him if he'd like to find the bar car; if he cared for a nip of the King's good scotch. He muttered that he would, and so off we went to find it.

Our train journey North was as to be expected, the Colonel made friends throughout the cars. Some shifted in their seats as he regaled them one of his many stories, but all seemed chipper and polite at the very least. Trains this far North are a different sort- filled with many more common people than highbrow types, which suits me fine, as they are from whom I stem. And since a Briton is a Briton to the old man, he fits in just the same. Yes, we made our way just fine winding through the Northern Kingdoms of my people. The Colonel craned his neck to see Stirling Castle, pointing and shouting that it was "plainly visible" when it was anything but. I agreed it was however, and complimented the Empire right along with him. He chatted. I listened. He plotted. I hummed. He pointed out this and that. The five sisters and Loch Lomond. He sang songs and whistled tunes about each of them. And to be certain, it wasn't so bad a journey at all.

Before long a conductor type announced our soon to be arrival into

Shiel Bridge, a small little village along the long line North. I'm not certain how much further it goes, really— anything this far North and West is strange to me. But here we arrived, some of the very few left onboard to disembark. I carried our few belongings as the Colonel strutted around, stick under elbow, smart in his uniform, puffing his moustache at this and that.

"Quite!" He puffed at a sign post before moving along down the platform.

It was a lovely late morning in Shiel Bridge; to our great fortune the sun shined and craned its way into the sky. Some birds chirped, the grass wet with either a late burning dew or fresh coat of rain. Ah- the smell of the highlands. Crisp! Dirt roads which wind off into the hills covered in patches of heath and highland grass.

"Lovely— the heath. Isn't it Colonel?" I asked and squinted into the sun.

"Heather, actually!" He put it bluntly.

"No— Heath I think. Note the needle like petals and…"

"Nonsense! Heather, my boy! We are in the highlands!"

"That doesn't— look here, heather has much flatter leaves and covers like a— A sort of moss really!" He waved his hand at me and kept up his stride. Just like a Scotsman to argue over highland foliage before waving off the advisory.

"Now then, my boy!" He started at me. "There is this matter of getting to the ferry crossing at Kylerhea! Shall we go into town for a cab?" He pointed his stick into the air and marched as if on parade. 'Town' is hardly what I'd say, more of a village, and now I did worry about our choice to cross here. Suddenly I was not convinced at all that we'd find a way to Kylerhea crossing.

"If we can find something…" I muttered fearfully to myself. The Colonel heard.

"What's that now, boy?" He said.

"Nothing, Colonel. I just wonder how much trouble we'll have finding a way to get to Kylerea from town!"

"Nonsense! Some good steward of the empire is BOUND to be happening out that way! Come now! Let's have a look!"

We searched the town in vain. Several people with horridly thick brogues offered little help, stating we would be best to walk. Finally, we stumbled upon a Shepard type whose accent I could better understand. Though the Colonel had been fascinated by every tongue we happened across, his fascination did little to aid our cause.

"Kail-Rhea? Nahhh. Tha's cross tha channel tha iz!" He stated when I asked him the best way to get there.

"Kylerhea? Across the channel? Yes, we are trying to get across the channel. What I mean is how might we best *get* to the crossing point at Kylerhea?" I attempted to commune as the Colonel mused about our new friend's highland ways.

"Nah yoo's won Glenelg." He said matter-of-factly. I didn't understand. He, clearly, didn't understand.

"Glen…nelg?" I questioned trying not to offend.

"Too, 'ight. Yoo won Glenelg naht Kail-Rhea. Canny get tah Kail-Rhea less ya's cross at GLEN-NELG!" I think I understood, some minor language barrier it seemed.

"Ahh! Yes! Okay, right! Sorry. Glenelg is the mainland side, yes! Sure! We are trying to get to Glenelg so that we might cross to Kylerhea! Yes." I was quite happy with my advancements with the locals. The Colonel seemed impressed as well, he bounced his eyebrows at me and the gentleman, smiling so.

"Roight." The local said and crossed his arms.

"Right. Well then. And the best way to get to Glenelg is?" I asked.

"Wolk." He said and nodded.

We argued, you can be sure of that. I promised the Colonel that it was his fault for choosing this place to cross over onto the Isle of Skye. I had mentioned to him and reconfirmed the idea several times, that we could have trained even one stop further to attempt a crossing at Kyle of Lochalsh. That crossing would have been much closer to the train platform! That crossing wouldn't have demanded we find a way to travel 8 miles down a country lane in search of a ferry heading out of Glenelg! WHERE EVER THAT IS! That crossing! Wouldn't have demanded we WALK— when a proper way to travel could not have been secured!

"But— Heavens no! We had to follow the words of your dear sweet

Grand-mama! Who insisted the only way to get to Skye was via the ferry at Kylerhea! Which! By the way! Is inaccurate from the start! Being that Kylerhea is ON THE BLOODY SKYE SIDE TO BEGIN WITH!" I shouted over the whipping wind.

Because, yes. It had started raining. Nearly the moment we departed our kind local, sure, the Scottish weather had moved in a gale. We had pulled rain slickers out and began our trudge. The Colonel held the brim of his hat and shouted back so I could hear him over the deluge.

"Do. Not. Belittle the name of dear sweet Grand-mama, Bertie! Not now!" he stammered, his moustache and large nose poking out from under his hood and hat. Like a giant walrus.

"You look like a WALRUS!" I shouted.

"A WHAT?" He shouted back.

"A WALL-RUS!" I shouted again. I wanted him to hear my insult.

"A BLOODY, WHAT?" He said through the sideways rain.

"A. WALL. RUS. A WALRUS!" I made tusk motions with my hands.

"WHAT IN GOD'S NAME IS A WALRUS!" He said back. Curse him.

I cupped my mouth and prepared to shout a vivid description of a Walrus to the Colonel, but as I did the rain died down and the wind cut off, as if someone had merely shut the window. Suddenly the sun shone again, birds chirped and a mistiness rose off the ground. We both turned and twisted, staring up at the sky straining to believe our eyes.

"Ah-hah!" I shouted.

"HAH-HAH!" The Colonel shouted too, he raised a triumphant fist. We stopped. Stared at each other straight faced- and promptly burst into laughing.

"Well, there you have it! There you have it, old boy!" The Colonel said, hunched over his knee caps. "Hardly a drop now! And surely only a few more miles left to go! Why! Why, I'd say, might even be a decent stroll in the sun!" He laughed and I did as well. The idea of a quiet walk to the coast not seeming so bad, just then.

"Yes. Well." I said. "Several miles left to go at least. Still. It is early yet. Can you manage it, old man?" I said, sorry about the Walrus comment by now.

"CAN I HANDLE IT. I SAY, WOT! AND WHAT IS IT WE ARE

94

IN SERVICE OF, BERTIE?" I rolled my eyes and went through the motions.

"We are in Service to the Queen, and with him the Empire of Britannia and all its holdings."

"RIGHT THEN AND AS SUCH."

"We are duty bound to see to its successes, by pain of death, or mockery in the streets…" I said as he mouthed along with me, bouncing a finger like a conductor.

"Right— mockery in the *County Lanes,* I think this time." He winked. The devil.

"Do try and keep up." I puffed with a smile and began to trod on. He pumped his hands, stepped back once or twice before bouncing on again forward with a smile.

"ON RAGGGGLAN ROOoooAAD! On an Autumn DAYYYYY!" The Colonel sang and stomped. He bounced and dipped his shoulders, swung his stick a few times and damn near danced his way along. This continued for several miles, I laughed when I could and sang when I knew a line or two. And he bounced and he jigged and he stepped— all the way to the channel.

"Ah-hah!" He shouted as we crested a hill and began our descent towards the end of the winding road and the water before it.

"And see here!" He shouted. "The ferryman's hutch! DAMNED DELIGHTFUL!" He nearly ran down the way towards it. I called after him to slow down, as any good valet might.

CHAPTER 15

A Crossroads at Kylerhea

When I caught up with the Colonel he was already knocking on the hutch door; a tiny little fisherman's type shack. Here we had arrived, at the very edge of the mainland, Britain; staring across to our challenge. The crossing here at Kylerhea couldn't have been more than a quarter mile from mainland to isle, but the water was deep brown and ominous. Almost as if the Earth had become molten and fluid, as most Scottish water is- thick with the runoff of peat bog and deep brown clay. The result being water almost as thick as the accent. Looming across the channel were the rolling hills of the Isle of Skye. Since we had arrived towards sunset the eeriness of the entire situation was not lost on me. Suddenly the weight of our task seemed very real, as if the journey here might not have been honest. As if the entire time we were merely on charade until the Colonel buckled and shouted something about me having finally called his bluff; that we do not, in fact, serve the Queen- and therefore don't have to solve a potentially dangerous crime occurring on some outlandish Isle in the far North.

But.

Here we were. And as the sun sets, I cannot help but shudder, feeling very much alone as I did just then. A glint of blue caught my eye and I turned to see what it was. Nothing it seemed. Just my nerves. The Colonel continued to knock.

"BLAST!" He shouted. "Seems no one is home, Bertie!" His voice was chipper, of course. He never worried about anything.

"Colonel-" I began. "Colonel. I have to admit— I find myself. Well. See, here— it's just that…" He slapped my back as if I were in a coughing fit.

"Out with it, lad!" He smiled. Annoyance began to stifle any nerves I may have had.

"It's just that it's getting late, old man! And now we have no ferry operator…I mean. Is it just me? Or Does it seem like we're at the end of the world here! Again we have no plan— AT ALL." My tone was collected; I will say that. I was not blaming him; it was merely the truth! We hadn't really gotten past the ferry crossing in our plans, had we? And now that we're here? Well. Of course this *is* how the Colonel does business, that much is plainly clear by now! But with the very real thought of having to confront grain thieves in short order— I was on edge to say the least!

"Of course we have a plan, Bertie!" He said as if it were obvious.

"Do we now?" I asked as if I had missed the part where we decided how we would tackle a Queen sized problem.

"Sure, sureeee! We simply must find a way to cross onto the Isle! And then we merely find out the end of this business of fairies!" I let out a few exasperated chuckles- was it really that simple?

"Is it really that simple, Colonel?"

"And why not?" He said with his hands on his hips, confirming to me, for the first time I think, exactly how he had done it in the past. At this point I had limited ideas on the 'Duties at home' the Colonel had tackled before. Some snippets of stories from his days with Hector Stuart. Now that I think on it- I'm sure he had had a hand in that Ghoul from Brighton old Barnsworth had mentioned earlier- But until that very moment I believe I still thought some sort of military protocol would show its face. That we might receive clear orders once we arrived in the Highlands, that another letter from the Queen's man might have arrived. But, no. That simply wasn't going to be the way of things— And why? Well— Why not, says he!

"Why not." I shrugged and looked about. "Why not…" I murmured to myself. Another blue glint caught the corner of my eye— I chalked it up to the setting sun, it was the time of day when seeing isn't such an easy thing to do.

"Yes. eee-yes." The Colonel said as he moved around the Ferryman's Hutch. My mind raced to accept the gravity of my current situation. I thought of myself, sitting in a cozy flat, sipping some tea and reading a book. Perhaps even soaking my feet in a hot tub…

"OHHHHH-HOOOOOO!"

The noise startled me. The Colonel as well.

"Great, Scott! What in heaven was that!" He stammered and looked about.

"Oh. HOOOOOoooOOO!" Again it came— like the high pitched belt of some mystical being. My spine chilled.

"What in heaven's name is that— Colonel?" I looked around for the old baboon but had lost sight of him. I moved towards the hutch— "Colonel?" I said again.

"OHH! HOOOoooOO!" It came once more.

"Colonel!" My voice began to raise as I jogged around the corner—

"HALLOOOOO! THERE!" I found the Colonel shouting and waving his hat. "I SAY! HALLO THERE!" I squinted my eyes to see past the man. A small raft was lofting its way from the Isle. It made a diagonal path; on board was one very large looking person pushing the thing with a very long pole.

"I say, Bertie! Look there! The boat! What luck! And such a BEAUTY, EY WOT! Reminds a man of the *Hornblower* almost, eh?" My nerves seemed to cool. These Highlands have a certain mystic to them, one finds themselves almost nervous in their presence the first time— But they cooled at the sight. It did seem a fine little craft.

"Oh-HOOOO!" The boatman hailed again, and even I began to wave.

───────

We sat watching the slow crawl of the ferry as it made its way towards us and towards land. The Colonel narrated the entire thing; Marveled on the man's ability to fight the current. Wondered how long he'd been a ferryman. Claimed he himself would have enjoyed to 'try the lifestyle,' as he put it. Still on edge a bit myself, I murmured agreement and awaited our man.

"Colonel." I said as the craft neared the shoreline. "Let's talk strategy for a moment, shall we?"

"What's that, now? Strategy? Again?" He said, hardly taking his eyes from the excitement at sea.

"Perhaps let's not let onto our business, straight off. Get an idea for this fellow first, we are—shall we say—on the front lines now…" I played my game towards the Colonel's weakness, careful to incite the old soldier inside him.

"E-yes. Yes. Quite right, old boy. Best to maintain…" He squinted his eyes and looked around. "…secrecy." Good. I had him.

"Good. Perhaps even leave out the bit on fairies? Since you've said it yourself, what the people believe is the truth? Why not maintain the idea that we have not heard the rumor of fairies at all for the moment, only that we are here to check on the business of grain in the North for the war effort?"

"Leave out the fairies— Check." He agreed.

"This way we might get some truth from the people without them knowing, see?" I tried to steer the man away from the fairy idea altogether, seeing how it went with old Fergus— My true aim being to keep the Colonel on track more than anything.

"Excellent idea, Bertie! Excellent. Yes. Best to let the people tell US the problem, eh?" He jabbed me with an elbow.

"Yes, my thoughts exactly." The boat scraped onto shore. "Hallo there! Hallo!" The Colonel shouted and approached, one hand up in greeting.

But the boatman did not respond. He leaned over his pole and eyed us with the most intensely weathered face I have yet seen. Wrinkled deeply at the ears and the eyes from what I can only assume were years of surf lightly splashing his face; leaving it tanned and tight. His beard was gray and dry from the same storied treatment— and his eyes a pale blue. He looked like a highland Pict of old— I imagined blue paint across his face, and we? The Romans I'm afraid…

The air remained as icy and as mystical as it had been before— have I properly explained? I don't think I have; I was nervous. The highlands are a strange and historic place- that much I know. How else does the idea of Fairies exist? How else does the idea make its way into the mind of one Barnaby Barnsworth, who himself had most certainly never been here, yet believes it possible still? And how else do I, of all people, standing on the shore facing off with some wild boatman, believe myself- if only for a moment, that yes— Perhaps fairies do exist in the highlands. It is for the very wildness of the lands here; the way it makes you feel. Should you find yourself here one day you may know it too— if not let me tell you again, the air is heavy with ancient ideas. This boatman being the wildest myself and the Colonel had yet found.

"Bertie—" The Colonel whispered. "Parlay with the man." I shot the man what I'm sure was a surprised look.

"What's your business, friend." He said to me in a deep, winded voice.

"We," I started and looked again at the Colonel, "we're on the Queen's business." I said, hoping it best not to lie but trying to give away little. Silently praying that by invoking the Queen's name we may avoid issue but wondering if that could be true. He tilted his head, but said nothing, continuing to lean on his giant oar. The Colonel looked cross at me for bringing up the Queen—but I thought it best, and in hindsight, still do.

"We aim to cross. We have business in grain." I said. He tilted his head the other way and answered—

"Not much for grain here laddy—try again." He didn't shout, he didn't even raise his voice, and yet it boomed. I eyed the Colonel in alarm, he shrugged—the toad.

"We— we were told grain efforts for the Army have stifled. Gone missing so to speak. We aim to find out why, and perhaps if we can, offer some help." The boatman laughed.

"The crofters have suffered— yes, I'll give ya that, lad. But it weren't for the Army, least I know. They've been cleared out, them crofters have— you lot and your bloody Clearances. Those yet remaining haven't got much to go on— rumor says bands of thieves have taken to stealing what's left..."

"And what sorts of thieves!" The Colonel interjected and I nearly screamed.

"Don't ask. If ya don't want to know."

"Fairies." The acorn said bluntly.

"Colonel—" I tried to whisper.

"Wot the locals say, so it is." The boatman said plainly. I attempted to bring the topic back around—

"I'm sorry, sir." I tried to restart. "If I may ask— What did you mean by crofters? And the bit on clearances? What did you mean? Who's being cleared out? And— well. Why?" He again tilted his head, this time towards me with a look of annoyance.

"Crofters, boy. Farmers. Keep to the land, raising small crop and yes— perhaps even grain. Used to be kelp— that's shot to shite. Now it's just about enough to keep 'em going, as well as their Yowe. But they've been cleared out— most of 'em. Some sent to the new world, others tah Van Diemans land. Why's I ask, so it is. Queensmen come round here— it's usually to clear out the folk or collect boys for the Army. And since you've got Army skins on, again I'll ask. What's your business, friend? Speak plainly and I'll decide who's taking a trip today and who's not."

I turned to the Colonel and gave him the same worried look he returned to me. None of this made any sense.

"It doesn't make any sense." I accidently said aloud. "We— We were told grain shipments were being disrupted...nothing about folk being cleared out?" I cut myself off and nearly whispered. "...the letter said." But I hadn't read the letter, had I?

The Colonel heard me, however, and added proudly-

"We have this letter, see here chap! From the Queen. We aim to help— And if you can promise sensitivity, I'll share it with you now in return for a trip on your boat!" He brought the letter from his pocket book and held it into the air. The boatman seemed to consider a moment and then-

"Inside." Was all that he said.

⚊⚬⚊

Inside the ferryman's shack was what one might imagine when reading about the lives of fishermen. I read Dickens' *David Copperfield* as a young man and believe that Mr. Peggoty's home was described similarly— I wondered if Dickens had been here. Peggoty's house was made out of an actual boat if I remember correctly. Cozy, in a crisp salty way, with a looking glass nailed up where the stern used to be, lined in oyster shells or course, and a bed with just enough room to squeeze into. This place was not far off— an entire life at sea was on display and the same smell of low tide you get on the docks in Liverpool existed here too. But— almost more honestly, if I could describe it. We sat at a weathered old table in a dingy excuse for a kitchen. Two salt washed windows overlooked the water with the Isle behind— it was beautiful and I thought of my mother. She'd have loved to have sat here and watched the sun go down. The boatman rummaged around making tea— and I thought of Abigail doing the same at the Swan.

The Colonel, I'll say, was all business. A side of the man I had only caught brief glimpses of. It thrilled me deep below my layers of worry. The letter sat, folded on the table, between the two of us. How badly I wished we could talk privately before our interview began; there was simply no space for that here. The boatman finished his work and sat the kettle between us, sitting with a great force of cracking and creaking from his chair.

"Now." He began. We said nothing. "Before we see this letter— from the Queen, says you. Let me say my piece. Reason why I'm so particular on who crosses and who don't these days." The sun dipped lower, nearly extinguished now. I wondered if we might cross at night, if that were possible. I wondered if we would find somewhere to sleep on the Isle if we did— I wondered if sleep would be available at all. I thought of Fishy-Bob curling up in my lap as I picked at some holes in an old armchair, reading Dickens and chatting with Abigail.

"Mah names Thompkin MacLeod. What do ya know about Clan History?"

"A fair bit." The Colonel said with a nod. "This man, Albert— is a MacGregor. And myself being a MacDonald on my mother's side, have grown up hearing the stories."

"Fine— Fine." He said. "Clan MacLeod have been on the Isle of Skye for generations. Before the disbanding of the Clans they held dominion alongside the Donald's. When I was born on this Isle we numbered well above 22 thousand. Today, our population has fallen to just about 16. We have always- ALWAYS." He pounded the table with a clenched fist. "Served the Queen. And the Kings before 'er! We have sent many sons to service under our Banner— And they have always returned victorious." He squeezed one eye shut. "Do ya know what they call our banner wee man?" He directed the question at me— I took minor offense to his insult.

Myself and the Colonel again eyed one another and shook our heads.

"Tis the Fairy banner." The Colonel's eyes went as wide as saucers, but to his credit his mouth stayed shut. I had to bite my tongue, for just a moment, to keep from laughing. The old codfish.

"Those who fight under it are protected. So the history goes. And so those who have gone, have always come home victorious in the name of the Crown. Well— says I. This would be a great and valuable resource to a Queen would it not? Our soldiers?" We both agreed with short nods- not daring to interrupt. He went on.

"So why does this Isle get smaller? Well, says I! They've cleared us all out, haven't they! One, two—ten at a time! At first we were told overpopulation had made the land infertile. Fine— fine. We accepted that! 'Assisted passages to the new world' they called em— cleared out the land for the lords. And sure enough, the yield increased. But what else! The landlord's coffers, that's what! But— fine, fine say's I. Makes sense, don' it? Tis a small island after all and the new world has promise, so they say. Fine. This was done all before my time, see? But I heard, we all heard— and so when it started again, we wondered the same. See when they came round to clear up the land again, it was the crofters who got the boot. Those cleared from the fields were sent to crofting villages, expected to make a living fishing and farming kelp. Once the kelp trade collapsed? Shite. There weren't enough to go round! Overcrowded again, they said. Not enough food to keep you here— Well we do alright, don't we? No— noooo. See you can't fool Thompkin MacLeod. I may not be a lofty clan laird but I knows when I smell something rotten. The young they sent off— America? Van Diemans— hell. OUT. The old, they sent to the poorhouses. Forced onboard the good ship *Midlothian* on punishment of imprisonment. And who made money off those who were left? Cause it weren't those lords being sent off Isle! Families gathered up- some as quick as a night's pass! Why— yah's wake up one morning and find your dah and mam put on a boat! And who's left! Who's left then! Small families, that's what! God knows they have had hard enough time keeping the food stock! Men and women workin' always! Kids runnin' amuck across the land! Our families, our homes! Upended! And who is to blame!" He eyed us threateningly but we gave no answer. I don't think he expected us to, we all knew the answer.

"The clans had the right to stay, that's clan law, that is! *Dùthchas* is the Gaelic word, have yah heard that? Clan Lairds were BOUND to uphold that! But your Queen, this Empire- convinced the lot of lords they were commercial landlords first, and far before any Clan leader! Our whole way of life, a way passed down for ages! Shot to shite. God's sake." He paused and rubbed his hands over his forehead, swearing as he did. "Aye. Those left here are making ah living scratchin' the fleas from the land. My father kept the boat— as do I, and so we stay. But the few crofters left— the true men of Skye? They make little enough to survive, and be sure that they will. But for what? Hardly their Isle at all if they can be sent off for nothing but lies, is it? The land yields enough, sure, but for the lords. Not much left over for those who remained after the clearances. The villages get more crowded, while the hills be chock full of lamb. Those lamb bear wool for the lords! And were left wondering how long it'll be till they ship more off because of it all. So again, I ask yea— What business do yah have here? Cos if yah come to report for more land clearance, yah won't get across on that boat there, I can promise yah that!" He folded his arms and sat back in his creaky chair, the snapping and cracking of wood being the only sound.

The Colonel bounced his eyebrows once, maybe twice before letting out a sigh. "We serve the Queen, MacLeod— that much we have said. Shall I say more; you must first promise this one thing." Again I say, the man was all business. I let him go, just as curious about what might come next as I'm sure MacLeod was.

MacLeod merely raised his eyebrows quick in return with a shrug.

"What we do, MacLeod— is of a deeply sensitive nature. You must understand this. What I say now must not be uttered to any one other person. Your passion for your home is as well placed as ours is for the empire— which, I say old boy, is why you ought to listen. Do I have your word? As a Scotsman? Not to let on to anyone as to why we are here?"

"My word as a Scot— is as good as gold." He spat on the floor.

"Well said." The Colonel spit too, before looking at me.

"Am, I? Right." I spit.

"Now then." The Colonel began, quite satisfied it seemed. "What we do, Thom, is this. We serve in the name of the Queen— without ever stating her name, see? Things that the Queen ought not to do, or ought not to be SEEN doing, is what we accomplish. We serve the Crown— in the shadows, if you will. So as not to insight backlash from bad political upheaval, you see?" MacLeod nodded but looked confused; the Colonel went on. "In this way, the Queen may accomplish her true ambitions without upsetting the delicate balance that is our Empire— And God save it. In the case of your depleting Isle—Well. It seems the Queen is of the same opinion as you."

I was learning as much as our man MacLeod was. I hung on every word— as if it were my first day on the job and I was hearing what my duties would be. Christ. How did I ever end up in the service of this nut? Why don't I ask more quest— because they don't get answered! There. I answered myself. The Colonel went on.

"It seems we are here to help keep it, I say!" The Colonel finished with a flair.

"You know what that sounds like tah me?" MacLeod said and crossed his arms. "Sounds like a bunch of horse SHITE!" He spit again. "Some foolishness to trick a wee isle man into getting you across. You'll size up the land, report to your Queen and clear off more of my kin!" I shrugged, crossed my own arms and awaited the Colonel's answer the same.

"Ah— and you'd be smart to assume such!" The Colonel said. "But see here, our proof! This letter—" he tapped on the folded paper between us. "Is written by my contact to the crown— a damn decent chap from Sussex, written by him but signed by the Queen Herself— And God save her! It confirms our mission here! As well as who sent us! And again I'll say, old boy— I believe it will align with your interests quite well, indeed." He raised both hands as if to show innocence—my mouth hung agape; I had never met this man before. This man, the Colonel, in seriousness. He was different. Powerful, even. I shook my head, the man full of tricks. Made me wonder what he could accomplish if he were always so sincere...

"Go on, then," the boatman said, "read it."

"Right. Now." The Colonel pulled out reading glasses, where on Earth he got them, I cannot imagine. I never knew the man to need them before. God help me. He unfolded the letter and made a show of the Queen's hand. "I shall skip to the relevant portions, I think."

"Read it all." MacLeod said plainly.

"Right. Very well," the Colonel replied. "Let's see he-ah! It reads... *'Archie: Trouble up North in the Highlands. Kelp trade gone sour- thieves rumored to be stealing from the locals. Trouble for the war effort if clan pool ruined. Can't say more. Locals will dispel details. Check at the tin'*—ah, the tin is a pub in Liverpool," the Colonel added looking over the brim of his glasses.

"Go on," he growled.

"Right. Where was I? Ah— *'Make haste. Trust the people's opinion as always. Discretion key, avoid land owners. Preserve the Isle for the war effort. Report as always. Signed*—' Well signed by the Queen, as you saw." He looked over his glasses again like an old professor might have when debating an assigned grade to an annoyed student. "So. There you have it. Preserve the Isle!" he said and waved a fist into the air smiling, as if that pathetic string of words would explain anything to anyone.

"Is this a joke? What am I supposed to take from that?" the boatman said angrily. I joined his sentiments, fuming suddenly. All of this? For that?!

"How on Earth did you get anything about grain from that letter!" I yelled.

"What? Is Kelp not a grain?" The Colonel said, confused.

"What? Why would you—" I began to shout before being cut off by MacLeod.

"Why in the hell should I believe you're here on a mission for the Queen, based on THAT BLOODY LETTER! It doesn't make any sense!" he shouted. We both began questioning the Colonel, both trying to outshout the other. The boatman said something about 'lies, bloody lies.' I added quips about the brevity of the thing.

"Youse can both turn right back round! I won't have yah on my boat!" MacLeod said.

"I say, to right old boy!" I nudged the boatman to agree— he looked wildly at me as if he were considering squeezing my head off.

"What in tha 'ell?" He shouted at me and raised a fist. I braced for the blow— the Colonel came to my aid.

"Now— Now! Now wait just a moment!" The Colonel stammered.

"It makes no SENSE!" The boatman said, and I agreed.

"Now, see here!" The Colonel tried to defend himself. The small kitchen became overwhelmed with noise.

"You've made it all up! Give me that letter— Give it here!" MacLeod yelled.

"I MOST CERTAINLY. WILL. NOT." The Colonel puffed out his moustache and half turned from the man to shield his paper.

"Let me see the bloody signature!" The boatman raged on, grabbing at the Colonel.

"I too would fancy a look…" I said and quietly poked one finger into the air as the two tussled around the table.

"YOU WILL DAMAGE THE NOTE!" the Colonel yelled. "THE

QUEEN'S DECENCY!" he went on. The boatman roared again. The table screeched against the floor—chairs creaked in agony. Tea cups cluttered against one another. The Colonel and the wild boatman half wrestled over the letter. I let them go for a moment. Truly— I was on MacLeod's side, and would have helped him wrestle the acorn had I thought he needed my help. He didn't.

"Would yah— Give me that! YOWOCH!" The Colonel bit the boatman's hand, I swear to you, he did. This caused the giant seaman to hurl backwards into the table, fully upsetting my tea glass and spilling its contents onto my lap.

"Oh— BOTHER! Hang— Hang on!" I said and rose. The two carried on like children, ignoring me completely. Suddenly I was more annoyed than I was eager to see the Colonel squirm. My decency caught up with me and I attempted to quell the squall.

"Hang on— HANG ON. HANG BLOODY WELL ON." I said and the room calmed. "It seems—" I said and patted my hair down. "It seems we need to take a step back." The men hushed and seemed to agree, tangled up like weed rats, they eyed me with differing looks. The Colonel looked like a gentleman who had just been harangued by a mob— the boatman? Looked like the mob doing the haranguing.

"Now MacLeod, see here. I am the Colonel's aide, and I admit I am just as confused as you at present. I promise you this— my part in this lunacy has been quite a bit more to endure than yours has at present. But if you'll let me question the Colonel for a moment I may very well be able to explain. Would you just—" he raised his hands as if to say 'Go on.'

"Thank you. Heavens. Now— Colonel. That letter is abysmally short, and explains very little. Actually? It explains nothing at all— especially to anyone who hasn't been with us every step of this boondoggle! I'm wondering myself how in heaven's name we ended up in this man's kitchen! I can't begin to imagine what he thinks! Show some couth, for heaven's sake!" He squinted his eyes at me. MacLeod only gazed in- amazement? I think? I couldn't guess what he was making of all this. "I realize of course that this is my fault, I should have read the letter myself in Liverpool. Too late for that at any rate— So. Let's take a step back shall we? Recap the letter? Trace out our steps a bit with Mr. MacLeod? This way we may all be satisfied with the truth- or not. Now. See here, what—" I rubbed my temples, my head started to pound just then. "What was that bit about the clan pool? Something about it being ruined again?" I asked him with eyes squeezed shut.

The men untangled themselves, the Colonel snatching the letter from MacLeod's hand with an angry look. He crossed his arms and slumped into his chair— he smoothed out the wrinkled note and looked up at me.

"Not sure, Bertie. It says just that. *'Trouble for the war effort if clan pool ruined'* there's nothing else about it." He seemed upset. I ignored it. MacLeod *was* upset- and since I was certain he could hurl the both of us out the window and into the sea— I was most concerned with his happiness just then.

"I wonder..." I whispered before turning to MacLeod. "Mr. MacLeod, you said the men of Skye have always served the Queen under this, this— This, Fairy banner— Correct?" He agreed with a short nod of the head. "And you said they are always victorious?"

"Damn right." He looked cross-eyed at the Colonel. "Their banner keeps them safe in battle!" he said and spit again. The Colonel, I say, spit again too. I rolled my eyes and continued, on to something I felt.

"Well that's just it then, isn't it!" I said. The Colonel's eyes flit with excitement.

"What's that now, Bertie?" he asked.

"It seems we *are* here to protect the men of Skye after all— or rather the man pool of Skye that is! The letter says kelp trade, did it not? Which the Colonel interpreted to mean grain, the fool." He tried to pipe up but I didn't allow him— I plowed on. "Hence my confusion, sure! But why I said we were here for the grain at first! But didn't it also say something about thieves stealing from the locals!" Both men sort of shrugged their shoulders, becoming strange allies against my deep thought. "Why, that's it then! We are here to stop the thievery! But not because the grain effort is bound for the Queen's soldiers—but that the men of Skye are bound TO BE Queen's soldiers!" They looked confused. But I went on, a total epiphany of the brain occurring. "Doesn't it say— *Avoid landlords*? The Queen can't be seen to incite bad blood with the nobles, but she can't afford to lose the men who fight under the— the uh? What's it called? The Fairy Banner, isn't it?" I said and pushed my hand through my hair. "No it all makes sense now, doesn't it?" I said as my pulse dimmed and the excitement melted away. I was sweating. My mind's grip on the idea slipping away.

"Explain it again." The boatman said.

"Okay, okay. Right." I laid my hands out on the table. "I understand your confusion, Mr. MacLeod but I believe it's just this simple. See we have been putting it together ourselves as we've made our way here— total secrecy as the Colonel said, basing our next move on the Colonel's initial weak interpretation of the letter combined with snippets of rumors we've heard from locals." The Colonel again tried to interject, I again plowed on. "But, now that I've heard the letter word for word myself, I believe our mission is this: To stop the thievery occurring on your Isle so that the lords have no grounds to clear off the locals. This way, the Isle of Skye is preserved, and the nobles are not upset. Men from Skye will continue to serve in the Queen's Army, the land won't be cleared of the locals and the lords will be none the wiser. See? Everyone wins- The Queen included." I sighed and added a weak— "Yes." Mostly confirming to myself why on earth I was actually here.

Both the Colonel and the boatman looked cross at me. The Colonel's lip curled as he attempted to follow my logic— MacLeod growled and moved his hands around.

"You're telling me? Based on all that? That this Queen wants to help the people here, STAY here?"

"Yes— Yes I think so. Seems she is a decent woman after all, doesn't it?" I said and winced, not sure if anyone noticed.

"Then why doesn't she just outright order it!" MacLeod demanded.

"Well," I said, and flipped my hand as if to sort of agree with the man. "You heard the Colonel. The Queen can't appear to take sides, can she?" The tension unwound just a bit. I pushed my hand through my hair once more.

"Too right!" The Colonel shouted. The boatman frowned.

"So, you're saying, the two of you— Were sent here, BY THE QUEEN, to stop the thievery occurring to the locals? And because of that? They will be able to stay on their Isle?"

"Yes. Yes, I think that pretty much sums up our business here, doesn't it? There won't be grounds for land clearances if the locals here have enough food to stay— and they will. If the thievery is stopped."

"No more clearances?" he asked and curled up an eyebrow.

"No more clearances." I said and hoped.

MacLeod turned his head and cursed. He seemed to mull it over for a moment before saying with a sigh. "Then yah will need ferrying to the Isle now wont yah?"

"I say, so we shall, old boy!" The Colonel said happily. The boatman grunted and rose from his chair—he seemed much more like an old man to me as he did. As if suddenly bent from the burden of his people.

"They say it's a Fairy, you know? Stealing from the locals," he added quietly and went to pour us more tea.

"Yes." I said quietly. "I'm afraid we have heard that. Perhaps that's an issue for another day, I think." I added. He sighed.

"Too late to cross tonight— We go in the morning. And lads?" We looked up. "If yer lying, I'll fly the Fairy Banner right up yer arses meself. Now- How bout a drink?"

The Colonel cheered in excitement and immediately the tension in the room dissipated. We chatted for another hour or so by candle light. The Colonel bombarded the man with questions regarding sea life. He did his best to answer them all, bless the man. I thought of the people of Skye. Of their wanting to stay. The idea of clearances, foreign to me and upsetting. But I will add, the idea that the Queen was against it as well did make things better. I thought of Abigail again— and promised myself I'd pen her a letter before bed in the Boatman's Shack; promised myself I'd do my best to help stop the thievery, that this little corner of our Empire might continue to exist— It is a mystical and ancient land; but it is still Great Britain.

And God save it.

CHAPTER 16

The Isle of Skye

I woke the next morning early and found my way down the narrow set of stairs to the kitchen again. Myself and the Colonel had shacked up on the third floor— which I wouldn't have guessed existed from the look of the place outside, but there you have it. The stairway lifted out of the kitchen, turned a few times, brought you to the boatman's room and then finally to the cramped loft I shared with the Colonel. Needless to say, I was happy to awake with the sun. The morning was crisp and cool; I didn't need to be outside to know it. The way the wind blew at the visible grass on both the Isle and on the mainland made a man shiver in a delightful way, staring at it over the steam from his cup of morning tea. I had left the Colonel fast asleep, being one of the first times in my career that I had actually seen him doing so. He slept with his mouth open, I discovered; his moustache pulling and pushing in the wind he made— I laughed over my tea in these delicate moments of quiet. A pang of nerves still existed in my guts, but I did my best to suppress them. I had penned a letter for Abigail last night as the Colonel chit chatted his way into slumber, and had just thought of a proper ending when my silence was disturbed.

"Be a bit of a rough cross today, I'd say." The boatman grumbled from behind.

"Dear me." I started. "I beg your pardon Mr. MacLeod; I didn't realize you were awake."

"Just MacLeod, Laddy. No need to be so formal." He rummaged behind me.

111

"How do you know?" I asked about the crossing with a nod, turning back to the window.

"See all them whitecaps? The waves pushing there? Means a strong wind's heading in from the North— pushing the water there. The closer they are, the harder she's pumping— We'd be best to start as soon as your man's awake. Does he sleep long usually?" I had to laugh.

"Not usually, no. Ah Mr. MacLeod— MacLeod, I mean. Can I ask you?" He looked up. "These clearances you spoke of last night— I just can't seem to get my head around them."

"Nor I, boy. Like I says, people accepted them at first— made sense. But now that the land is plenty open? It just don't stand to reason. Our villages are full and crowded, but why? Cause they made em that way when the fields were cleared! Now the isle is wide open and the people starve in the towns. All while rumors fly saying they'll use that as an excuse to ship more off. They've sent away the old now, true. But soon, we fear it'll be the hard working youngsters— Aye. It just seems like the taking over of an Ancient Home from the people who live there, don't it? My Ancient home— that is. All's for more land ownership and money tah the landlords. Doesn't make sense at all." He continued working in the Kitchen. "You boys like your eggs?" He asked bluntly.

"The Colonel will be pleased, yes." I laughed a bit. "It's just that I wonder how the people are faring- by the sounds of it, I imagine the blood is a bit...delicate, at the moment." I tried to be delicate myself.

"Delicate would be an understatement. These days the locals won't take too kindly to anyone in uniform they don't know— too much mistrust. And how could yah blame 'em? You boys will have a rough go at it, I'm afraid. They're scared, true. And leery of outsiders. Kids are growin' up lacking a proper home. They rove the hills wild and abandoned. Parents forced to work the day, payin' them no mind. It hurts the old folk left, and scares the rest of us solid. So if you'll be doing this, then yah've got to be smart about it. Keep low, see? Don't let on to your business here. I've got some clothes that'll fit more or less, that's a start anyways. I canny get ya all the ways to Uig, so youse'll be on your own fer most it— but I've got a cart cross the way there that'll take yah as far as the town of Portree. We can find yahs some lodging for the night and a way to Uig from there..." He continued to scrape around the small kitchen, a sense of sadness hanging behind his tough exterior.

"Why do you help us?" The question overwhelmed me. He stopped his work and looked up, but not at me.

"Skye is me home. Like my dah before me's and his before him. I want the people to stay. I don't want it to change. Thing is?" He looked me in the eyes. "I believe yahs." He nodded. I did the same. He went on. "That man of yours, the Colonel you call him. Well. Damn if he don't seem sincere. Crazy? But sincere. Figure— if it's true you want to help? Can't hurt, can it? I'll not be convinced you're here for the Queen— but that don't seem to matter does it? Long as yoo's are telling the truth about helping, don't matter much to MacLeod who sent yahs." He went back to his work.

"For what it's worth MacLeod— I'm a highland man myself. My mother raised me in Inverness. I can't say for certain where the Colonel is from but I can speak to his sincerity. For everything he is— the man is certainly loyal. I do believe he will do whatever he can to preserve this empire- even the smallest bit of it." He laughed.

"The smallest bit— too right. Your man is many things— But. I like him. And you. How the hell is it you ended up here? A bloody Colonel and a Captain? I can't for the life of me say. But I won't mind it, says I."

"Well. To be honest your guess is as good as mine—" I laughed a bit as well. "I do believe we are here for the Queen's interest, as far-fetched as that may seem. The Colonel? Well. He saved my life in the Afghan, and then my career by taking me as his aide. Since then? Well. It's been an odd journey to say the least."

"It's good enough for MacLeod if yah can promise me one thing. A Highlander to a Highlander." He said.

"Anything," I said.

"Don't balls it up. Find the thief— end it. Don't give them landlords more reason to send us off."

"I promise we will do our best. I wonder if you won't do something for me as well?" He nodded and asked what it was. "Can you post a letter for me?" He laughed.

"You two are a wonder, that's for certain. Post a letter, sure. Cross me heart as a highlander, if you help my Isle, I'll post your letter." We laughed and agreed on our pacts. He went on.

"Eggs, first. Clothes second. Then we'll see about getting across that gut, aye? Go and wake your man."

I did what I was told.

———◦◦◦———

We finished our eggs and a few more glasses of tea before setting off. MacLeod was right, the wind was pumping. She blew hard against me as I leaned on the railing of his little boat. The sea splashed against the tiny ferry and threw mist into your eyes, making them water. MacLeod pushed and pulled on his stick behind the tiny sail mid craft. The Colonel stood like a figure head on the bow, a complete laugh in the clothes outfitted to him by the boatman. One leg perched on the railing himself, he looked like the English version of one George Washington crossing the Delaware. He squinted into the surf, nose and moustache protruding. He was surely the spitting image of Queen and Country.

"You look like John the Baptist!" I shouted over the surf.

"Not now, Bertie!" He scoffed back and continued his hard stare into the sea.

"I have some beetle bugs here in my pocket if you're hungry, John!" I laughed and shouted. He merely shot me a glare before continuing to ignore me. I couldn't help myself. I had been giving the Colonel a hard time on his choice of outfit since he donned it. MacLeod had presented several options- he had gone with the long leather boots, fishermen's chaps and a sheepskin jacket over a long sleeved sweater. He had chosen to keep his military cap, however— something he was quite stubborn on. I convinced MacLeod it could be worked into our story and so he was allowed to keep it— to his great pleasure. I had modestly chosen a blue striped shirt and black knit fisherman's cap. I thought it would match our ruse— That we were fishers who had landed on Skye for a few days and thought it best to enjoy the Isle before heading back to sea.

"Won't be long now, lads!" MacLeod Shouted, forcing the Colonel to turn back a moment before returning to his ever important task of staring fast ahead. I had to laugh to myself. The man completely believes in his cause— the right man for the job, indeed. It's no wonder to me, just then, that he is continually called for 'duties at home'. What Queen wouldn't continually use the force that an acorn can bring against nature! I certainly would…

"Get ready to scrape!" MacLeod shouted again. The Colonel braced— as did I, and we arrived with a soft thud onto the Isle of Skye.

"LAND HOOOooOO!" The Colonel shouted— too late, I was sure, with a visible roll of the eyes from MacLeod. The Colonel leapt from the boat and splashed into the water before trudging the several small steps to dry land. I carefully exited as to not wet my boots and turned to catch the rope MacLeod heaved at me. Here I was, living the sea life. We together pulled the ferry onto shore a-ways before the boatman seemed confident she would hold. The Colonel strutted around the Isle huffing at this and at that. As myself and MacLeod worked I heard him call to a seabird— 'Damn good work there, lad!'. I shook my head as the bird flew off.

"Now then." The boatman began. "Welcome to Skye." The Colonel hurrahed him. I smiled and thanked the man.

"AHHHH!" The Colonel said with a stretch as if we had just crossed the length of the Atlantic. (We hadn't come close of course, we weren't at sea more than 25 minutes, even WITH the hard wind) "DAMN GOOD!" He went on. "A MAN CAN ALMOST SENSE THE FAIR FOLK ABOUT! WOULDN'T YOU SAY, BERTIE?" I wouldn't have, I'd wished he would get off the idea of fairies.

"You'll be best to stay sharp— the locals here keep the fairies well in mind, so they do. Don't know if I believe much myself— but you do feel the mystery don't yah?" MacLeod said to the Colonel's deep, deep fascination. Somewhere in my depths I shuddered to understand his meaning.

"And how will we know to see one, MacLeod?" He stated.

"Ah— well. Shite. Some folk say they look like little peoples, they do. Some people say if a blue glint catches your eye, well then yah've seen a fairy. All hogwash if yah ask me." He grunted and finished heaving a pack onto land. I shivered a bit. Blue glints— bah! Just fairy tales for small children is all, says I! The Colonel, I knew, felt very differently. Heaven help me.

"We'll walk the way up the path there. Down the next draw is my home— we can fetch the horse and cart there. It'll be a few hours ride to Portree, I imagine. Won't get there until near dark." All very good I thought. Finally, a decent plan, and a man to help see it through.

"Capital! Capital!" The Colonel shouted and began his hike up the path— sheepskin jacket wild in the Highland breeze.

We made a good pace considering myself and MacLeod were loaded down with several bags of his. The Colonel marched on ahead— bless him. We crested the hill and took in the view, it seemed the entire Isle was visible. Like one large raised table, sitting over the ocean, cliffs for its legs. Down the hill sat a lovely little cottage that I'd have loved to have gone inside of and stayed for the rest of my life. Pity that we had work to do. We arrived, unloaded and sat for a moment while MacLeod rummaged inside the house.

"Right. That's it then. First things first, MacGregor? The letter." He put out his hand and I stuffed my letter to Abigail inside.

"She'll make it to post— or my names not MacLeod." He put the thing inside his jacket.

"A letter— To who!" The Colonel said wildly. I'd had hoped my exchange would have been done outside the ear of the Colonel- that was not to be the case.

"It's...Just. Abigail, of course!" The Colonel smiled from ear to ear, the devil. "Just to keep her informed, you old Baboon!"

"Suuuure! Sure! Best to let her know we've arrived, lord knows. Myself and Hector were SO prompt with letters in OUR day!" He ribbed and laughed, I ignored him. MacLeod busied himself with the horse cart, ignoring us both.

"Ready then, MacLeod?" I said and walked away from the sniveling old man. He giggled and followed after me.

"Ready, on." He said and climbed onto the driver's seat. The Colonel and I clambered into the back on top of a pile of hay and straw. I began to itch immediately; the Colonel began to laugh and toss bits of hay in my direction. I frowned at him from my uncomfortable position.

"Portree, first. On we go— Here lad!" The horse bumbled forward and the cart creaked on behind it. At least we were making progress I thought. We continued on for some time mostly in silence until I couldn't stand the hay any longer. I climbed my way into the driver's seat and sat next to MacLeod. The Colonel wriggled his way as close as he could get- he sat leaning in the hay as if on parade. The day was warm, the sun shined and a few clouds dotted the blue sky. The wind chilled a bit- but in a refreshing sort of way. I imagine the Colonel might have even sweat a bit in his chosen outfit. I laughed to myself again. As I sat next to the wild boatman I will admit— I felt very ancient. As if I had gone backwards in time; I cannot overstate the feeling one gets on this Isle. Her rolling green hills, bits of browns and yellows. The dark hills beyond rising and leveling themselves into mountains, and the sun— no matter the time of day, always seeming to hang on an angle. As if high noon would never come; that at any point throughout it was always near dusk on the Isle. I decided this was the true course of mystery, that the idea of fairies only continued to exist because of the way the day made one feel here. Happy at that, my shoulders loosened and I cracked on a bit with my companions.

"See there— that mountain there!" MacLeod said as I snapped out of my dream state. He'd been attempting to get the Colonel to see a specific set of hills the old nut simply could not locate.

"Tha one that looks like a man laying down!" MacLeod went on.

"A man lying down?" The Colonel squinted and shaded his eyes. "AH! AH-HAH! Yes! Why there's his nose, of course! And such a pronounced forehead! I do see it! Look there, Bertie!"

"I see it, Colonel." I said.

"Right— there ya go. Looks like an old man, don't it?" MacLeod said, proudly.

"Looks sort of like a thumb, to me." I said bluntly.

"Nonsense!" The Colonel gaped. "It's the face of a man, to be certain!"

"Not the face of a fairy, Colonel?" I said slyly with a grin, attempting to insult.

"Could be!" was all the man returned, bless him.

We continued on at our slow pace; the morning turned to afternoon though the sun hardly changed at all. MacLeod continued telling old legends and fairytales and even I paid close attention. Best to gather all the information we could, after all!

"Here, now! Here's a boy— good man!" MacLeod shouted to his nag- it was a pleasant journey.

"What a fine beast, I say, old boy!" The Colonel chirped from his hay stack.

"Oh— right. Call's him Willy Wallace, I do. Fine creature. Hates the English."

"William Wallace! I say!" Shouted the Colonel; I was thankful his comments ended there. The Colonel had surprised me since we'd arrived on, or even near to, the Isle. His overstepping comments, down. His demeanor, though still a solid dose of buffoonery— were none the less more reserved. I never thought I'd see him out of uniform in my life, and now here he sat- the spitting image of Skye, surprising me over and over again.

I say, we married on as such for several hours. The sun grew warm and I nodded off against the giant man's shoulder with the voice of the Colonel pecking at my ears.

The cart creaked and rumbled on. Willy Wallace whinnied from time to time. And I continually dozed, lost somewhere in that sleepy state of half woken and half not, determined for whatever reason to seem awake but failing at that. I felt myself nod and bob several times but did nothing to rouse myself.

A thump and crunch of gravel coupled with the distant chatter of an unhinged Colonel finally forced me awake with a start.

"This one, here?" I heard the Colonel shout.

"Jus' wait fer a moment." A grumbled reply came from MacLeod.

"Where are we? Uig?" I said and started to move. The world had gone dark on me, the large shadowy figure of our Ferryman worked with the bridle of his nag. Our cart had stopped on a cobbled street lit with several oil lamps up and down its lengths. It seemed a charming town, but somehow darkness amplified an edge of unease.

"Naht yet, no. Portree." MacLeod grunted. "Gotta stop fer the night."

"Right." I said and shimmied down from the driver's seat.

"I say, MacLeod- is it this one?" The Colonel said again, materializing at my elbow. "Ah Bertie, good lad! Awake I see? Capital. This one here, MacLeod?"

"Fer God's sake man, wait a bloody moment!" He continued to work with the nag, I rubbed the sleep from my eyes.

"What are you looking for, Colonel?" I said wearily.

"The Pub, of course!"

"Mhm. Right." I shrugged.

"MacLeod! I say, man! Just point out the right door would you?" The Ferryman returned a grunt and threw his hands into the air.

"Fer God's sake." he rumbled over. "Yes. It's tha' door you've half pushed open the last several times yahv asked! Just wait a bloody moment before yah go in, won't yah!"

"Well yes, sure! I suppose we might wait, it's just that I can't imagine why—" The large man cut him off.

"Listen here, now." He jabbed at the Colonel. "You're in the seat of the Isle, lads. What you say and do will travel round this rock faster than shite through a goose, ya hear me? Make one slip and this whole place will deem ya clearance agents and ya wont do shite for no one. Lease of all, me! And god knows the locals will call hell on me fer bringin' ya here! So, BE smart. Stick to yer story, ya hear me?" He looked mostly at the Colonel with one bulging eye of concern.

"No— yup. Course'!" We both spat out in some form or another nodding and crossing our arms like school boys.

"Wouldn't dream of letting you down, old boy!" The Colonel added with a flair.

"Right." He didn't sound convinced. "Well? What are ya doing here?"

"We…" I started, confused.

"We're here in the name of the Queen to settle some business with a fairy, of course!" The Colonel said smartly.

"No damn, ya! Imagine ya don't know me! Stick to yer story, God's sake! What are the two of yas doing on this bloody Isle?" He raised his voice.

"Ah— yes, I see! We? We are here! We…" The Colonel eyed me as if asking me to finish.

"We're fishers." I nodded. So did the Colonel. "See, our boat is moored here in Portree. Thought we'd spend a few days on land before heading back to sea."

"Christ. This was a mistake." MacLeod swore. "Right. Anyways, it'll have to do. That door is the pub— go inside. Have a drink. Try out your story. There are rooms uptop fer tonight, I'll see about getting you to Uig in the morning. Good?" He raised his hands. "Good." He finished and strode off.

We both watched him stroll away, his large figure growing more and more shadowy as he went. I turned to eye the Colonel, clown as he was in his sheepskin.

"And where are you going?" The Colonel asked into the darkness.

"Tah find ya a ride to Uig!" The boatman shouted back, mixing in a healthy amount of grumbling and murmuring I couldn't quite make out.

"Well— more for us then, eh Bertie?" He said with a rib from his elbow.

"Now listen here, Colonel." I said and waved a finger at the man. Slowly waking up my annoyance was growing, helped neither by the fact that I'd slept when I should have been awake or by the growing amount of night time bugs swirling around the streetlamp light. "MacLeod is right— you've got to be careful NOT to mention ANYTHING!"

"Anything?!" he sputtered.

"Anything!" I went on jabbing with my finger. "Not fairies, not the Queen, not the Army! NOTHING! Nothing but fishing!"

"Nothing but fishing?" He gasped.

"Not a word! About anything else! Least well be thrown from this Island!"

"And what about whisky?" He shot up a finger of his own. "Surely I can mention that, can't I?" His question was sincere. The Dog.

"Whis…Yes. Sure, alright. Whisky is fine." I begrudgingly admitted.

"Well then! And what problem did you think I'd have with that?" He laughed, I did not.

"Every problem in the world, Colonel! Every time we go somewhere and agree NOT to mention the Queen or Fairies or whatever, you always do! I admit I may have mentioned the Queen to MacLeod first, now that I think about it! But you brought it up to Fergus!"

"Tut, Tut, Tut, young Bertie." He said and waved a hand at me, turning towards the door. "I am a simple fisherman, landed on an unfamiliar Isle, with dreams, not of mischief, but only for a good and stiff drink!"

"Yeahhh…" I said with squinted eyes.

"Come, along! Come along, First mate!" He winked and nudged me. "See here, I'm already in character." My mouth hung open.

"Colonel…" I said and grabbed him as he pushed the door open slightly. "Perhaps just a bit more strategy, we—" He cut me off.

"No, no. My mind's all made up, would you just let— Let me." We scuffled a bit. The door opened and bumped shut again. Opened slightly more, and thumped shut again.

"Bertie, God's sake. For God's sake man! You're! You're panicking me, man!"

"What if this place is packed!"

"We…" he said and struggled out of my grip. "…Don't know that!"

"Yes— But. WHAT. IF." I was so worried the man would tramp down the door and announce his arrival in the name of the Queen. Fear forced me to linger on, I'm not proud of it! Refusing to accept the challenge I KNEW lay behind this door!

"WHAT. IF. WHAT." he said and lunged forward, now fully embraced in my arms.

The door clanged open, we collapsed in the doorway in some great heap, and for all my concern about seeming inconspicuous, I believed I had just ruined us. Slowly we both seemed to lift our eyes tangled together as we were, and to my shock the bar was completely empty. Save for one young looking barman with greasy black hair wearing a look of concern behind very thick spectacles.

"Welcome to the Queens Larder!" He smiled.

"The Queens, what?" The Colonel said from the ground. We scrambled from the floor and dusted ourselves off. The Colonel glaring at me with an eye of 'I told you so' written all over his face.

"Larder!" The Barman said happily. "Like a cupboard!"

"Right." The Colonel said, though I'm sure he didn't understand the name of the place.

"Don't recognize you lot! Will yah be havin' a drink then?" He said, still very cheery.

"Ye—" The Colonel started before shooting me another glare. "I should say, YES. My good man!" He strode toward the bar, built into the side of the wall, passing the many empty sets of high topped tables as he did. Careful to dust himself off further in a great display of annoyance towards me. I lagged behind, bitter I admit.

"Archibald Reginald Korn." He said. "CAPTAIN." He looked sideways at me. "Of the fishing vessel ABIGAIL STUART." He smiled at me now, showing off. I didn't give him the satisfaction. "And this is my val- My, uh. Vale. My. He's my… Well, my first mate, I should say." Nearly slipped up there, but he caught himself, I'll give him that. I eagerly watched him go on. "Bertie McGregor! Bertie! Won't you join me for a drink!" He extended his hand and I shrugged, smiling slightly. Look at you go, old man.

"Aye, Captain." I grumbled and did as I was told.

"Wonderful, that!" The Barman said. "And what will yah have then? Uh. We have ale!"

"A Whisky for me, I think! The boy will have Ale." He actually did have the air of a fisherman. That man, full of surprises he always is.

"All out of Whisky, I'm afraid!" The thick spectacled barman announced. I laughed, nothing to worry about now, is there?"

"Ah." The Colonel said. "Just an ale then I suppose." Two drinks were freshly poured and sat before us. We slumped into our barstools and tried to look as salty as we could. The barman merely smiled at us and seemed to wait for us to drink.

"Uh-Herm." The Colonel said. "Nice, uh. Nice isle."

"How's that? Skye? OH YES, LOVELY PLACE, THA!" The barman smiled more.

"We uhh…We've just moored here. In Portree, that is." I looked sideways at the Colonel. He matched my confusion and shrugged. "Thought we'd enjoy the isle a bit before sailing on, see." I finished.

"Lovely!" The barman said.

"We uhh…We're not from here. Clearly." I said raising my hands, trying to read the barman, carefully trying on our story.

"Right!" he quipped and smiled.

"Right…" The Colonel said, squinting, seeming almost annoyed with the locals' lack of concern for our being here.

"Don't you want to know why we—" The Colonel began to say.

"FISHING. Fishing! Like I said, Ker— Uh HERM. Captain. Like I said." I looked at him with wide eyes and mouthed 'let. It. go.' from the corner of my mouth.

"Oh— OH RIGHHHHT." He winked. "Right. Ah-hah. Like my uh. Like my FIRST MATE said. Fishing!" The Colonel added nodding at me when he announced my title again.

"Sure, fishing! We get lots of fishermen here, sure! Well not so much these days, see what with the clearances and that whole nasty business, seems to have slowed everything down, it has! People leaving so much as they are now. No, sureeeeee. Sure! Fishermen, yes! Lovely, that!" The man said and rambled slightly.

"Right. Right well. Clearances. We'd sure know nothing about that, would we now, Bertie?" The Colonel embellished. I rolled my eyes and fought the urge to slap my own face.

"No. No, certainly not. I say, old boy, you wouldn't happen to have lodging here at the Queen's Larder now, would you?" I said hoping to change the subject.

"Oh, sure! Sureeeee, we have rooms to rent up stairs, sure enough! And would ya be after a bed then?" He squinted. The Colonel and I looked at each other.

"ee-Yes. Yes." The Colonel said, both of us nodding.

"Two beds, actually." I added to be sure.

"Lovely! I'll run up and see to them while you lads enjoy your pints, won't I!" He smiled and left us confused but nodding. In no time at all we were completely alone in the pub, the man scurrying off to prepare us a room. The Colonel gave me a puzzled look.

"Well. I say." He spat out. "AND WEREN'T YOU SO WORRIED, BERTIE! My GOD. He didn't seem to care at ALL, did he?" He began to laugh. I joined him, slightly at first.

"Well— how was…" The Colonel's laughter started to roar. He jabbed me with a fork he'd found somewhere. "How was I? OUCH. Bugger! Stop. STOP THAT! WELL HOW WAS I SUPPOSED TO KNOW!" I shouted and defended myself, laughing with the man.

"How were you supposed to know the locals would be so simple, I DON'T KNOW!" He roared. "Oh, Colonel. Oh. What if. What if. What if." He made chirping noises, mocking me.

"Confound you, old man!" I laughed. "Though— Though I will, say! Nice bit of work there, wasn't it! My God, I nearly thought you a fisherman myself for a moment! If it weren't for that bloody sheepskin!" We laughed. We sipped our ales.

"My sheepskin! Don't you. Don't you dare, Lad!" He jabbed at me with his fork some more. I found a spoon and attempted to paddle him back.

"I happen to LOVE my sheepskin jacket! I do! You bugger!" We battled on with our utensils laughing and whooping about our fears of breaking character.

"Oh! Oh HELP ME. HEAVEN HELP ME HE CAN'T DO IT!" The Colonel mocked me more. We laughed more.

"I don't know what MacLeod was on about! I mean. I mean he mentioned the clearances- But, he didn't think twice about us being involved, did he?" I asked. We laughed. The Colonel said MacLeod's name and waved a fist. He reached across the bar and poured us two more ales, promising with a wink to have the barman add it to our tab.

"I say!" The Colonel announced sloshing his drink as he did. "That Ferryman of ours is ALL WORRY. LIKE YOU! PISH!" He touched his nose. "He doesn't realize he's alongside the QUEEN'S OWN MEN! Does he!" We laughed. "Does he, boy!" He pushed his glass against my shoulder— I agreed. Oh how we laughed.

"THE QUEEN'S OWN MEN, IS IT." A booming voice came from behind us.

Startled, we both flinched, myself so badly my shoulder was left sore. Hunched low, the Colonel looked at me shocked, as if to say— 'What have we done?'. We turned, slowly, the both of us.

"ALL WORRY AM I?" MacLeod said, arms crossed, his figure looming exceedingly large in the tiny bar room. The Colonel audibly let out a sigh. I winched further, not sure if it were worse for us or not that it was our friend who had caught us.

"My word, MacLeod! You nearly frightened us to death!" Said the Acorn.

"What did I say about letting on as to why you are here!" He shouted and approached us.

"Well— not to let on to others, is what you said!"

"AND WHAT IF I WERE SOMEONE ELSE."

"Oh— Heck. Seems the locals aren't worried about visitors at all! Are they, Bertie? Not judging from their Barkeep, I'll say that!" I wished he hadn't involved me. The Colonel didn't seem nervous around MacLeod at all. I was horrified by the man.

"YOU." He pointed at me. I gulped. "YOU I EXPECT BETTER FROM."

"COME NOW! Come now, MacLeod! Sit! Sit! Have a drink! Relax!" The Colonel slapped his shoulder, far too at ease.

"You be careful, wee man." He said, almost reluctantly, to the Colonel. "Not everyone here is so easy going— least of all those who have had family sent off. They won't be so careful around visitors. You just be DAMNED careful!" He slumped next to me at the bar.

"And were you able to secure us a ride to Uig then, MacLeod?" I asked, careful to change the subject again.

"No." He harrumphed.

"Ah." Said the Colonel, his gaze dropping.

"Right. So. What now?" I asked.

"So." He grumbled. "So I'll be taking you there myself in the morning. Most likely by boat."

"HUZZAH!" The Colonel cheered. I chuckled. And as it happened, the wild boatman cracked a smile himself— even if it went as soon as it came.

CHAPTER 17

The Town of Uig; A Highland Town

"This box loading is preposterous!" The Colonel complained again as we struggled down the small promenade that made up the coastal front in Portree.

"Yes but isn't it a lovely little walk along the houses here Colonel?" I asked and struggled with my own heavy box. Portree proper sits on the side of a hill; a short walk down the way leads one to the actual town port. Almost hidden from town, if standing in the main square, a neat little row of sea houses curves its way along the water at the base of a cliff. Truly picturesque. Truly lost on the Colonel, forced into hard labor as he was.

"Oh bugger these HOMES." He said still struggling, not at all used to the act of hard labor but unable to argue with the large ferryman now calling the shots.

"How on Earth we have been reduced to the hired hand— I CAN NOT IMAGINE." He went on. I rolled my eyes.

"UIG." MacLeod boomed from the deck of a tiny fishing craft. "IS WHY. YOU DO WANT TO GET THERE DO YOU NOT?"

"CERTAINLY YES. Why on Earth don't we take your cart..." He trailed off.

"The use of this ship better fits your purposes, damn ya! As I've said! ALL MORNIN! Not to mention it's an easier trip! And tah use it for your purposes means usin' it for its true nature! My man allowed us to use it ONLY IF WED HAUL HIS LOAD! THAT MEANS PACKIN IT. AND NO ONE RIDES FER FREE."

"Yes— yes! The Colonel dumped his load onboard and waved his hands. I was beginning to love the ferryman for his ability to control the Colonel. I could never have imagined the Colonel lifting heavy crates onboard a fishing vessel, and could never have made it happen myself. MacLeod merely raised his voice and declared 'This is the way it is!' and off the Colonel scurried. To quote our barman from the Queen's Larder— Lovely.

"But what I don't understand is how this will make any sense! We'll arrive in Uig as fishermen, and you'll haul off back here with the boat!" The Colonel continued complaining, though MacLeod had made the plan clear several times already.

"We'll arrive at night. You'll slip into town and tell the people a nice handsome chap from Portree dropped ya off in his cart as part of your little tour of the place, and I'll be rid of yah! As we well decided last night, yah bugger!"

"I find your plan full of HOLES, MACLEOD!" The Colonel shot back. Likewise, was I beginning to admire the Colonel's persistence at challenging the giant man. What a happy company we made.

Our evening last night had remained quiet. The tiny pub never gained another patron besides our company, leaving us free to scheme and plot. MacLeod had let on that he might be able to secure us a boat to travel round the Isle and into Uig Bay. The plan being that he would drop us off and be gone, leaving us stranded to solve the issue of the thievery alone. That problem for a later date, it was decided however, and satisfied the three of us went off for an early night to bed. He awoke us early the next morning with the good news of a successful securing of the vessel— and condemned the Colonel with the news of having to load it first in the same breath. I found it all quite agreeable of course, though the Colonel was not convinced of the labor portion, leaving him irritable and stuffy.

"No matter, the boxes are loaded now, aren't they Colonel? Wasn't so bad at all!" I chirped happily, the coastal scene very much awakening a sense of charm inside me.

"Speak for yourself! I've surely damaged my spine, I have! How, now, will I possibly outwit a FAIRY!" He squalled and huffed, short of breath.

"SHHH—Hush! Hush!" MacLeod waved. "Climb onboard and let's be off then, before yah's let on to the whole bloody isle why yer here!"

"OH, AND LET ON TO WHO, MIGHT I ASK!" The Acorn cried.

"I've hardly seen ONE PERSON ON THIS WHOLE ENTIRE ROCK." I laughed at his ever growing despair and quietly pushed him onto the short gangplank.

"You'll be seeing not but stars if yah…" The boat grumbled into silence.

"WHAT'S THAT NOW?" The Colonel said through huffs, finally catching his breath.

"Nothing— Nothing, Colonel! He said nothing!" I gingerly prodded. The boatman laughed and made his way to the front of the boat. I followed, leaving the Colonel on the small deck gasping for air still.

"She's no Brixham Trawler but she'll do for our needs, she will." MacLeod said and worked at a hunch. "Based on the Brixham she is, should make a fine speed- 9 knots I reckon! Imagine we'll pull into Uig before dark! We have the gage, young master Albert!" He seemed excited; The entire affair fascinated me, never having been much on the seas myself, and certainly not as a potential deck hand. I felt like a small child, watching his father work, but it didn't bother me at all. How deeply I long for learning, as is well known to these pages by now.

"You are quite comfortable on a boat, I see MacLeod."

"Oh, aye. Been at sea both man and boy!" He worked pulleys and tossed directions at me. I began to enjoy myself thoroughly. I unhitched our mooring ropes, careful as I did to ask questions. The Colonel came round slowly, apprehensively; eagerly eyeing our progress. Slowly our boat began its march through the choppy waters. We seemed to glide, the wind casting coolly over me on the dark and gray morning. As we floated away from the harbor finally a Portree native appeared, shuffling away from us toward town.

"I SAY!" The Colonel shouted with a wave of his hat. "RULE BRITANNIA!" I elbowed him violently. His greeting was not returned however and off we sailed regardless, into the Sound of Raasay, as the Ferryman denoted, promising us a short trip into Uig.

I think I could go on in this journal for some pages regarding our journey to Uig via the sea. Mostly I think I shall spare that now, being that my true intention here was to muse upon my life in the service of A.R

Korn. However, I will say this— rarely before or since have I enjoyed a journey so well. The sea is infectious I think. In its vastness it resembles the great unknown that man has long written about and wondered about and so surely there is a deep primal desire to be near to its edges. But for those who have made it their lives to set out upon it? They seem to regard it differently. It is precious to these people, men like MacLeod. It makes up their entire lives, the sea. In most cases it seems, it either feeds their families or provides for them a way to do so. And so they regard it with a deep sense of home. And because this is surely true— they keep it well. And they are very apt to showing it off to those who come to see it. Like showing off something they've made, it is infectious in this way. It is simply impossible to walk the coast or witness a sunrise or, in my case, sail across it, without feeling that deep sense of home yourself. Even if you do not yet call it your home, they have made it so for every man. Perhaps it *is* primal? Perhaps it is human nature. Certainly it is human nature to wonder about the sea, but I do wonder if it is not so to go further, to be upon its vast nature. This is how I found my way to Uig. Dreamily wondering of its mystery, allowed into its secrets by a man whose very blood has been washed amongst it. I muse, indeed. But I will go no further for the sake of brevity— and for the sake of our mission, for we arrived in Uig late into evening, the stars beginning to spot the sky.

A long jetty poked its way far into the harbor, affected by the tides. We moored onto its posts, one of the very few crafts to do so. Looking beyond, the town seemed nothing more than a tiny village; small lights began to ignite the hills affixed to the fronts of thatched houses and buildings.

"IS THIS IT?" The Colonel squawked, quite ruining my dream state. "Doesn't seem much, does it Bertie?" He elbowed me, the clod.

"Right. Uig." MacLeod said. "Best to get them crates on the dock now, tomorrow morning someone will surely be round to collect on the shipment, I can avoid the mooring fee and you twos can slip into town and find a room to stay in." The evening air cooled us as the darkness set in.

"Bugger." The Colonel declared. We set to work flopping the heavy things onto the dock. Before the last barrel was set to port night had arrived. Distracted as we were, we failed to see a lantern approaching, bobbing its way through the night and towards us. It wasn't until the thing was half way down the dock that I finally noticed it- elbowing the ferryman who stopped and squinted in the direction I had nodded. The Colonel stopped his work and gasped, slightly. As it approached I made out the figure of a man, wrapped in a cloak. He held the lamp high above his head.

"That you, Archer?" the figure asked. We three eyed each other, not sure how to answer.

"How does he know my name?" the Colonel whispered. The figure moved the lamp from side to side, craning to see it seemed.

"Archer, he said." I shot back.

"You sure, Bertie? Could have sworn he said, Archie…"

"For god's sake man, yes. And who the devil calls you Archie anyways!"

"Fergus calls me Archie! I sa—" I cut him off.

"I hardly think Fergus Dillwyn is present here in Uig!" I emphasized each word, our whispering becoming quite hostile.

"Shhhhh. Shuh— SHUSH. Let me think!" MacLeod waved his hands at us.

"Archer? That you?" the voice said again.

"Ye— Yes? No, I mean. Friends of Archer, that is. MacLeod is my name, we've taken his shipment for him today." He announced uneasily. Our eyes were as wide as saucers.

"Ah— wonderful! Well come aground, man!" the voice said happily and approached.

"Richard Mackenzie is my name! Harbor Master, Uig! At your service! That'll be the post I gather? Excellent, that!" He spoke.

"Thompkin MacLeod," said the Ferryman, extending his giant bear paw to the man on the Jetty. "My, uhh? My crew, Archie Korn and Bertie McGregor." I laughed out loud at the Colonel's given name before catching myself, a wonderful bit of improvisation by the ferryman. Quickly my laughter turned to fear, hoping the Colonel had caught on, praying he wouldn't announce himself captain of some other fishing vessel thus making himself completely out of place onboard MacLeod's ship. But he didn't— to my shock and surprise. He merely shot the man a smart nod and a wrinkle of his moustache before looking cross at MacLeod. Well played yourself, old boy, well played. I thought.

"Wonderful, wonderful." the local declared. "Couldn't imagine who on Earth would be docking so late into the evening! No matter, no matter!

You'll be staying the night then I reckon? Charlotte will have beds sure enough, she will!" He waved at us to come aground and started motioning to the shore. I shrugged at the Colonel who returned the motion and we all three of us clambered onto the deck, beginning our stroll with the harbormaster. MacLeod looked particularly uneasy, looking back at the ship several times as the harbormaster chattered on and on about all manner of things.

"A deckhand!" whispered the Colonel.

"SHUSH." I said.

"IT WAS ALL I COULD THINK." MacLeod shot angrily in equally hushed tones.

"SHHHH." I spat. The children.

"And, and? And why did Archer not make the journey himself, then?" The man stopped short and asked, looking up at MacLeod.

"He, uh. Wasn't feeling well." MacLeod improvised again.

"Pity, pity." Was all the happy chap said before leading us on again. No one seemed at all suspicious and I, like the Colonel, began to wonder if there was much to be concerned about at all regarding the locals and their disdain for government agents. Then again, I suppose our outfits left nothing to be suspicious of, did they? I made a mental note to congratulate MacLeod on that bit of genius later.

"Here we are, here we are lads. Uig. Welcome, welcome." He shuffled on, leading us off the dock and up the dirt street of town. It seemed this main street made up the bulk of the village, with small pockets of houses hanging over the place in the hills beyond. The harbormaster continued talking as we walked, the three of us grunting small responses to his many quips. We approached a well-lit building that, to me, looked like the most prominent place in the village. It was marked 'The Charlotte' and even in the dark I could make out its pale green colour, a hotel I assumed. From the various carts and pack animals hitched outside and the noise coming from inside, I gathered this place was well worn by the various locals.

"Afraid yah'vv caught us on a bit of a busy night, town meeting going on inside, that is! Most of the locals have come round- but they'll be plenty enough to eat and drink and Charlotte will have plenty o'beds yet for weary merchant men! I'll bring yah right 'round to Char-Lott!" He shuffled us up to the door, hung his lantern and weakly pushed the giant thing open.

Inside was a desk built into the wall, much like the swan, off to the right was a bar scene warmly lit. Several people sat around the outside on high stools, more had gathered in chairs in the center of the room, several turned their heads at the sound of the door but paid little mind to our arrival. The bar itself was off to the left, where stood a barman listening intently (as was everyone) to a woman speaking from the far end of the room. At the desk leaned a thin woman with tight wrinkled skin, worn from the salt air I assumed, as most were. She leaned and listened with a look of concern greeting our arrival with a small nod before listening in again.

"Tha' boat?" she questioned for a second.

"The very same, Archer's shipment. And— and? And will yah be after ah room then, lads?" He asked.

"Sure enough." MacLeod said, looking around nervously.

"Bit packed tonight lads, some of tha crofters 'ave come round fahr tha meetin'. I've got one room on the tird floor, just up those stairs." She said, still listening to the speaker, motioning to the stairway that shot up to the left of the desk. "It'll be just tha one bed I'm afraid. That alridt, then?"

"Sure, sure." MacLeod said, still uneasy. I rolled my eyes at the thought of one bed, cursing my luck yet again.

"Right." She said and turned her attention to us fully. "At'll be One Crown for the room, and?" She looked at Mackenzie who nodded. "Two shilling fer tha mooring fee. That alridt, then?" MacLeod nodded for us, I could sense his anger at having to pay to dock after all.

"I don't suppose you'll be paying then would ya?" He looked angrily at the Colonel and pulled out his wallet.

"I— I. Well, Bertie would have my wallet, see—" he squirmed, the man never dealt in cash.

"Mmm." He said and handed over the payment.

"Lovely. That'll be your key, then. Room 14, up tha stairs here and you'll be two more flights. Make yerselves at home, course. And wea be having ahr meeting then, but if yer after a meal yah canny find ah spot at tha bar there n'Duncan will see to yahs, alridt?" She smiled. The Colonel's mouth hung open but he said nothing, merely gazed at her accent in wonder.

"Right. Thanks again." MacLeod said and nodded at us towards the stairs.

We clambered up the stairs, careful to pass out several thanks a piece as we did, still doing our best to remain inconspicuous. Charlotte eyed us kindly enough; she seemed concerned with our awkwardness more so than anything else. Up one creaky flight of stairs we found the first floor. After several moments of bumping into one another we found a second flight and subsequent floor before finishing our climb and arriving outside the doorway of room 14 level three, ours for the night.

"Would you? Would— MOVE IT MAN." MacLeod said as we all three tried to pass through the door at once; stumbling into the cramped quarters we fanned out as far as we could. Very quickly we three men let loose a mighty sigh in various ways and forms. The Colonel drug his hands across his cheeks.

"AND WHAT, I SAY— WAS THAT? The Colonel shouted.

"Ohh, WHAT?" Spat the ferryman, or should I say 'merchant' now? Looking cross and he too struggled to unwind.

"I WAS TO BE THE IMAGINED CAPTAIN. NOT SOME— SOME, CREWMEN! WE HAD A PLAN!"

"Is that really what you're upset with?" I asked, spotting the absolutely miniscule bed.

"IT WAS THA BEST I COULD DO UNDER THE CIRCUMSTANCES!" MacLeod shot back. Frustration showed as we all came to grips with the new circumstance. MacLeod would have to stay, it seemed.

"Really, gentlemen— Have you had a look at this bed?" I asked the room.

"You were supposed to shove off!" The Colonel again.

"I'D LOVE TO. IN FACT! BEST OF LUCK TO YAH!" He made a motion as if to leave, but stopped short.

"Oh yes, MHM. I say. You're in it now, old boy! Talked yourself RIGHT into our story, you have!" The Colonel crossed his arms and pouted. MacLeod did the same, steaming.

"Gentlemen, really. I do think we are surely blowing things out of proportions here. No one seems the slightest bit concerned with our being here— I am sorry MacLeod that you've been pinched in, but what's the harm in staying, eh?" I tried to reconcile.

"My ferry is what! I've got a life tah live, yah know! And I'm telling yah, we've been lucky thus far, if these folk thought fer a second you were here for clearances ohhh they'd! They would!" He spoke hurriedly.

"Oh, they'd what!" The Colonel said, still angry he wasn't allowed to play the role of fish captain.

"Im tellin' yahs!" MacLeod shouted.

"Enough. Enough! Look here— We can still make this work. MacLeod can stick around an extra night and tomorrow we'll announce he's leaving to return Archer's ship or what have you! Meanwhile we can announce our deciding to stay until the next shipment for having fallen in love with the town!" I raised my hands at the two angry men. "Good? Aye? Good?"

"Hm." Harrumphed MacLeod.

"Hmph!" The Colonel matched him.

"Honestly! Have you forgotten why we're here?!" I asked with gusto. "Serve the Queen!" I looked at the Acorn. "Save your Isle!" I looked at MacLeod. "Is that not enough?" I looked around. "Is that not enough?" They slacked their folded arms and eyed each other like toddlers forced to apologize. "For goodness sake! We've hardly been asked to do a thing yet! Lose one night! PRETEND to be a deckhand instead of a captain! Heavens! Is it really so bad? Aye? Is it really so bad? Well? IS IT?" I surprise myself at times.

"Aye. It? Right." MacLeod coughed out.

"I suppose. I suppose not, then." The Colonel added.

"Lovely!" I said and threw my hands into the air. "Now for God's sake— have a look at that bed!"

The air seemed to fizzle, just for a moment. And then? Slight laughter. Growing laughter, and finally a healthy laughter from the three of us.

"I will not be the middle!" I said between breaths.

"Well surely MacLeod can't be, can he!" Spat the Colonel.

"You're the smallest!" The ferryman shouted and pointed at me through his own fits.

"You cheeky bastard!" I said and pointed back. "I am! I really am! Confound it!"

"How about?" The Colonel choked. "How about MacLeod? OH. ERM. THESE ARE MY DECK HANDS. I say!" The Colonel squinted and laughed, searching for our approval. How quickly the man can change pace. We laughed on until out of breath, finishing by coughing awkwardly and patting our chests and bellies.

"Hrrm. Yes. Well." MacLeod said. "I suppose one night here won't kill me will it? Bit of nasty one to be sailing through the night anyways, eh?" He slapped his ribs.

"Sure! Sureeee!" The Colonel called and reached into his sheepskin to check a pocket watch I didn't know he had. "Half seven, I've got. Are we up for a nip of the King's then, lads?" He was suddenly deeply sincere and honest, hand on hip.

"I'd be lookin' fer dinner myself." MacLeod said and looked at me. Both men looked at me. I smiled. Here I was, three floors up in Uig, three floors up in the empire, in a company I would never have imagined when I started my career at Sandhurst, so many years ago.

"Yeah. Yes. Yes, to both!" I said and shrugged. "We'll just have to be quiet I'm sure, what with their town meeting or whatever they've got going on down there— those Uigans."

"Ahh, yes! The meeting! Is that what you'd call them, Bertie? 'Uigans'?" He squinted at me as we all moved towards the door. I laughed.

"I'm not completely sure, Colonel." I said with a chuckle. He slapped my shoulder and we found our way downstairs much happier men.

———— ◦ ————

I admit we made a surprising amount of clamber as we arrived back on the main floor. The wooden stairs, MacLeod's girth and the Colonel's constant chirping combined to make quite the racket. We passed Charlotte's disapproving frown offering various forms of apologies as we passed.

"Sor-ree! SO-REE, there!" The Colonel half whispered and tipped his hat to a few people around the room. I looked down in shame and bumbled my companions along. The speaker had changed to a gentleman, middle aged, he briefly paused before continuing his speech; something about local farming. As he spoke we tried to be as unbothering as possible, but this seemed fruitless. There wasn't enough space at any single table, nor were there three open spots in a row along the bar. There must've been forty-some head in the place— we half-whispered and pointed with our hands in an effort to communicate.

"Let's split." I mouthed.

"Wha?" The Colonel mouthed back.

"Where do I?" MacLeod said without even attempting a whisper.

"Would. Would you jus— SIT. COLONEL SIT THERE." I whispered in sharp breaths pushing the Colonel into a seat at a table shared by two heavy ladies in bonnets. MacLeod I directed to the bar where two high seats were open. We plopped down, the Colonel objected whispering something about wanting to sit at the bar. I shot him a glare and we settled, the meeting continuing with the addition of several pauses and stares in our direction.

The speaker continued to go on about some local farm issues, I only half listened as the barman, Duncan, I presumed, was whispering about what we'd have. I ordered a pint and the stew, as did MacLeod.

"Bertie!" The Colonel whispered from his low spot behind me. "A whisky for me!" He shot a finger up. He did whisper, bless the man, but it was high pitched and abrasive nonetheless. I nodded and rolled my eyes at him.

"A whisky for my friend there— and will you bring him the stew as well?" I am the man's valet after all, though I hate to admit it. Had I not ordered him food he'd have found his sustenance in his drink alone, and that I did not want to deal with this night.

In short order our drinks arrived, as did the Colonel's behind us. He sat happily sipping and I did the same after a moment of checking on him, confident the man was happy and would make no further fuss. As our food arrived we continued to sit quietly listening to the local happenings. The stew was good! A healthy thick Highland serving of meats and vegetables, smothered in gravy. I happily thought of my mother and eyed the Colonel behind me every so often. He ate and drank, quite chipper it seemed, smiling and raising his eyebrows a few times at his company of plump Scottish ladies.

"I say." I heard him once declare, dabbing his lips with a napkin and chasing with the dram. Had anyone given the man a true look over they'd never have believed him the salty deckhand he claimed to be. I rolled my eyes and took another swig myself, finally seeming to relax entirely.

"And wha' will we doo then— AYE!" The speaker's voice rose, causing me to turn and acknowledge him. I caught MacLeod's eye of concern as well. "Once this bloody FAIRY has taken the LOT— there be none left fer us! And we'll be cleared out, damn certain!" He shouted, the crowd grew restless with his outburst adding in some shouts of their own and I noticed the Colonel's face to my great, great dismay.

That word. I know he heard it. There was no way the Colonel had missed it.

"FAIRIES!" The man speaking shouted again. "WILL BE THE RUIN OF THIS ISLE."

"Oh no…" I whispered. The Colonel's head swiveled around, suddenly deeply concerned with the meeting. He met my eyes, I tried to scream at him with my own— 'DON'T SAY A THING.' He squeezed his eyes shut and clearly gulped his meal down.

"DON'T. SAY. ANYTHING." I mouthed, hoping the sudden uproar in the room would make me invisible to all local eyes. He shook his head. Closed his eyes. Rubbed his temples. Good grief did the man struggle. He put more stew in his mouth and lowered his head.

The locals continued their uproar. Some shouted about fairies. Some swore and cursed pointing at the speaker.

"You can't believe it! Fairies! HONESTLY!" One shouted.

"IT IS A FAIRY, THA! I'VE SEEN 'EM!" Shouted another.

"QUIET! QUUUUIET!" came a roar from the front of the hotel. It was Charlotte, the old gal who seemingly owned the place. "Let tha man speak! God's sake!" I met MacLeod's gaze of concern again, matching my own, as it was. We swallowed as the room calmed and settled. The Colonel was visibly sweating. Heaven help me.

"Thank ya, Charlotte." The speaker said and leveled his hands. "Now look here! I don' know fer certain if it's a fairy, god's sake. But I do knows the damned thing SEEMS like one! My guess! It's some trick to confuse us and provide reason for more land clearances!" More uproar from the gathered towns folk, the speaker raised his hands to calm them.

"Probably— hell. Probably some thief hired by tha Lords to act a fairy and steal our crop! Three head of sheep I've lost! Three this week! Sherman's lost more, he has!" The townsfolk continued to add in shouts of agreement or challenge. "Well I agree!" He shouted. Just then I felt so out of place, but no one seemed to even acknowledge we being there.

"They'll clear us out when we can't keep enough food, they will!" one of the older gals from the Colonel's table sadly shouted.

"That's well said!" Duncan the barman added over my head.

"Damn right!" The Colonel shouted from a hunched position, keeping his back to the speaker as he did. I eyed him sternly and shook my head as if to say 'don't you get involved'.

The conversation in the room continued, the Colonel's quip going unnoticed.

"Well what are we to do!" Another older woman shouted meekly.

The room erupted again. Shouting and pointing. Several arguments happening across the place all at once. The original speaker waved a finger in the face of two men nearest him. Several younger men and women shouted in the corners of the place.

"IS— IS IT A FAIRY THEN!" someone shouted.

"IS IT!?" Another replied.

"QUIEEEEEEEET!" Charlotte roared again.

"Thank ya, Charlotte! Thank ya!" The speaker said as the room got quiet.

"Well? Is it true? Is it a Fairy then, John?" The meek old woman from before eagerly asked.

"I… I do believe… it may be. I can't say for certain!" Some chatter rose in the room, he raised his hands. "But I, I, I— I hardly think that matters, does it! We've gotta nip it either way, haven't we!"

"Well aye, sure John! But how! Bugger seems untraceable, don' ee?" A Shepard type added in. The room again rose up with murmurs and shouts and I noticed one of the old plump gals from the Colonel's table rise and begin to speak. This man John tried to dull the crowd. The Colonel eyed it all wildly from his stew. God help me.

"Johnathan Gable!" She shouted. "Let me speak!" The room shouted to let her speak.

"Alright! Alright, there Mrs. Lindsay! Go on then!" He dabbed sweat from his brow.

"I've been here in Uig me whole life, I have! Since you were a wee lad yourself!" She jabbed a finger at the speaker. "Me dah tended the fields above and me husband toiled for kelp, god knows!" The crowd murmured agreement like a catholic congregation. "Me dah, himself! Was sent off, as you know. His fields now hold flock for the landlords, but no Lindsay lives upon it! Hmph!" She nodded. More murmurs from the crowd. "For years, then, more fields were cleared and more tenants moved here! Myself and my husband among them! And good as this town has been to find room, we are plumb oot ov it! The kelps gone sour. And no work for makin' money now, is there! It's the best a man can do to cut turf for the fire there! And now that so many have gone off, we can't hardly keep track of what we have, can we!" The crowd shouted. "Children run amuck in the streets and hills! The place is falling to ruin! So it is, there!" Some men stood and waved their hands. I swallowed hard, watching the Colonel sweat it out. Don't say a word you great buffoon. "So my question to you Johnathan, is this— how are we to take seriously this idea of fairies when the very real threat is Clan Chiefs turned bruuuuTAL LAND-LORDS!" The crowd erupted again. This poor fellow John raised his hands and continued to sweat, trying to calm the crowd.

"Now—" He shouted. "Now wait a minute! I never— I NEVER SAID!" He waved his arms frantically. "I never said for sure it was a Fairy! Just that this thievery is making things worse! God knows!"

"Let's call it a Fairy then John!" Mrs. Lindsay began as the shouts continued. "Let's call it a fairy thief for we've none else to explain it! What then is to be done to keep our children a-home to grow up in! Cause if we be chasing tales and thieves instead of tryin' else whys to fix our problems, then I'm not for it, no sir! I'm not fer it one bit, I'm not!" She shook her head and sat back down at the Colonel's table. He reached across and squeezed her hand; I nearly jumped on him.

"Right!" John shouted. "RIGHT THEN! We call it a fairy, sure! For the time being that is, to be done with it. But let us be clear with our true intentions! This thing is only causing more harm! And before we can rebuild our families and dig in, well. I think— Well I say it must be dealt with!" He dabbed at his forehead again.

"What of the Children, John!" A small looking mother said from the back. She wore tattered clothes and was as frail as a small branch. "My husband's gone off to England for work! Sure his wages are sumthin' but no school means I've to keep an eye on 'em all day! Between the chores and the work, they've taken to raisin' themselves!" The crowd shouted.

"She's right!"

"God knows!"

"I— I, know!" John patted the air with his hands. "But we've no school master to teach them now, do we! Too many young people have left! And none are coming here, now! What— What are we to do?"

"We've got to do something!" One shouted. The scene was chaos, I felt like a toad.

"Look—" John said. "Look here. If we are too sure up this town then I think first, we have to stop this thievery! Who would agree?" he seemed desperate.

As the scene unfolded I continued to eye the Colonel, sure he was about to explode with questions and answers. He'd open his mouth, turn his head to hear some shout, take another gulp of whisky before closing his mouth again. He was too far from me to kick.

"This fairy must be stopped!" Another meek woman said as the uproar grew once more. "Least we see more land clearances and things get worse!" The room descended again into a cacophony of sound. Everyone seemed to rage on with their own opinion of fairy or not, and how it was to be solved regardless. They shouted about the children, and the fields. Some shouted about their homes and how long until they were removed from them. I honestly didn't know what to do. MacLeod and myself merely watched in shock as the meeting went on. But the Colonel was not the same kind of man...

"SEND A MAN!" He shouted and stood, for he *was* a true man of the empire.

The room grew quiet as if in the presence of some booming godlike figure, faces turning to squint at the stranger dressed in sheepskin and wearing a soldier's cap.

"Send a man on. Solve your problem!" he said again and nodded. It was quite the triumphing scene, I'll say. That is, until the place erupted again in shouts and curses leaving the Colonel standing among the chaos like a general surprised in his battle.

"WHO IS 'EE!"

"AH SIT DOWN!"

"And who are you!" I heard someone shout.

"He don' know!" another said.

"I say!" The Colonel shouted and joined the fray as if a local himself.

The place continued to fall apart, the Colonel continued to battle and MacLeod asked what we should do.

"Finish your stew, I think." I said and turned back to the bar and my meal.

"What?!" He shouted. The roar went on. I ate.

"QUIIIIIIET!" Charlotte shouted again, I didn't even need to turn to know it. "LET THA MAN SPEAK!"

"Thank ya, Charlotte, thank ya!" This John fellow said again.

"Naht yoo, yah silly bastard!" She said, as I continued to pay mind to my stew only. "HIM!" I didn't need to look again to know that she pointed at none other than the Colonel.

"HIM?" John said, confused, and I understood him briefly even never having met the man.

"Let 'em speak." she said. And speak he did. I sipped my drink.

"Thank yee madam. Thank yee. Ah-hem! My name is Archibald Reginald Korn! I am a Col— Ah. I'm a merchant man, myself! Been at sea both man and boy, I have!" Good start, I thought. I saluted him with my drink without turning around and took a giant gulp.

"And I may not be from your little village!" The townsfolk's murmur died as they listened. "But I do know the highlands! From top to bottom! Islay and Inverness! And I know this!" He shot a finger high into the air. "A wee folk fairy is not but mischief and thievery! And I'd be willing, to see to the bugger myself, I would!"

I mockingly mouthed 'oh would you, now?' as I continued to forcefully ignore what I knew was coming, draining my glass and tossing a finger up to Duncan for another. Madness.

"And why would ya do tha, now?" Charlotte asked from the front of the place. I can't say for certain but I did imagine her arms to be crossed.

"Well!" Said the Colonel. "For Scotland, of course! See I am a Campbell, on my mother's side..." He turned to address Mrs. Lindsay as if a side thought. "And I—"

"For Scotland!" One man shouted and threw up his hands.

"He isn't even from here, John! Who es 'ee!" Another shouted.

"Ah!" The Colonel pivoted. "Well! It just so happens that I am an expert on fairies and foul folk! Having nipped a Ghoul before in Brighton! And a nasty toad of a thing once in Egypt!" Some half-truths, I think. Mostly lies, I'd say. But I smirked and nodded my head, not bad for an unhinged old nut.

"See here! I'm a bit of an expert on Fairies and I do know about your trouble with clearances! And it just so happens that I am accompanied by two of the finest highland men who have yet tripped this empire! One of which is an absolute EXPERT on the subject of weefolk! I say! Let us have a shake at this mischievous little rascal!" He finished his soliloquy rather weakly I'd have said, and would have critiqued his performance quite harshly were I writing for the press. But I merely nodded to myself yet again and prepared for the next question, which I knew was coming.

"For God's sake! We don't even know if it is a Fairy! It's nonsense, is it!" one shouted. John raised his hands and curiously eyed the Colonel.

"And who are these two companions of yours then? This— This expert on fairies!" John asked.

"AH, of course! Why? BERTIE MACGREGOR!" He shouted and pointed. The room went dead silent. I gulped, turned and weakly raised my glass, coughing a little as I did.

"Alright there, everyone?" I asked the room.

After several minutes the uproar the Colonel caused died down yet again. I couldn't pick out most of the yelling but I will say I heard many insults of insanity and lunacy etc etc. The Colonel argued on of course and I finished another drink. MacLeod shot eyes at me and the entire place. What a mess.

Finally, Charlotte called the place to a respectful lull once more allowing this John Fellow his chance to question the Colonel.

"And just where did you say yah've come from again?" He asked.

"Inverness!" The Colonel replied, naming my home. Again, only a half lie. Well done old boy, surprising me more and more.

"And what brings you here!" Shouted another voice.

"Oh they've brought Archers Shipment in they have, the man's sick himself!" Mackenzie said. (I recognized his voice)

"Why would you want to help us!" Mrs. Lindsay asked, sounding confused. But many echoed her question and shouted similar things at the Colonel.

"Because!" He said and began. "Because I love this bloody empire! GOD SAVE IT!" Some booed. He went on regardless. "And I'd stand to see this highland home preserved, as I've said! I know of your land clearances and would help keep you here! If I could! If WE could!"

"Do ya speak for all of them, then!" Someone demanded.

"mmm. Ee-does!" I said over the brim of my glass, participating again. Quite determined to stay out of the Colonel's show as I should have done so many times before on this bloody trip.

"What's in it for you, then?" John asked and the room got quiet.

"Well." He seemed to think. Careful now, old boy, I thought. "How bout a drink?" He said slyly and winked.

The locals eyed each other. Some smiled and laughed quietly. They just couldn't seem to believe it— of course neither would I if I had never met this buffoon before, but there it was. The man offered his service, we waited to see if they'd take it.

"Mister." Charlotte began, coming to the front of the room. "I've been living here in Uig since I was a wee lass. Me dah owned the place, named it fer me. I took over when he passed. Hell. Point is. It's me hom. It's our hom. Yah say yah heard about tha clearances, and I believe yahs. But this…Thief. Fairy? Whatever it is— It's right bit more than a local bit of mischief. It's damn near the end of us wee folk livin here. We've been robbed blind for months now— can't no one seem to catch the thing, end it. Hell. I thank yee fer yah offer. But how do you expect tah do what we can seem tah? And more ovah, why shud we trust yoo?"

The room grew solemn, as if they all thought deeply about the seriousness of their situation. I sensed their grief, and suddenly found myself as concerned with it all as the Colonel clearly was.

"You're worried there'll be claim to send people off if the thievery isn't stopped, correct?" He asked. She nodded, as many around her did. "And you can't seem to commit yourselves to the task, since, as you've said, you have enough trouble keeping your homes about you without running around searching for a thief, yes?" They considered him.

"Then so are we. Highlander to highlander. Let us try and catch your fairy, preserve this bit of home. I can't promise we will, but it won't hurt to give it a shot, will it?"

I looked around at the many faces, noticing for the first time their features. Young faces, old. Scraps of beard or full bushels. Bonnets. Dresses. These were the good folk of home, and it was no wonder to me just then why we were there.

"I suppose...no. It canny hurt, can it?" Charlotte said and smiled. John smiled from behind her. Many in the room smiled and nodded.

"Will you have our help, then? Will you?" The Colonel asked.

"Aye." Charlotte said. "Aye we will." and nodded. She seemed to speak for many.

The room erupted into cheers and suddenly my drink was sloshing all about from the many hands that slapped my shoulder. Another drink was pressed into it. MacLeod got the same. The Colonel was surrounded by fans and fanfare all wishing us luck and good fortune. Mrs. Lindsay kissed his cheek, he went red as the Devil and smiled.

"Well then Fairy Master!" John shouted to me above the roar. "Drink up, tonight! Tomorrow we'll see what yoos can do!" He laughed and shouted and the bar roared on around us.

CHAPTER 18

The Hunt in Uig

"God my head hurts." The Colonel said, head in hands, hunched over the now quiet bar.

"Serves you right." I said as I swirled a spoon in my tea glass. "Quite the show you put on last night."

"What did I promise again?" He audibly sighed and rubbed his temples

"Oh you know, nothing major. Just that we are fairy masters who can solve their problem with the slightest of ease, is all. Fairy Masters. Is what you said. Whatever that is." I continued to ignore his soft sobs of pain. He'd gotten far too carried away with the party that ensued last night after his blind promise.

"You're upset with me." He shrugged.

"Please." I scoffed.

"Come now, Bertie. I'm wounded, have pity!"

"Colonel. Really. You are not. And furthermore my issue is this-though the plan was to eventually tackle this fairy problem... I'd just have liked to have...slowly gotten on with it. Ease into it, you know!"

"Not exactly our way, is it lad?" He rubbed his temples.

"Hardly YOUR way, is a better way to put it. And where is that boy Duncan with our eggs!" The bar was empty. The locals had mostly gone home after last night's absurdities, and the three of us were sent to bed with the promise from John to be 'round in the morning for a chat'. We had been roused early by Miss Charlotte, as she is called by her patrons apparently, for a promised breakfast prepared by this Duncan chap. Who I admit I did like, but was rather slow about his work.

"God knows." The Colonel said. "Damn happy to be here waiting though, eh wot? Better than poor MacLeod out there finalizing that shipment with what's his name!" He laughed.

"Mackenzie." I spat and sipped my tea.

"Ah, yes." The Colonel murmured. "And who is it we're waiting on for a chat, again?"

"That man, John."

"Right. RIIIIght." He looked up. "And what do we know of him, then?" I slapped down the paper I was attempting to read.

"We know nothing more of him then he of us! You hardly gave us any chance at all to get to know anyone around here before prattling on about going to war with this fairy!"

"And how about that, Bertie?" He asked, ignoring my insult.

"Yes! How about it!"

"No— no, no. I mean the Fairy! How about that! Turns out it IS a fairy after all!" His eyes were wide.

"Hardly, Colonel. Seems most believe it's a ruse of some sort."

"Fairy, I say. Best to keep our wits about then, eh?" He squinted and looked from side to side. I pursed my lips and focused my attention back on my tea.

"Sorry lads, forgot about yahs!" Duncan said returning with a plate of food a piece before whisking away again.

"AHHH! There's a lad! Splendid, splendid!" The Colonel chirped and rubbed his palms suddenly healed of his large head. Just then the door banged open behind us causing us to turn, MacLeod came bumbling into the bar area cursing under his breath.

"Shipments. Finalizing. MACKENZIE." He muttered.

"Alright there, Mac!" The Colonel said with a mouthful of egg.

"SHUT IT." He said, ripping the toast from the Colonel's plate. "An hour I've been on that dock working and here I find you— you! Eating! Move!" He pushed the Colonel's chair down the line with a screech and joined us at the bar. I lifted my brow and turned back to my paper and tea.

"And a good morning to you, Mr. MacLeod." I said nonchalantly.

"Oh aye, a good morrow indeed!" He shoveled egg into his mouth. "Has that twit John been round yet?"

"Not as of yet." The Colonel said cheerily without a concern in the world.

"Great then I won't have missed what in the world it is that we are supposed to do about this FAIRY YAH VOLUNTEERED US TO GET AFTER." MacLeod was clearly as sour as I was with the way things had gone last night.

"Oh for heaven's sake, you as well? Do I not recall a speech from Bertie before dinner last night about why we are here? It is the Fairy isn't it!" The Colonel asked.

"That's not the point! I was supposed to be out of here! Now I'm sacked up with you two chasin' some DAMN fairy tale!"

"Oh please, man." The Colonel scolded. "You'd have stayed on your own anyways. And furthermore!" He raised a finger but was cut off by the door banging open behind us again.

"HALL-OOOO! HALLO THERE! And how are our Fairy Masters today! Large heads I presume!" It was the fellow John. He laughed and made his way into the bar area. "Morning Char-Lot!" He chimed as he passed the desk.

"Alright there, John?" The Colonel asked.

"Alright as rain, lad! Quite the time we had last night, eh!" He slapped the Colonel who winched.

"Erhm. Yes. Yes, quite!" The Colonel coked an elbow and balled his fist with a weak smile.

"So lads! What's the plan, then!" John said and eyed us eagerly.

"Colonel?" I asked, raising my eyebrows.

"The plan. OH RIGHT THE PLAN! Yes. Well. Catch this Fairy of yours, of course!" He sputtered.

"Wonderful lads, wonderful." He eagerly eyed us more. "And…" His demeanor shifted to nerves. "And, erhm. And how will you be going about tha' then?" He smiled a toothy, though uneasy, grin.

"Well…I.. I suppose we'll, just—" The Acorn stammered.

"What can you tell us, John?" I took over. "Where has this fairy been spotted?"

"Ohhhh. Well. All over I'm afraid." He balled his hands again and rocked back and forth, shaking his head.

"Right. Well." I said. "I suppose we'll…we'll just set off and start looking then, won't we lads?" I asked my company. They shrugged with large eyes, not sure if that was the proper answer either.

"Wonderful!" John said. "Let's have a look at some maps then, shall we!"

"Fine." I said and the man was off to find them for us.

We finished our breakfast talking over maps hand drawn of the area surrounding Uig. The scale seemed drastically off and mostly guessed at, but the map at least provided us a general idea of the place. And so, although it was less than perfect, it would suit our purposes. John explained the general geography and places of interest where people had been robbed or had claimed to have seen this fairy. It seemed to me that our search would make a crescent around the town of Uig on the coast; the town itself being the point on a compass, were you to draw a half circle around it.

"Right. So there's Uig here on the coast. Balnaknock, here to the West. The Falls of Rha here, to the North. And Earlish, just there to the south." I tapped and looked at John for confirmation.

"Right." He said and nodded.

"Right." I said. "So we'll just consider that our target area then, shall we? Search the places in chapters. First West, I think. Then to the South and finally to the North. Surely we'll run into him at some point."

"I don't know Bertie...Could take days!" The Colonel said, holding his chin.

"Yes." I said, annoyed. "Several I'd bet. Hopefully we'll run into the bugger before having to search the whole area, right?" I said and flattened my hands.

"Right!" The Colonel said happily.

"Wonderful, lads! Really Wonderful." John seemed convinced. Happy to have three complete strangers agreeing to search high and low in order to solve his problem. "You almost seem like a military man, yourself there MacGregor! Have you ever served in the Army?" I eyed my company.

"I— No. Just handy with a map is all. Like the Colonel said, we've uhhh. We've had a few run-ins with things like this before...in our uh. Travels. Unfortunately," I cleared my throat and made a motion as if to dust off my hands.

"The Colonel?" John asked to my horror.

"Oh! Uh! Yes— Archie, I mean." I said through gritted teeth, forcing the name I had never used out of my mouth. "His nickname, see—" I began to explain.

"Right! Well, anyways!" John said and moved on with a sigh of relief from us all. "We are all just damned delighted you've agreed to help us— being that we are strangers to you, and all. But it's like me mah always said, god rest her! Highland Hospitality goes in every direction!" He smiled. We smiled. There was a brief, almost awkward pause.

"Right." MacLeod said and smiled with his teeth. It seemed insincere but it worked.

"Right. So. And what will yah do when yah find him, then?" John asked with a suddenly nervous face.

"We. We will— Ehrm." The Colonel said.

"We'll just have to find him first, won't we?" I said flatly.

"Right. Well. Good luck then, lads. You think you'll head West first towards Balnaknock, then?"

"I think so." I answered.

"Well. Wonderful, that. Do be careful though lads. There hasn't been much violence…just. Well mischief, shall we say? Come back round for supper and we'll have your report then, won't we?" He laced his hands together.

"Great." I said and he smiled. "Well lads, lets uhh. Let's be off then, shall we? See if we can't find us a fairy in the highlands."

"Rule Britannia." The Colonel whispered.

———◆———

It was a typical rainy misty, gray coloured day in the highlands. We trooped out of the Charlotte and just started walking West. We tramped through Glens and over hills. We walked through mud and rain puddles. We searched high and we searched low. We tried to seem inconspicuous, we tried to seem like merchants laden with goods to prompt a fairy raid. But, nothing— Morning turned to afternoon, the weather did not improve and our spirits worsened.

"Christ, we've been walking all day. Where in god's name are we?"

MacLeod said, quite soaked, as we all were. I checked the hand drawn maps again.

"Best I can tell— we're sort of? South of Balnaknock? Or not quite to Balnaknock really, but still sort of South of it anyways. Confound it— I have no idea."

The Colonel was ahead of us, cresting some small hill. Hand on hip, borrowed rain jacket flapping in the wind. He was very serious and it did little to help mine or MacLeod's morale.

"Tally ho, lads! There's the Hill! CHARGE." And off he went, pathological in his pursuit. MacLeod trudged up from behind me.

"I'm gonna kill him…" He muttered and followed after the Acorn. I sighed and did the same.

Our search continued for the remainder of the day though we saw neither hide nor hair of a fairy or thief. We made it very near to Balnaknock before deciding it best to turn round for the day and return to the Charlotte for dinner and rest for the night. Upon returning to the Charlotte the sun had gone down and the place was full again with locals eating their dinners in the bar area.

"ALRIGHT THERE FAIRY MASTERS!" John shouted and greeted us when we clanged, sopping wet, through the door. "Any luck?" We shook our heads, and he frowned. "Well— Come on for some sup then, will yah? Tomorrows another day!"

We nodded and joined the small crowd in the warm dining area.

The next morning started in very nearly the same way the one previous had begun. We ate a sloppy breakfast of egg and toast served by the slow, but kindly enough, Duncan. The Colonel chirped on about this and about that, as if we hadn't spent the entire day before tramping over the highland Isle of Skye. Already my old wound panged and throbbed in my shoulder and catching a glimpse of the wet weather outside I was sure today would bring more of the same. MacLeod ate silently beside me, his fork and knife seeming so small in his giant hands, his shoulders looming silently over his plate. He seemed to fizzle and burn with every comment the Colonel made.

"So it's South today then is it Lads?" He asked for the second or third time.

"Yes, Colonel." I said. "We'll make for the town of Earlish, as I've said. See if we can't run into the bugger somewhere between here and there."

"Capital. Capital. Pass the salt Mac, my dear man! There's a lad!" He ate and smiled, the devil. The salt shaker seemed to tense and strain under the Ferryman's grip as he passed it with a grunt.

"Rain again." He spat.

"What's that, now?" The Acorn said with a mouthful.

"I said it'll be raining again today!"

"SUUUURE! BUT IT ALWAYS RAINS IN BRITAIN!" He howled. "It's just like I've always said! Isn't it, Bertie? An English pot grows best in the—" But I cut him off.

"RIGHT. Let's be off then, lads!" I said slapping down the maps I'd been studying, an attempt to diffuse the tension as I did.

MacLeod slapped his legs and rose, reluctantly, but as if by duty. The Colonel shoveled a few more heaps of egg into his mouth before rising and trotting to catch up with us as we pushed through the door.

"Good luck, lads!" Charlotte said as we left. I turned and gave her a nod as the door swung shut. She seemed to almost smirk— as if to say, 'you'll need it'. We would.

And so off we tramped again! This time to the South! Again we merely started walking the moment we left the warmth of the hotel. It rained the morning on. Misted through the noon hour and started and stopped throughout the afternoon. As cold and as gray as the day previous, and just as the day previous we found no signs of a fairy or thief. We walked up hills and down into small valleys, we traversed our way around several peat bogs. My feet were soggy wet and my skin had the moist feel of sweat under a raincoat. I was not the happiest of men and it seemed MacLeod fared no better. Himself having the hood of his raincoat high over his head he squinted and scowled his way through the fields.

"Have a look at this, lads!" The Colonel shouted from atop a small knoll. "Looks like a promising field beyond there, shall we have a look then!" He turned and pursued before we could answer.

Judging from my poor maps, we had made it very near to what the thing labeled as 'Earlish'. Though I cannot confirm it actually being a town as we never found any sign of it; still the Colonel kept up his spirited chase, the rain or poor luck never seeming to bother him.

As the afternoon turned to evening and the sun began to set MacLeod had had enough. He cursed the weather and the fairy and begged us to return to the Charlotte. The Colonel was convinced after we coaxed him with the promise of a dram and so we three again, returned in defeat.

⸺◆⸺

The regular locals manned the bar area of the Charlotte again as we tramped back in, dripping wet. John frowned at me when I shook my head with a grimace, waving us over for dinner anyways. The hotel was warm and lit the same with a fire in the hearth and lamps high around the walls. We fanned out, the three of us, and tried to regain our health. The Colonel went right to Duncan at the bar and stuck up three fingers; though I couldn't hear what he said, I knew a whisky was bound for my hand. MacLeod slumped into a creaky chair at a small table, splashing the same plump little ladies from the night prior with rain drops as he did. And I made my way to John, leaning on the far end of the bar.

"No luck then, lad?" He asked quietly, his same nervous expression taking over his face.

"Not today John, no. Sorry to say. I'm beginning to wonder if this fairy of yours is real at all." I took off my jacket and sat in the stool next to him.

"Ah— don't be daft. The buggers out there, sure enough! Just a matter of time, it is! Come now lad." He let the word lad drag on a bit with a shrug of his shoulders. I smiled at him and took observation of the place. The Colonel was laughing and moving his hands as he talked with Duncan, three drinks in front of himself. MacLeod smiled and chatted with the plump ladies, fussing over him and his jacket. The other patrons chatted and ate or saw to their drinks, it was a happy scene after such a long day.

"What's that, lad?" John asked, catching my smile.

"Oh— It's. It's nothing. Nothing John. Just. It does feel like home here, is all. I've been marveling to myself as we tramped your hills here the last few days, how quickly your town has taken to my company."

"Ah, it's the highland way Lad, isn't it!" He smiled and winked. I frowned, just then, thinking. It had to be said.

"John— you seem like a sort of authority figure here. Can I be honest with you?" He raised his eyebrows and tilted his head.

"Well— I. Sure, sure my boy. I do try to be a sort of govnah 'round here, I do. What's on ya mind, then?"

I blurted it out.

"My name is Albert McGregor, I'm a captain in the Queen's Service, late of the 72nd Seaforth Highland Division. And Archie there is a Colonel himself, I'm his aide— see? And—" He raised his eyebrows letting out a deep sigh as he did.

"And. And, well. I. See, here's the thing, we're not here for land clearances! We're not, I swear it! We actually, well? It's sort of a long story to be honest, and uh. Well, Erhm. See here, it's just that we sort of work for the Queen, actually! Well, sort of anyways! More like her administration, that is! And well, we heard about the thievery problem and we!" He laughed and raised both hands to calm me.

"Calm down, laddy. Calm down." He said and patted at the air laughing.

"Calm down?" I sputtered.

"Yesss. Yes, calm yourself, boy." He puffed out a few more laughs and went on. "Charlotte had her suspicions, she did. You didn't take us for common enough wee folk did ya?" he laughed and put a hand on my shoulder. "No, heavens. We suspected something the moment your man stood up, we did. I'll be honest, I thought you boys would size up the land and quit after one day— I did! Report back or what have yah. Be off, anyways, so to speak! Charlotte thought we'd never see yah's again. Tough ol' gal, tha." He shook his head.

"You don't, ah? You don't suspect we were here for land seizure then?" I asked as I hunched over the bar.

"Nahhht at all, boy. Naht now, least anyways!" He shook his head, a serious face gripping his expression. "One day in this highland weather is one thing, sure. But to endure two such as yah have? Nahhhht at all, boy!" He shook his head and a weight I had not realized existed lifted from my shoulders.

"Charlotte had her suspicions, then?" I half chuckled.

"Oh, aye. Tha' she did! Said for sure you were here to size up the land— we've had noses round here before, we have. But I says, let's see. Let's seeeee. I'll tell yah the truth, I didn't believe that man Archie of yours to be insincere at all! Damn way he has about him, he does…" He trailed off and squinted his eyes. I had to laugh.

"That he does. As sincere as any of them." I said as he nodded and made sounds to agree.

"Anyways, we thought after one day of course yah'd have yer report and yah'd be off either way. When yah set off again this morning, and then came back to us again this night? Well— says, I. Can't say for certain why they's here, but it damn sure must not be to clear us off!" He nodded again, the happy plump man.

"Right, well. Your weather is terrible." I said and nodded with a smile.

"That it is, Laddy! That it is!" He laughed and put an arm around my shoulder with a squeeze. "And, and— And, would yah be in a position then to tell me why it is you are here?"

I cocked my head. "To be honest, John. Besides to solve your problem I'm not entirely sure. We do serve the Queen, and we have been sent here to help, that much is for certain. But why us? I suppose it's because the Queen doesn't want you gone." He laughed a bit more.

"Well. S'good enough for ol' John. God knows the people 'round here are right tore up with it. And for certain if it don't find a happy ending…I do worry we may well be sent packing for lack of food for the pantry!" He looked at me, concerned, but chuckling.

"We'll find him, John. Make sure the next lads who do come round to size up the land won't have any reason to send some of you off." He placed his hand over my forearm.

"Aye. I believe yah, lad. I believe yah. Tanks. Tanks." A tear welled in his eye and he coughed removing his hand. "So. So then, it'll be North in the morning, aye?"

"Yes sir. The falls of Rha— see if your fairy isn't up there." I looked around the bar, checking on my fellows. They happily chatted and drank on. Good.

"Good, good man." John said. "Just one thing, Bertie."

"Sure."

"Don't let on who yah really are. Most folk won't believe yah, feared as they are. Let's keep that business of the Queen and the military between us, shall we?"

"Of course, John. No problem, at all."

"Ah— and one more thing, Captain?" He asked.

"What's that?" I said.

"I wonder if I might join you tomorrow? Have a go at it myself?" He wrung his hands sheepishly.

"That'd be fine with me sir." I said with a smile. He slapped my shoulder once more, and left me to order a drink.

———— ◆ ————

Later that evening we returned to our small room on the third floor, unwinding for the day. MacLeod sat in a chair near to the one small table in the room, unlacing his boots. The Colonel sat on the edge of the bed doing the same. I made myself a sleeping area on the small oval carpet at the foot of the bed; the bed of course not having room for all three of us. (MacLeod and the Colonel shared the bed, a story all its own. Lots of lines drawn, as one might imagine) The Colonel sang to himself as he swayed and attempted his task, having had several whiskys. MacLeod wrung out his jacket one last time and hung his worn out old socks from the edge of the table. What a scene, I thought.

"So John knows we're military." I said casually.

"HE WHAT." shouted the Colonel, MacLeod looking up shocked.

"HOW?" spat the ferryman.

"Well, I told him." I said, plainly.

"BERTIE. HOW COULD YOU!" the Colonel scoffed, puffing out his moustache, genuinely concerned.

"Turns out he and Charlotte had their suspicions anyways, I just sort of blurted it out, really." I shrugged, maintaining my nonchalance.

"Oh well! Wonderful! And how about THAT! Am I the only one around here who cares to stick to the plan!" the Colonel said, placing his hands on his hips and shaking his head.

"YOU?! Stick to the plan! Mister stand up and volunteer us for a bloody SNIPE HUNT!" Roared MacLeod, always eager to jab at the Colonel. His favorite pastime by now. I laughed and continued to pat at my bedding, smoothing out the creases. The Colonel and he argued briefly, shouting about snipe hunts or real detective work etc etc. MacLeod threw up his arms and cursed and confident their spat was over I calmly went on.

"Yes, well. As I've said, they sort of guessed it themselves anyways.

155

Thought if we were truly land agents we'd have gotten what we needed by now and cleared off. Knew we were honest when we went at it another day in this abysmal weather." MacLeod scoffed and said something about that making sense.

"Well. Fantastic." The Colonel said going back to his boots. "You both thought it'd be ME who soiled the secret! WELL. Let the record SHOW. I SAY WOT." I laughed.

"Oh, and John will be joining us in our search North tomorrow." I added.

"Oh for god's sake— And now a bloody CIVILIAN will join the hunt!"

"MacLeod's been with us this whole time!" I said.

"NOT THE POINT, BERTIE!" The Colonel went on. "We are in the service of the Queen! We can NOT be slowed down by some— some! SOME UIGAN." MacLeod laughed. I sighed.

"Yes. Well. What harm could it do— we've two days out in the countryside and not a single sign of this thing to show for it. We might benefit from a local eye!"

"Two days! BAH! I once spent TWO MONTHS in search of the North-West Passage with Hector Stuart and we DID NOT complain!" For the life of me I could not imagine why the Colonel was so against John joining us.

"You never went to no Pole!" MacLeod spat. "I SAY." The Colonel answered, aghast. They wound up to argue once more.

"Enough. Enough!" I said patting the air. "For God's sake, calm down you two. It's just John and Charlotte who know our true identities and it's hardly cause for concern! John will join us tomorrow, end of story. He'll lead us to the Falls and god willing we'll find this fairy and be done with it!" They grumbled their reluctant acceptance.

"Well I don't like it!" The Colonel said, wrenching a boot from his foot.

"Fine. Noted." I said. "Now, the real issue tonight is this— what on earth is our plan should we actually find this thief tomorrow?"

"Fairy." Said the Colonel.

"Fine. Fairy. Whatever it is. What is our plan?" I asked again.

"Simple." Said the Colonel.

"Well?" Asked MacLeod. The Colonel scoffed, stopped his work on the second boot and looked at us with one hand on his hip.

"MacLeod will simply knock his thick head against the fairy's own and we'll drag him back here unconscious! Let the good people of Uig do what they may! I say!" He was clearly annoyed.

"Why you—" MacLeod said.

"Alright!" I laughed. "Alright." The Colonel eyed the large ferryman slyly, the devil. "You are a very large man indeed, MacLeod. Perhaps you *can* subdue the thing." I added. MacLeod merely eyed us both angrily.

"Oh right, sure. Make old MacLeod do everything, fine! And what good are you two then!" He asked.

"Well…" I began.

"Damn good distractions, we are!" The Colonel said happily.

"Aye, well that's fer damn sure." The large man grumbled. I laughed again.

"Well, then. There you have it. That's settled too. Now, I'm going to sleep, thank you very much! Try not to kill each other tonight. I am on the floor after all!"

The two men pushed and shoved into bed. I fell asleep listening to them argue about whose toe was crossing onto whose side. The absurdity of it all.

CHAPTER 19

North this time, to the Falls of Rha

I awoke the next morning earlier than I had the few previous. I admit I had within me a sort of vigor which I had been lacking thus far. I attributed my happy resolve to the unburdening of our mission with John last night and was eager to see him with us on our hunt later that morning. I quietly got ready for the day, careful not to rouse the sleeping bed fellows I shared my lodging with and made my way down the stairs to see about a spot of tea. Charlotte whispered a Scottish good morning and told me where I might find the kettle hot; tea in hand I made my way outside into the cool gray of the rising highland morning.

The air was sharp and wet, the mist swirling in from the port, and I strolled, I dare say, to lean on one of the posts that held up the jetty. It were not so bad a spot at all, tea glass in hand; I admired the morning and almost felt at home. Not a bad mission after all I'd say. I was not entirely convinced, as of yet, that we would in fact find this thief or fairy but was still comfortable it seemed with my current position regardless. For the first time since we left India really, I felt we had a proper idea of what we were after. In my mind it still might have come to nothing, but to say we were accomplishing our goal? I was quite content at that. For better or for worse, none could have said that I had failed at my post in service to my dear and dreadful Acorn Colonel.

"Alright there, Captain!" The voice startled me from my morning visions. It was the fellow John, approaching from my left side through the mist engulfing town.

"John, my good man!" I began. "You look ready for a fairy hunt!" He strolled with the aid of a walking stick, a small pack slung behind his back. His dress was classic— A deep green and red kilt with the sash of the thing thrown round the shoulder of his thick shepherd's sweater.

"Looking smart yourself, there boy!" His chipper matched my own. It felt almost as if we were pleasure hunters, off on a pretend trip in search of a local mystery, as one touring the place might do.

"Aye. Well. It'll be a long day, I'm certain. You're sure you want to come along then? Not that we wouldn't be delighted to have you!" I added.

"My dear boy! Yeees! Yes! Can't have the locals saying we men of Uig didn't do our part can we? Charlotte have the kettle on, then?"

"She does indeed, sir! I'll be in in a moment!" He smiled and strolled on, some parts of his outfit clinking and clambering as he went. Bless the man— from that time on, when I thought of Uig, I thought of him. He was the embodiment of the highlands; as the Colonel was of his Empire. I loved them both for it. He led these people, whether they had asked him to or not. And his love of his home was charming to me, and only added to my morning devotion on the docks of Uig town.

I spent the better part of an hour as such— and was only too happy to do so.

When I finally pushed my way back into the hotel I found a familiar scene. The Colonel and John sat in stools laughing— the Colonel heaping eggs into his mouth between shouts and quips. Big MacLeod leaned further down the bar explaining something to Duncan by the way he moved his hands. I stood for a moment and watched before the Colonel finally saw me and raised a glass for a proper good morning.

"Bertie, my lad! In from the cold are ya!" He seemed as happy as myself. Good, I thought. "John was just telling me about The Falls we shall trip this day! Weren't you, my good man!" He ribbed John who let out a soft whistle and a laugh.

"Is that right?" I asked. "I suppose you've been there before, have you?" I said and approached.

"Oh aye— I have! Many ah time! Lovely spot, that is!" The Colonel half cheered with a mouthful of egg.

"How long a walk, would you say?" I asked the man.

"Ohhhh— the better part of the day I'd say, to be safe!" He said with his classic look of concern.

"Right, well. If you lads are ready, then. I say we head off at once."

"CAPITAL, LAD! CAPITAL!" The Colonel declared and shoveled the remainder of his feast down before dusting off his sheepskin coat while rising. "Look sharp there, Mac! And to arms!"

Some half hour later we were all fit enough to push through the door and out into the morning- happily we found the morning sun cutting its way through the mist.

"AH-HAH! The sun! A good omen, I say! We shall find our fairy this day, and be sure of it!" The Colonel announced with squinted eyes and hands on hips. "Tally HO!" He promptly turned sharp left and marched.

"This way, Colonel." I called from behind, taking John's lead heading to the right and into the hills.

"RIGHT!" He marched back, arms swinging. I imagine John wondered just then how long he could keep up that pace and vigor from the look in the man's face. I hadn't the heart to tell him- all day.

And so we marched! Yet again! The third day of our search beginning as had the rest. John led us first along the road and well out of town. We passed several houses nodding and wishing good mornings to the few who kept them. They whispered and waved, surely commenting on this being the mad company of strangers who had promised to find their fairy. The Colonel issued many Huzzahs and Hoorays, as was his way. And I will say, though we did not find a trace of any mischief well into early afternoon, I found day three to be much more enjoyable. The sun was warm in the cool air, and if one stopped to rest in it, which we did often for the benefit of old John, who huffed and puffed— then one would almost find himself beginning to sweat. The march was easier this time too, we rarely seemed to leave a proper road and therefore had less of a challenge gallivanting over hills and glens as we had previous when we lacked a native guide. I began to enjoy myself.

"My!" Huffed the fellow John. "My. My. My. Is that true?" He asked me while leaning over his walking stick, referring to a tall tale the Colonel had been telling.

"OF COURSE IT IS!" He shouted from on ahead.

"Perhaps, I think yes." I whispered to the man with a smile and a wink.

"Bollocks." MacLeod said, without a whisper.

But the Colonel kept on without hearing and so we walked, until we were very near to the Falls themselves.

"It's…It's not far off now lads! Just to the top here and back down around, see the river cuts through those hills just there!" He pointed and huffed. I must give the man credit, he doggedly kept up our pace, determined as he must have been, and we did enjoy his being there. Having an outsider seemed to keep the relative peace between the Colonel and MacLeod, reluctant friends as they were. I would equate their relationship to that of family— forced to love one another by blood. Our blood being our shared mission of course, but the effect was the same. I laughed and continued to pull myself along the way.

"Ah-hah!" The Colonel called from ahead. "I hear them! I say! I hear the falls! Tally Ho, lads! Not long now! Not long!" The man streamed ahead and down the hill before us.

"For God's sake," MacLeod said and moved to catch up. I hung back with John, matching his slow pace.

"Is. Is your man there always so…energetic? I wonder?" He struggled to puff out his words. I had to laugh.

"Yes, I'm afraid it is his way." I said. John nodded and paused briefly to catch his breath. "I do wonder though John, we seem to be no nearer catching this thing than we were three days ago. Is there anything about the sightings from before that seem to match? I mean— what usually brings about a run-in with this thing? Whatever we're doing, it doesn't seem to be working. Does it?" He seemed to consider my question a moment as he began his march again.

"I'm afraid there really isn't, Bertie. I'm sure you must think by now we've made it all up!" He huffed.

"Nonsense, that it does exist? Sure enough that much is clear. We've heard about it as far off as Liverpool. Rumors and whispers among locals, of course, but still. There has to be *something* out here. But how to find it…"

"Well— I'm afraid mostly it's just been assumptions, see? Someone will wake up to a missing flock of ewe. Or a damaged and ransacked garden- and they'll? They'll simply blame the fairy, they will! But old Sherman claims he saw the bugger make off from his place one evening round dusk— and of course Mrs. Abigail Walker has a similar claim from the window of her front room!" He shook his head. From the road ahead the Colonel could be heard whooping and shouting with some sort of glee- I assumed he found the Falls.

"Look at em!" I heard him echo from below.

"I don't suppose we ought to have a visit to old Sherman's place? Should we?" I asked.

"Well, sure. But yah came damn close enough to it when you went out round Balnacknock I'm certain!"

"Bugger." I weakly stated.

"Bugger, indeed." He said and stopped. "Ah! Why? The Falls of Rha!"

I turned from John and saw them, magnificent I must say. The falls of Rha are aptly named; there are two of them. A sort of double waterfall flowing down from the hills. One fall fell from up above where the river made its way down through the hills into a small pool, before falling again to the elevation I stood at with John. Wonderful view, I admit, I don't mind to restate it. MacLeod leaned against a tree with crossed arms watching the ever youthful Colonel scampering all around them. He shouted and whooped like a small boy, and I had to laugh before turning back to John. He himself eyed the beauties as if they were made by his own people, and sure enough to me? They were. But they did little else to help our cause, as no fairy seemed present.

"Have a look here!" The Colonel shouted from above. "This pool looks VERY MISCHIEVOUS. A great spot for a fairy, I'd say!" He splashed around out of my view. He began shouting for the fairy to come out and I saw MacLeod roll his eyes.

"Well, whatta ya say, lad?" John asked.

"It is lovely John, sure. But I don't see a fairy or a thief, do you?"

"No...No I do not." He sighed.

Beauty be damned we both seemed to accept the fact that no fairy would be found this day or at these falls. For the lovely morning, the lovely stroll, and all the loveliness of the company here at this spot, my mood soured and the gravity of the hopelessness of ever finding this thing began to weigh on me. It seemed impossible that we would ever find one thief in all these hills surrounding Uig.

"John!" The Colonel shouted from above. "Have a look at that pool, man! Fit for a Fairy, I'd say! Come on, man! Have a look yourself!"

John rolled his eyes at me and sighed before beginning to scramble up to the pool made by the first of the two falls. I ambled up to MacLeod and joined him, cross armed, watching the boy at play.

"Whatta ya say, Mac?" I asked.

"I say there aint shite here." He spat.

"No. I'm afraid you're right." I said as he raised his eyebrows to agree, arms still cross. I went on. "I wonder— How long can we go at it before we call it what it is? Not that we have anywhere else to be- It's just that I'm beginning to wonder if this was all just rumors and fantasy after all."

"Aye." Macleod said. "But good luck convincing your man there." He nodded at the Colonel who by now was flinging water down onto John as he made his way up the rock. I chuckled, but behind my laugh was that ever growing sense of hopelessness again. How would we convince the Colonel to give up? I could not imagine. But I was his valet, it was my personal duty to keep the man straight! As I had done before and intended to keep doing, however painful that might be to me! But the weight of that task did burden me, I cannot lie, and so worry began to set in.

After an hour or so of standing around the Falls the Colonel finally agreed to begin our walk back to the Charlotte. For the first half hour or so we all agreed over and over with him on both the beauty of the falls and the potential there for fairy activity. I hadn't found the means to broach the subject that hung over the three of us- that perhaps it was indeed time to call it quits. My feet ached from the days of long marching and even though the sun still hung in the sky, I felt wet to the core.

"Perhaps tomorrow we march back out here and set a snare for the little Devil! We might set several more around to the East and South! We can circle round them all until we get the bugger! What do you say, Bertie?" The Colonel chirped as we walked, the sun showing signs of early evening.

"Colonel, I—" I stammered.

"What's that now Bertie, bit of the soldier's blues, aye? Don't worry, my boy! We'll catch him! We will!" He didn't pick up on the read of the group.

"Oh just tell the man, boy!" MacLeod grumbled.

"Tell me, what?" He stopped.

"Colonel, I. I just wonder if perhaps it isn't time to call it quits? We've spent three days and hiked through the entirety of the region! Maybe... Maybe there is no thief..."

"Of course there isn't!" He puffed out his moustache and placed both hands onto his hips.

"Oh?" I said.

"Because it's a BLOODY FAIRY!" He crossed his arms.

"Oh come on, man!" MacLeod said.

"Colonel, really. Wouldn't our efforts for the Queen be better spent elsewhere?"

"NONSENSE! Nonsense, Bertie! Our task is here! Here! John! John— Surely you must agree with me!" He looked at our local voice.

"Oh— Well. See here, I do! It's just. I can't imagine you lot would want to keep traipsing these hills with nothing to show for it!"

"BAH!" The Colonel swatted at the air. "Three days in bivouac and you all want to call it quits! I say! Why, Hector and myself never called quits! Not when the ice from the pole was CHOKING IN AROUND US! AND LET ME SAY THIS!" I loved him for his devotion. He was devoted, if nothing else. He went on giving many other examples of forgoing brevity in the name of the Queen and we all shrank and tried to hide our eyes for the shame of not being able to agree.

"I say. Bertie. Would you return to Abigail without a story of victory? I mean it!" I pursed my lips and tilted my head.

"Who is Abigail?" I heard John asked MacLeod.

"Some girl. I don't know." They watched us argue. The Colonel asked me who I was in service of. I tried to reason with him. We argued back and forth as the others stood by.

"It is a wonder though." I heard John say to MacLeod, both men cross armed and watching us.

"What's that?" The large man said, amused.

"I thought for certain you lot would find this thing at the Fairy Glen."

"The what?" MacLeod asked.

"The Fairy Glen? You know! The Fairy Glen! Out towards Balnaknock!" MacLeod shrugged.

"Never heard of it." The Ferryman grumbled.

"You didn't check the Fairy Glen?" I heard him say between the Colonel's shouts of duty, courage, honor.

"Hang on, the what?" I turned to ask him.

"The Fairy Glen!" He said. "The one out towards Balnaknock! You lot didn't check there?"

"No— We. I've never heard of the place!" I shouted back.

"What's that, now? A fairy's what?" The Colonel piped in.

"Oh for god's- The FAIRY GLEN. It's on your map, it is! It's out towards Balnaknock!"

"Right! We've heard that! I don't— I don't know. No! It isn't on the map!" I said.

"Check the map." The Colonel said and reached for my pockets.

"No— Would you. Stop." I slapped at his arms.

"Sure enough it is! Look, here. Look!" John said and reached for my pockets the same.

"Okay, alright. ALRIGHT. I'll get the map!" I swatted them both off and fumbled into my pockets in search of the maps John had given me three days prior.

"Here, here they are, here. See here." I unfolded the map, the three men gathered round to crane their necks. "See there. Nothing about a Fairy Glen on this map!" I slapped at the thing.

"Ah." Said John. "Well. Well it ought to be!" We all looked at him cross but said nothing. He shrugged.

"Right." I said. "Well what is it!"

"Oh well, it's just— It's called the Fairy Glen! Sort of a local wonder, see? Spiral rock formation on the ground, little rock tower, looks like a castle, see? Like a little Fairy's Garden!" He explained.

"Just sounds like another place for visitors to ogle at, like your falls were." I said candidly, not bothering to be careful with offense.

"Nonsense!" The Colonel shouted. "I want to check this fairy glen!"

"Colonel, we've been all around it! If it were there, surely we'd have heard it— or it would have made itself...KNOWN! I don't know!"

"I want. To check. THE FAIRY GLEN." He crossed his arms and looked away. I gritted my teeth.

"FINE! FINE! Tomorrow! The Fairy Glen! But if it's not there, and I DOUBT IT WILL BE! Then we call it quits and not another word about it!"

"Really?" He turned and squinted at me.

"YES REALLY!" I shouted again.

"Wonderful!" The Colonel exclaimed, all smiles again, as if we hadn't just argued up and down the hills of Uig.

"Say it." I said.

"Say what?" His arms still cross.

"Say we'll be done if we find nothing there."

"Hm!" He puffed out his moustache.

"COLONEL."

"Oh YES. Yes, sure. The Fairy Glen or bust." He stuck his tongue out at me. I forced myself to ignore it.

"Right." I said. "You." I pointed at John. "You show me where exactly this thing is on the map, and tomorrow? We go."

"Yeh— Yes sir!" John shouted. I slapped the map back into my pocket and began to walk again. The rest of my company joined me.

"Bertie?" The Colonel chirped from behind.

"What." I asked without turning, keeping my pace.

"Are you upset with me?"

"No." I said and smiled, though I didn't let him see.

We returned to the Charlotte, ate our dinner and planned the next day's final attempt to locate and capture a thief who might be a fairy.

BOOK III

A Study in Fair Folk

CHAPTER 20

The Fachan

It would be quite inaccurate to describe my knowledge of the Highland hills around Uig as anything other than poor. Days spent wandering them does less for a man's ability to describe them than one might guess. For they are a dizzying labyrinth of greens and browns. The mist obscuring what the sky convolutes— the whole of the world seeming exactly the same, no matter how many footsteps you might count or acknowledge. I had studied the map for hours that night, going over and over the spot John claimed this Fairy Glen was hidden, trying to mark out reference points which I might find useful the following day. I had found the spots, the reference points, but no matter how many times I counted steps, measured previously compassed lines or racked my brains to decipher where we were, we continually found ourselves lost and were therefore forced to retrace our steps often.

The mist was heavy thick that morning when we left the Charlotte, and rather than wait another day for better weather I had stubbornly chosen to go— damned determined as I was to prove the Colonel wrong and be done with it. A decision I greatly regretted at present. For we were lost yet again and it was nearing the noon hour, at least. I walked, distractedly conscious of each step, glancing between my feet and the map, surrounded by the mist and fog. Damp, is how the world seemed. The Colonel carefully walked a few steps ahead of me, obscured in mist at times, and the man MacLeod kept up the rear.

"Bloody POINTLESS." MacLeod said several times throughout the morning. We had woken quite disheartened, save for the Colonel.

John had chosen not to accompany us as he had woken himself sore and uncomfortable from the day's hike previous. I continued to curse myself for not waiting another day, but every step I took frustrated me further and demanded I see this place found and found empty of fair folk or thieves. We were making our way along a small path we'd found after our second or third time traipsing along an unmarked road. Upon its discovery there was a brief moment of excitement in which we imagined we'd discovered some secret way to the Fairy Glen, but as we tip-toed the broken path, fit more for a goat than a man, our hearts sank once more.

"This is bloody bollocks. This path leads nowhere! It's hardly fit fer a man!" MacLeod shouted. I sighed aloud, fearful our group was splintering once more, worried for the cause I might have had in it.

"Oh, rubbish!" The Colonel shouted back. "Maybe not for a man SUCH AS YOU! YOU GREAT LUMMOX!"

"WHY YOU—" MacLeod said and raised a fist over my head, shaking it at the Colonel.

"Gentlemen, please!" I said. "This is not helping matters!" I tried to reason with them though I felt every bit of MacLeod's frustrations. It did seem quite pointless by now.

"No. Nope. I'm done! I am! I won't go no further, madness, tha' is! There is no Fairy Glen! Four days we've been doing this! No more!"

"I say, you don't know that!" The Colonel shouted back.

"I know it! DAMN FOOL. You go on, then! Find it yerself! I'm done!" MacLeod raised both hands and turned, beginning to walk back the way we had come.

"MacLeod, please!" I shouted. "Please, wait! Wait a moment!" I begged.

"I will not— I've had it! Bloody mistake coming here at all..." He walked on. I turned to the Colonel who's face showed concern for only the briefest of moments before settling into a grim expression.

"Let him go, laddy! Let him go!" He scoffed.

"Colonel— Damn it! We need him!" I ran after MacLeod, careful to avoid several rocks strewn across the path.

"Mr. MacLeod! MacLeod! Please— would you wait a moment!" I shouted catching up to the hulking figure.

"Bah!" He spat when I grabbed at his high shoulder.

"Please, MacLeod, Please. We need you." I breathed.

"HARDLY!" The Colonel shouted from up the path.

"Please, Mac." I begged. He squinted angrily at the man.

"Yah won' find this Glen, boy— Shite. Even if yah do, there won' be no thief about it. Look around yah, bloody fog is socked in so thick yah canny breath for lack of it!"

"Let's just find the end of the path, then. We'll be done soon enough and back to the Charlotte!" I continued to plead with the man.

"Can' do it, lad. I'm sorry. I am sorry. I'm soaked through. Dog tired. I can' go one step more. Find your glen, and then find me back in town. I'll get yah to Portree in the morning, and be done with it all." He turned to walk away, shaking his large head as he disappeared into the mist. My shoulders dropped as I watched him go, feeling totally helpless and alone in the hills around Uig. I didn't believe we'd ever find this thief, but should we get lucky, we were now absent one large and foreboding ally. We were alone again. In my wallowing, a hand reached into my view and wrapped itself around my shoulders gently squeezing…

"The warrior's path is often lonely, my boy." It whispered. I turned and caught the Colonel musing at the sight of the man's departure as if it wasn't his fault at all.

"COLONEL! Damn it! We needed him!" I shouted.

"I say! Hardly!" He placed his hands on his hips, a classic.

"Hardly! HARDLY! And what will you do if you find this thief? Ask him nicely to surrender?!" I was quite ruffled.

"Please! I say, two strapping men of Britannia such as we! Nooooo! No— We shall be fineeee! We'll manage! We will!"

"But MacLeod is our friend…" I sighed.

"Yes, I say, our very large and very grouchy friend. Noooo! No my boy, he'll have his feet up in the Charlotte before evening and we'll be back soon thereafter, thief in hand! MORE GLORY FOR US, I SAY WOT!" He laughed, I couldn't believe it.

"We'll never find this Fairy Glen, Colonel. And even if we do manage it, I do not believe we'll find any sign of our thief there." I put it bluntly, shaking my head.

"Course we won't lad!" He winked. "Because it's a FAIRY!" He nudged me with his elbow and carried on with his walk. I sighed and tried to catch up, turning one last time to see if MacLeod had changed his mind. He hadn't, it seemed. I jogged briefly to catch my charge.

"You do remember your promise, don't you, Colonel?" I asked.

"What's that, boy?" He shouted over his shoulder interrupting a passionate whistle he'd begun.

"Your promise— The promise you made should we not find this fairy!"

"We'll have to find the Glen first, I think!" He shouted at me as if an afterthought.

"Right…" I whispered to myself.

Our progress along the goat path slowed and sped at the whim of the tiny path. At times we had to clamber over rock and tree branch until the way began to narrow further with the addition of a second rising hill; before long the path resembled a small canyon, but this did little to damage the Colonel's spirits. I grew more hopeless all the while.

"I say, Bertie! I've been thinking!"

"What's ah— What's that Colonel?" I asked as I shimmied between the rock faces.

"About Fergus!"

"Joy. And what about the old sod, then?"

"Well. Not so much him, rather something he said. What was it he told us about Fairy's again?" He stopped and took a breath. I considered his question and cleared my throat.

"Uhhh. Not much, really. He. He sort of explained the different types, didn't he?"

"Riggght. Right." He puffed out his moustache. "And do you remember any, then?"

"Ahh. Well. Not really, if I'm honest. Do you?" he sighed, pursed his lips and shook his head.

"Right. Uhh. Something about the sort who live near water, wasn't it? And the ones with the little red tunics?" I offered.

"Yes, but wasn't there something about one sort having just one eye? Wasn't ours supposed to have one eye? I've not heard that up here, come to think of it— Have you?" He asked, puzzled. I admit I was too.

"No, actually. I haven't heard that either. Was ours supposed to have just the one eye? I don't remember." I honestly couldn't. We kept walking, confused.

"Sureeee, Sure! Didn't somebody say that? Who said that? Not Fergus, was it?"

"Uhh? It was Barnsworth, wasn't it? Back at the Tin?" I added, causing the Colonel to chuckle.

"I say— It was Barnsworth, wasn't it? That damn fool!" He laughed on. "Seems he got that one thing wrong, didn't he? Silly old Barnsworth... Poor sod. Bugger, though. I could have sworn Fergus said something about it too."

"He did, I think. He had a name for it— The Fowlin? I don't know. Something strange, at any rate. You were quite fixed on it; I'm surprised you don't remember."

"No— No. It wasn't The Fowlin, it was something else. Come now, Bertie! Surely you remember!"

I laughed. "I'm certain I do not! I'm still not sold this thing IS a fairy!"

"The Falcon, was it? No— No, that's a bird." He stroked his chin and thought about it. "The Froley? Nooo, no. The foxly!" he snapped his fingers. "No. Confound it, wrong. What was it!" he was laughing.

"Oh who cares, Colonel. What does it matter, anyways?"

"The Fachan!" He shouted. "That was it, wasn't it!" He laughed and eyed for my approval. I laughed a little with him.

"Right. Yes, that was it. The Fachan. Really wonderful." We strolled on, the path bending ahead of us.

"The Fachan? Yeees, ee-yes. One eye. One eye...I say!" He made scratching sounds for a second before igniting the end of his pipe, puffing out several small clouds denoting deep thought.

"Where on earth do you keep that thing?" I asked. He began to answer before turning his gaze to the path ahead of us with a squint of both eyes.

"I say, Bertie. The path is widening out! My god...MY GOD MAN! LOOK!" He pointed, a puff of tobacco smoke escaping his mouth as he did. I turned to look myself, and indeed the path opened itself up to none other than a Glen. The sun shone brightly from the far side of the thing; not a spot of mist obscured our vision. A little rock formation towered over the Glen, resembling a walled castle, and a rock formation spiraled on the ground before it...

"Dear…GOD." The Colonel whispered before breaking into a run. "WE FOUND IT! BERTIE! LOOK HERE! WE FOUND IT! WAHH-WOOHOO! YIPEEE! WOULD YAH LOOK AT IT!" He danced around the spiral circle; I caught up, staring in disbelief.

"What…on earth…" I couldn't believe my eyes. It was just as it were described to us, a perfectly hidden glen complete with an over looming castle and an unexplained spiral formation. The Castle was truly just a rock…but damn if it didn't resemble a small fairy's home. And the spiral was the same, rock pieces pressed into the ground forming the shape some 40 feet in diameter.

"WOULD YAH LOOK AT IT!" The Colonel shouted and danced.

"I— I see it! What on earth do you think caused it?" I hate, even now, the phrasing I used.

"WHY. FAIRIES OF COURSE! What else could explain this perverse shape!" He danced and spun round.

"Perverse shape? Colonel it's a spiral…" I said, mostly thinking to myself.

"UNNATURAL, BERTIE!" He began to walk the shape with long over exaggerated steps. "I wonder how it works!"

"How what works?" I asked.

"THE SPIRAL!" He answered, of course.

"How it wo— Colonel I don't think it's meant to do anything! It's just… well most probably it's some sort of ritualistic shrine from a past peoples, denoting, perhaps weather patterns? Or maybe the stars. I wonder…" I trailed off, mostly talking to myself.

"NONSENSE! IT'S A FAIRY THING! COME! COME HERE, LAD, LOOK!" He shouted and moved towards me, grabbing my shoulders and pushing towards the shape on the ground.

"See— See here, boy. It's almost— why it's a path! See! You start at the open mouth and if you follow it—" He pushed me forward and guided me through the shape. "You sort of…Why you sort of get to the end of it, don't you!" We arrived at the end, or rather where the spiral meets in the center, where the largest of the rocks was pressed into the earth. We climbed on top, the Colonel searching all around.

"Well?" I said.

"Hm. I thought that might do something…" He stroked his chin again. "Curious, very curious." I laughed.

"You've lost it. And furthermore, I don't see a fairy here. Do you?"

"Well, my god! It's got to be here somewhere, hasn't it! Let's have a look up at the castle, shall we!" He ran off.

"Colonel, I— I should hardly think that will make a difference! BE CAREFUL!" I called after him as he began to climb towards the thing.

"COME ON, BOY! THE CASTLE!" He scampered up the rock and I chased after him, much more careful and deliberate in my efforts. We arrived at the top and leaned on the formations, and though they did resemble a fortress of old, in truth, they were simply just rocks.

"Rocks." I said.

"Hmph." He puffed. "Quite the view though, aye?"

"You're stalling." I spat.

"Stalling what!" He shouted.

"Oh give it up, old man! There's nothing here! It is quite fantastic, I'll warrant you that! Much better than those falls, but I don't see another soul around! Do you? Colonel, isn't it time!" I trailed off.

"Stop that." He said. "I won't hear it."

"Colonel. We tried." I shrugged as a hard wind swept up the rocks chilling my skin.

"We haven't tried hard enough, clearly!" He crossed his arms.

"Come now, old boy. That can't be further from the truth. You know? I'd bet the fire is lit at the Charlotte— Perhaps we head back there for a whisky? We can talk about what to do, sure. But Colonel, really I think it time—" He cut me off.

"What's that?" He asked, a look of concern on his face.

"What?" I asked and looked around.

"Nah— Nothing." He said. "No! That! Can't you hear it?"

"Hear what?" I suspected a trick.

"That sound! You don't hear that!"

"No! What is it? What are you talking about!" He looked around, his face of concern still evident.

"I swear I heard…laughing…" He squinted his eyes.

"Laughing? What are you getting at? Is this some point you're trying to prove? It won't work, Colonel. And to be frank- Oof!" He pushed his hand into my gut and held up a finger.

"There." He said. A chill went up my spin. Laughter. In the hills around us. Quiet. Faint at first, but growing.

"Wha— Colonel? What is that?" I grew nervous.

"Steel away your nerves now lad— I fear...the thief grows neigh..." He squinted his eyes shut tighter and looked around as if prepared for war. The faint laughter continued.

"Colonel... I. It's the wind. That's it! Hah! Can't you tell! My god. It's the wind whipping off the rock face here! My god, I will admit, you did worry me for a second there, Colonel. My god, my god. Ah-hah. My. Let's be off this rock then, I—"

"BERTIE! LOOK!" He pointed towards the spiral. I followed his hand, slowly, nervous, afraid even. And sitting in the center was...was a person. Rather a small person, but a person nonetheless! A cloak around its shoulders, and a piece of cloth tied around his head, covering one of his eyes. He slowly looked up, and I nearly fainted, too shocked to speak.

"My god..." The Colonel whispered. "It's him...I can't believe it. It's him. IT'S HIM! THE FACHAN! THE FACHAN, BERTIE! IT'S HIM! CATCH HIM! CATCH HIM, BERTIE! RUUUUUULE BRITANNIA!" He galloped down the hill to my utter despair, sheepskin fluttering in the breeze, his military cap catching the glint of the sun. It was marvelous, for the briefest of moments.

"COLONEL, NO!" Was all I could manage. But the man was off and running. And I, to my own great credit, ran after him, though it was of course, much against my character. We bounded! Taking great leaps at a time. The Colonel closing the distance between himself and the creature yet unknown! Myself, closing the gap between me and my charge. The Acorn landed with a soft thump onto the damp ground, falling to his knees for just a moment, before regaining his stature and charging again!

"RULEEEEEE BRITANNIA!" He sprinted, myself behind, matching his speed, not at all certain who I was after or what would happen next! The creature laughed and stood to face our advances! It was A.R Korn who reached him first, throwing out his arms and diving towards the thing! He missed! Landed with a thump and turned to yell at me!

"CATCH HIM, BERTIE! CATCH HIM! HE'S COMING YOUR WAY!" It ran at me, startling me and throwing me off balance.

"JESUS CHRIST!" I shouted and threw out my arms!

But it was just too poor a showing. The thing side-stepped, evaded and ran for the hills. Pathetic as I am, I turned, slipped and watched him scamper up the cliff towards the castle before jumping down the other side and out of our view.

I lay in a heap. Defeated and sore, full of shame. The Colonel slammed his fist on the ground cursing. "DAMN! HE GOT AWAY!" He shouted. He scrambled back up and started running towards the castle again.

"Wait! Wait!" I cried and tried to stand. "Hang on, just wait! Let's plan this thing out!" I begged.

"Plan this thing out, man? The battle is here! Quickly! QUICKLY NOW, LAD!" He rushed past me and began to clamber back up the rock face. He slipped. Lost his footing a few times, and gave up, pounding the wall with a fist as he did. I dusted myself off, caught my breath and coughed as the Colonel came back to my aide.

"Alright there, lad?" He asked, trying to heave me onto my feet. I brushed him away and leaned over my knees, still on the ground.

"Yes. Christ. My wound, you see?" I offered weakly.

"MY GOD, BERTIE. IT WAS HIM! THE FACHAN!" He stared in disbelief at the rock wall again. "Did you see! My god! One eye! And the way he MOVED!"

"Now? Now, Colonel. We have no way of knowing if that was our thief!" I said.

"MY DEAR, BOY. IT WAS A FAIRY! HOW ELSE WOULD HE- WOULD HE HAVE...BLOODY MATERIALIZED LIKE THAT!" He was delirious.

"We don't know that! We weren't looking, Colonel! He might have been...hell, he might have been a little Shepherd boy! One we've just scared halfway to death!" I didn't want to believe it. I wanted to offer— rational! Concrete explanation! But the Colonel wasn't having it.

"What do we do?!" He spat. "Should we give pursuit, lad!" He looked around.

"No— I. No, I think we ought to report back. Find MacLeod— Damn! Find John, tell him! Tell him what we saw, maybe he can confirm whether or not…" I trailed off, still very shook up from the battle, I couldn't catch my breath.

"Nonsense! Nonsense, boy! We haven't the time!" I rubbed my eyes as the Colonel shouted. "My god, man. LOOK."

I stopped rubbing my eyes and looked up towards the castle where the Colonel was pointing. To my profound horror, there stood, silhouetted along the cliff, not one, but many figures. Some seemed to wear masks made of burlap. Some held sticks or clubs. All wore the same cloak the figure before had donned. And there stood the leader, one eye covered, cocking his head.

"Oh my god…" I whispered. "There must be, Christ. There must be twenty of them. What do we do- DON'T? Don't say anything!" I whispered sharply, waving a hand at the Colonel.

"Don't. Make. Any. Sudden. Moves. Laddy." The Colonel said through pursed lips. "They have us outnumbered…" He squinted.

"YOU DON'T SAY!" I spat. And I will tell you, I was quite afraid. The situation, not bearing much difference to my combat experience in the Afghan, had deteriorated so quickly my head spun. Suddenly I found myself, lost? In a fairy world I didn't want to believe in. Reason was slipping away, rational thought seemed more irrational with every face I caught standing on the cliffs above me. Images of my men retreating? The sound of battle returning to my ears! What in the world was happening? The Colonel was all iron though, and seemed to read my concern. He readied me for war…

"Bertie. What is it we are in service of?" I swallowed hard as he asked. But seeing no way out, I obliged the old nut, for it was he and I alone now it seemed.

"We are in service to the Queen. And with him. The Empire of Britannia." I struggled to get out.

"And as such?" he hunched his shoulders and squeezed his fists shut.

"We are—" I began but lost my voice catching the faces of more hooded things above.

"WE ARE!" he shouted.

"WE ARE DUTY-BOUND! Tah- to see to its successes…" I swallowed again.

"By pain of death!" he shouted.

"BY PAIN OF DEATH! OR! OR MOCKERY IN THE STREETS!"

"RIGHT THEN. YOU THERE! FACHAN!" He pointed at the thing, who I now believed was indeed, the Fachan. "ARE YOU THE FAIRY WHAT'S BEEN STEALING FROM THESE GOOD PEOPLE!" It cocked its head to the other side.

"SPEAK." The Colonel shouted. "OR WE ARE FOR YOU!"

It raised its hand and pointed at us without a word. His band of followers let out yelps and whoops of all calibers and descended the rocks towards us.

"Oh! Oh GOD!" I said and stood, finally, pushing my shoulders against the Colonel.

"COME WHAT MAY! HOLD THY GROUND, YOU SOLDIER OF ENGLAND!"

The wild crowd approached with speed, they surrounded us whooping and hollering. Encircling us, they waved hands and jabbed at us with sticks. Myself and the Colonel bumped into each other and slowly inched backwards toward the spiral. They lunged and whooped, but never got close enough to touch. We inched and inched, lunging back in an effort to scare off our assailants the same!

"They!" I shouted. "Are they?! CHILDREN!" I shouted over the gale.

"DON'T LET THEM CLOSE! AH! YAH BUGGER!" he waved a fist at the crowd! We inched closer to the spiral.

"COLONEL! WE! WATCH OUT!" We had our backs to one another now, fending off the gang of miscreants.

"THE SPIRAL! CARE- CAREFUL! COLONEL!"

I tried to step over one of the rocks making up the formation, but in the struggle, I misread the size of the thing. My foot just barely grabbed the edge of the stone, bearing the weight of my body it slipped. I grabbed for the Colonel but felt myself fall. A sharp pain in the back of my head put out the lights, and I saw nothing more.

CHAPTER 21

Fairy Games

I awoke in a crumpled heap. The waning sun forcing my eyes to squint shut, I tried to ease them open. The Colonel was making his usual comments—something about the Queen. Britannia. His promise of swift retribution. What on earth?

I sat up and rubbed the back of my head. The seat of my pants and the tips of my knees were damp from the dewed and cold earth. I was uncomfortable.

"AH! BERTIE! AWAKE AT LEAST!" The Colonel shouted, unseen yet by me. "TELL THIS FAIRY HE SHALL NOT STRIP OUR HONOR, YET! I SAY!" My head pounded as I rubbed sense into myself. "UNTIE ME YOU DOGS!"

"Colonel what are ya—" I said and looked up. "Oh! Oh, goodness me. Oh dear god." I found The Colonel tied to a pole of sorts stuck into the earth at the center of the spiral. His arms were at his sides and ropes bound him round and round. I should have laughed at his moustache twitching back and forth in discomfort, if not for the cascading realization of time and place gripping me at present.

"Oh my...I—" I said and looked around at the entire scene. "Right. Hello there." I said to the Fachan standing over me to my right. Surrounding the spiral was his gang of fairy miscreants.

"RUN BERTIE." The Colonel shouted. But I did not obey, I merely sat and observed from the ground. I forced myself to steal the nerves, which I take great credit for, even still. The Fachan, however, said nothing. Eerily he cocked his head at me.

"Um. Right. Well. I see you've tied up my charge, there." I tried to remain calm. I didn't want to incite further aggression. I had not yet heard the thing speak, only the Colonel, who continued to squawk like a trapped swan.

It would be of pertinence to this account, I think, to restate my opinion on several matters at present in our narrative— I still did not believe this creature to be a fairy. He looked like an adolescent to me, of no more consequence than an irate school boy— but the Colonel believed it true, and the thing itself gave no notion of disbelief in the idea either, and so, I played along. Perhaps there was some doubt in my mind... Regardless, he did not answer me.

"Might I ask why?" I squinted up at him. The Colonel continued to shout curses and threats.

He didn't answer me still, the creature. Instead he started to laugh! Confound the thing he laughed into fits! His band of fairies joined in; the Colonel's eyes grew wide and then cross with anger. He fumed. Still I gave them nothing.

"Right. Well, if you won't answer me— I'll just untie my charge here and be off, won't I!" I stood and dusted my knees off, doing my best impression of a school teacher.

"BERTIE! ATTACK, LAD! ATTACK!" The Colonel shouted. I wished he wouldn't, he had no concept of my game. I took a step towards him.

"I don't think sah!" The Fachan shouted as several of his gang raised their sticks and clubs— I raised my own hands in defense and backed off a tad.

"Alright— Alright there..." I began. "But I must say, you're not giving me much to go on here, lad."

He laughed again, that childish laugh, full of mischief.

"Your friend tah is a loud one. Had tah tie em oop." His voice was light. Though his accent thick in places.

"I see that— good for him, says I." I stated and crossed my arms.

"BERTIE!" the Colonel chirped in.

"You shouldn't have crossed over tha," the Fachan said.

"Crossed over?" I asked.

"Soldiers 'av nah business in the fairy world!" He pointed.

181

"How do you know we're soldiers?" I asked.

"Yah's not frum 'ere. Him's shoutin about attacking this and that. Why did you come to this place!" At this he crossed his arms matter-of-factly. Now was my chance, I felt. I took it. I began to stroll about, just a tad.

"I admit we are soldiers— it's true. Very smart of you. We came here in search of a fairy THIEF. I see now we've stumbled across a gang of mischievous BOYS instead!" They booed and sneered, the Fachan became visibly upset.

"We are not boys! I AM THE FAIRY THIEF! Yoo do naht believe, aye! We'll tie you up next we will!" He made a movement as if to threaten me. Again I raised my hands and backed off.

"Well now, wait a moment!" I said. "I may yet be convinced— but you've not given any reason for me to suspect you of anything other than mere children at play!" The Colonel continued to huff and puff. "If you are a fairy...prove it." I tried to seem as confident as a headmaster.

"I SAY, YES. PROVE IT YOU BUGGER!" Shouted the Colonel. A nearby fairy jabbed him in the gut. "OOF- I NEVER!" He added.

"We don 'av to prove nuffin." He spit. "We'll tie you up and leave yah's stuck here in the fairy world, we will!" The Colonel's eyes went wide, as if petrified by the idea of it. Confirming to me that he too believed we'd somehow crossed into this Fairy World, as the small thing had put it. An annoyance, but something I thought then that I might use to my advantage.

"Tell me, Fairy Thief." I started at him. "How can we be certain you are what you claim to be? Myself and my Colonel here happen to be masters on the subject of Fairies! Aren't we Colonel!"

"Yah— YES. YES WE ARE. MASTERS. INDEED." He puffed.

"Having studied under the tutelage of Professor Fergus Dillwyn, GREAT fairy master himself- We happen to know everything about your kind. Tell me. Why should I believe you are the fairy thief were after?" He seemed to grow self-conscious, if only for a moment. My plan, though wildly off the cusp, was falling into place. At least I hoped, I admit I was hastily forming it within my own head. It would be untruthful for me not to add, that I was not nearly as confident as I was projecting. The balance of power must remain neutral, I thought! I had to keep him on the defensive until I could figure a way to slip out of the snare I now found myself in. Would you believe the war I fought in was more concrete than this! My goodness.

"You know ov tha Fachan, aye. See I've got one eye!" He shouted. I had him. So he did think himself to be this Fachan, eh? This I could use. Use to anger and frustrate! Yes, this would be my plan.

"YES! SURE! YES! BUT TWO LEGS THERE! AND TWO ARMS!" I shouted and moved forward. "What Fachan has that!" I struggled to remember everything Fergus the twit had actually told us about fairies. One of everything! So I remembered!

"Tha's not the truff of it! IS IT LADS!" He shouted and his gang agreed with a roar. "ONE EYE!" He shouted, growing angrier.

"Oh aye, SURE! BUT WHAT OF THE OTHER QUALITIES!" I went on, stalling perhaps!

"WE HAVE THEM TOO! DON'T WE LADS! WE DON' TAK KINDLY TAH STRANGERS! NOR SOLDIERS! WEARING OUR COLOURS ALL THE TIME! NOR WILL WES LET YAH TAKE ANYTHING FROM OUR WORLD WITHOUT AH CURSE!" He showed his hand, some same knowledge as me regarding fair folk! My thesis thickened! My plot? The same!

"SO THEN! YOU MUST BE A FAIRY!" I shouted! The tension grew.

"I AM THE FACHAN!"

"THEN YOU MUST HAVE WITHIN YOU THE ONE FAULT ALL FAIRIES CARRY, AYE?" I egged him on, he stumbled a bit with his words.

"AYE. We...AYE! YES! CURSE YAH!" I didn't believe he knew what I was going for, and of course the Colonel surely didn't, he watched the back and forth eagerly, eyes bouncing between me and the Fachan.

"WELL THEN I HAVE YOU. A GAME! AND YOU MUST NOT DECLINE! A GAME SHALL DECIDE OUR FATE!"

"Ah game?" He struggled out.

"OH YES! SURE, IF YOU'RE A FAIRY! FAIRIES CAN'T SAY NO TO GAMES, CAN THEY!" To be honest, I'm not sure exactly if that's what Fergus had said...but it seemed to work.

"Ah game..." His face turned into a sneer and his gang began their childish giggles again.

183

"A game. Yes. Yes, I say." I stammered. Quite at the end of my train of thought. "And— And, and, AND IF!" I raised a finger. "If we win! Then. Why then you must surrender to us and let us leave your fairy world!" I nodded my head. At last my plan had come full circle. I would play a game to save my acorn. Just then the gravity of that very thought struck me, and I must have turned pale white, for the Fachan laughed into a roar, clutching his sides.

"Well!" I said, trying to remain confident. "What say you!"

"Aye. Ah game. And if we win? We tie YOU up little man, and yah's both stay here- FOREVER!" He shrieked with joy. His fellows echoed him. A chill ran up my spin.

"Right." I gulped. "And what shall be our game then?" I asked, nervous as to what he might suggest.

"DARTS!" The Colonel shouted.

"Darts?" I said and turned to him. "Darts? Colonel, I can't—"

"Darts?" The Fachan said with a cock of the head, watching me.

"YES. I SAY, DARTS!" The Acorn said again.

"Colonel, please!" I shouted, upset he had butted into my play.

"WELL WHY NOT!" He said.

"I say, Fairy Thief— I wonder if I might have a word with my companion?" He paused and smirked, nodding his head at the Colonel. I shrugged my hands and accepted his ruling, stumbling over to the spitted nut.

"Uh— Excuse us there, won't you chap? Thank yee." I said to the fairy guard; he squinted and walked off towards his boss. I put my nose nearly against the Colonel's and began to feverishly whisper.

"COLONEL FOR GOD'S SAKE WOULD YOU STOP. YAH— YES! NO. NO! NO I KNOW YOU WANT TO HELP. BUT MY GOD, DARTS? WHAT ARE YOU TALKING ABOUT!"

"BERTIE YOU KNOW THE GAME I SAW IT! I SAW IT IN EDINBURGH! BONGO TAUGHT YOU HOW!" He furiously whispered back.

"DEAR GOD COLONEL THERE ISN'T EVEN A BOARD HERE, I ONLY MEANT TO- CHRIST I DON'T KNOW! DISTRACT THEM OR SOMETHING! I THOUGHT MAYBE— HELL I DON'T KNOW THAT THEY'D GET TIRED OF US AND LEAVE! MAYBE

A…a foot race! I don't know!" My mouth could hardly keep up with my panic.

"Come now, you? A foot race! We'll be stuck in the fairy world forever!" He cried.

"WE ARE NOT. IN THE FAIRY WORLD! AND HE IS NOT THE FACHAN!" I poked him in the chest as I spoke.

"THEN WHAT IN HEAVEN'S NAME IS HE!" He almost shouted, ruining our game of whispers.

"HE— GOOD GOD MAN! HE IS A CHILD! AND HE'S GOT THE WHOLE LOT OF THEM CONVINCED THEY ARE FAIRIES! WOULD YOU JUST—" But I was cut off by the Fachan again.

"WELL!" he shouted from over my shoulder.

"Uh- Just one moment!" I said, attempting cheer.

"IS IT DARTS, THEN!" he went on.

"YES." The Colonel shouted. "DARTS FOR OUR FREEDOM!"

"Colonel!" I said with even more fury.

"Come now lad!" he whispered. "The eye! ONE EYE! DEPTH PERCEPTION!"

"I— What? How did…" I stammered.

"Did Bongo not teach you to throw with BOTH EYES OPEN!"

"I— Well, yes! He did! But, how did you?"

"I WAS STANDING RIGHT THERE!" He whispered and puffed spittle over his moustache. "You can do this, lad!"

"But— how? I don't—" I shook my head.

"WE PLAY DARTS!" The fairy shouted. I turned and saw him, cross-armed and smirking, several of his kind doing the same behind him.

"Oh, for god's— And how will we play darts then?" I said angrily.

"ROCKS!" The Colonel shouted.

"ROCKS?!" I said looking back at the old man, tied up as he was.

"YES, I SAY! ROCKS! LITTLE ROCKS! SET THERE ON THE SPIRAL! THREE OF THEM! First to knock them off at seven paces!" He went on, confident and smirking.

"Seven paces?" I stammered. The fairy seemed to consider this though, turning and murmuring with his brood.

"DEAL!" he shouted and laughed. They all started to laugh again, their fiendish giggle.

"RULE BRITANNIA!" The Colonel shouted and shook, creaking the pole he was bound to. I swallowed hard, and nodded. What else could I do?

———— • ————

It was decided that several large rocks would be piled high enough to make a platform of sorts, and that we would each place three moderately sized stones on top. After which we would select a smaller stone to use as our dart. The first to knock all three from the platform would be the winner. I stood, arms limp, in complete disbelief as the Fachan orchestrated his troop to set the pitch. I rolled my eyes as the Colonel issued several 'huzzahs' for their efforts. And I thought, for the briefest of moments of an old phrase- 'A noose around the neck of my career'. Confound you Albert for not listening. The sun hung in the sky and a small stone was pressed into my palm by the grubby hand of one of the fairy band.

"Right." I said. "Well let us be clear on the terms then, Fachan." He looked at me sideways, standing before the platform as we both were.

"Should I win—" I began. "You lot must surrender and take us from your fairy world. Back. Uh. Back to our world, I suppose, if that's how it works." I didn't try to hide my annoyance now.

"Yah won't win, wee little man. But aye! We agree to that term don' we lads!" They cheered. "So long as you agree yah'll be tied opp and left when yah lose!" He laughed and laughed.

"Yes, yes. Fine." I waved my hand. Confident I would not allow such a thing without running away first— or perhaps some other adult reaction. I am a grown man of consequence after all! Damned as that notion seemed at present! The Colonel remained hitched to his post, the buffoon.

"Right. Well. Me first, or?" I asked. He gave a little bow and pointed his arms at the makeshift dart board. His fellows giggled insistently.

I sighed. "Right, then." I lifted my hand, squeezed an eye shut and flung my rock with a pitiful amount of zeal. It missed. And tinked off the side with an annoying amount of crescendo. The fairy band erupted into laughter and I felt my face turn red and sizzle.

"BERTIE!" The Colonel shouted. "WHAT WAS THAT!"

"What?" I shrugged and turned. The Colonel twitched his moustache and violently closed one eye again and again. I had to chuckle myself.

"Oh…right." I laughed as the fairy strutted up to take his first heave.

"NOW SEE THIS LADS!" he chucked his dart, a small stone of course, and over confident, missed as well.

"HAH!" I shouted and pointed. Some excitement growing inside me. "Yah won't win with an arm like that, will you now!" He gritted his teeth at me in anger and his gang booed and hissed.

"Lord, heavens— Alright! Alright, my turn again!" I lifted my stone and rocked it back and forth. Careful not to close either eye, I focused on my target— a moderately sized stone.

"Come on Bongo Ryan." I whispered and let fly. In a moment of still pause and silence she sailed! Glorious! And landed with a thunk! Knocking my target from the platform!

"HUZZAH!" The Colonel Cried and, ashamed as I might be to admit it, I slapped my hands together and joined in his applause.

"HOW BOUT IT!" I cried— enjoying myself for a moment. Only a moment!

"BAHHHH!" The Fachan roared and stuck out his tongue. "MOVE OVAH— MOVE! MY TURN!" With his one eye covered he let fly his stone, another sad and pitiful miss!

"RULLLLLLEEE BRITANNIA!" The Colonel cried and I laughed.

"Well, now. One to nothing, is it?" I confidently jabbed. A mere grunt from the Fachan and I danced up to the line. Completely enjoying myself now I even hummed a small tune, meant to wound and insult.

"The sheep is in the meadow and the kyyeee is in the CORNNN!" I whistled and sung strutting up and raising my stone. "And— UH!" I let fly with both eyes wide open and would you believe, a second moderately sized stone clunked from the platform.

"HEYYYY!" I shouted, feeling the days of stiff archery competition returning to my throat. It happily sizzled. The Colonel rocked and creaked his pole laughing and laughing.

"WAH-WOO! WEE!" he cried. And our Fachan burned and burned with anger more.

"YOU'VE CHEATED!" he cried.

"Oh- Come now! Not at all! Please!" I stoked. "It's only two to zero, come now! Have a toss!" Things were going well. He gave a 'harrumph' and stood to toss. His fairy band egged him on, small children at play.

"Careful there." I said. "Yah've only got the one good eye, Mr. Fachan." He made faces at me before turning back to focus. He aimed. And missed.

"Ahhh— YUP!" I said as I watched. I burst into honest laughter, as did the Colonel. The Fairy band grew restless as their leader stormed from the line.

"WELL!" I said. "Just the one rock left then, is it? Suppose I'll knock her off presently!" I raised my eyebrows and strolled back to the firing line.

"I SAY, BERTIE! LET HER FLY!" creaking and rocking from the acorn.

"YOU MUST BE CHEATING!" cried the Fachan. But I ignored him and took my post. Careful to use both eyes and to focus, I let my stone fly and surely knocked the final rock from the platform.

"NOO!" he cried and turned. I dusted my hands off and turned to face him, laughing slightly. The Colonel rocked and cheered and creaked his post.

"Welllll, Fairy friend. It seems I have won. And now you must surrender to us and return in haste to the living world, won't you!" he sneered and crossed his arms. "Come, now." I said and placed my hands on my hips. "Are you not a fairy! Are you not all Fairies?" I turned and asked the group. "Then you must honor your agreement! Well? WELL?"

"No…" He said. "You must have cheated! HOW! HOW DID YOU DO IT!"

"I used both eyes." I said with a wink, tapping my nose. This however, only seemed to anger the boy more.

"Cheater!" he cried. "CHEATER!" he pointed. His gang joined in. Cries of 'Cheater' and of 'fake' grew around me. I turned and tried to protest, hands still on my hips. The Colonel pursed his lips and looked on with wide eyes.

"Well!" I said. "Will we be going now!" I had plans in my head to lead this band of mischievous youth all the way back to Uig— but that was not to be the case.

"You cheated!" cried the Fachan again. "AND YOU FORGET!" he went on and I sighed. "FAIRIES ARE FULL OF MISCHIEF! GET HIM LADS!" he pointed and a roar erupted from the band.

"Now— NOW WAIT A MOMENT!" I raised my hands in a moment of panic and desperately made the first decision that came into my head.

As the wild band of miscreants charged— I turned to the Colonel, and charged at him instead.

"Bertie?" he stammered. "BERTIE!"

And then a thunderous crack! As I leaped full-bore into the Colonel, wrapping my hands around his frame. Together we crumpled onto the ground, his pole snapping in several places. We lay among the ruin, damp, dusty and bruised.

"GOOD SCOT!" The Colonel gasped and pushed at me, his hands now free from the slacked rope. "I SHALL NEVER RECOVER!" He groaned.

"GET UP, COLONEL!" I shouted. "GET UP!" But it was fruitless, my attempt to free the nut was not quick enough. A thud on my back and the squirming hands of a grubby fairy child began to assail my face! It pulled at my ears and lips. Another latched to my side with a thump. A third landed on the Colonel's face below mine. More piled on!

"MMMMFAHH!" piped the Acorn who then heaved upward with all his strength! The pile of us lifted for a moment and seemed to pause before crashing back onto the ground. An impressive and unthought-of show of strength by the Colonel, but I could not stop to wonder! I scrambled to my feet and shoved my way to the Fachan, grabbing him and falling into another pile of small dirty bodies. We wrenched and squirmed in a mad fury of fists and elbows! I thought of the tin and of the similar scramble once had there! Clutching at the Fachan I rose and pushed my way from the crowd.

"Enough!" I shouted. "Enough! I have your leader!" I held him under my arm as he struggled to beat my grip.

"We have your Colonel!" he spit between gasps. And to my horror, he was right. I found the Colonel at the mercy of the band, stick at throat, several sitting atop him.

"Stop!" I shouted.

"Let him go!" A grubby faced child said.

"NEVER!" shouted the Colonel. "LET THEM HAVE ME BERTIE!" he added solemnly.

"Wha— Colonel!" I said

"What?" he said plainly.

"I'm not going to give you up!" I said half laughing.

189

"Well why not!" he asked.

"LET ME GO!" The Fachan struggled in my grip. I squeezed tighter, quite at a loss with what to do.

"LI— LISTEN!" I shouted as several other fairies edged closer. "NOT ONE STEP CLOSER! I- I MEAN IT!" I shook the Fachan, I admit. Poor little bugger. But the situation was deteriorating even more so! I didn't see a way out, not without knocking several over and simply running. But that option didn't see the tramps caught, did it? And then what was the point of this whole charade! The band grew closer, the Colonel gave a somber nod- as if I were meant to dispatch the thing and let them have us! I shook my head at him violently! Desperate! More desperate than I was in the Afghan! Watching my men retreat up the hill! Wound panging! BUT NO COLONEL TO SAVE ME NOW!

"DON'T MOVE AH MUSCLE!" came a rough voice. "NOBODY MOVE!" It came from behind- somewhere down the path the Colonel and I had come through. I shook the Fachan as I attempted to see what came next! And to my shock, cresting the path, were the hulking shoulders of one wild and salty ferryman.

"MacLeod!" I breathed. "And JOHN!" who scampered behind the giant figure pumping his arms to urge on his chubby frame. "MERCY!" I cried.

"DON'T YAH MOVE AH INCH!" cried the giant who arrived at the huddle of bodies. Shoving aside several boys he heaved up a piece of the pole and slapped in his palm. "Don't yah move yah buggers," he cautioned.

"I SAY! MACLEOD!" the Colonel said from under a pile of fairy youths.

"What! WHAT IS THE MEANING! WHAT IS THE MEANING OF THIS!" John huffed as he caught up. He wore a tweed suit today, a pocket watch strap dangling from his jacket. "WHAT." He coughed and struggled to catch his breath. "I SAY WOT!"

"THE FACHAN!" cough the Colonel, seemingly feeling the weight of the small bodied feet. "WE HAVE HIM!"

"Seems he's got youse…" said MacLeod and I had to laugh.

"NONSENSE!" the Colonel shouted.

"IS THAT." John said and rumbled toward me. "IS THAT— WHY!" He grabbed the chin of the Fachan and jerked it from side to side. "MY

GOD!" He shouted. "WHY! It's wee Alastair MacTavish! And- And who? Who are these lot?" He turned and looked into the tiny dirty faces.

"You know this boy?" I said without releasing the Fachan.

"I'M NOT ALASTAIR! IM THE FACHAN!" he cried and squirmed.

"Nonsense, nonsense boy! You're the grandson Bram MacTavish you are! I know who you are! My god have you been the one stealing from the locals! Alastair! We thought you to be gone!" I looked at the Colonel, who shrugged from under the pile. I looked at MacLeod who smiled and shrugged the same. I had so many questions.

"How do you know this boy, John?" I asked again.

"Why! Know him! His Grandad was cleared out on the *Midlothian*, he was! Alastair— we. Boy, we had no idea! We thought. We thought you'd gone off with him! Stealing from the locals! Why if your grandad could see you now!"

"YAH WELL HE CAN'T CANNY?" the presumed Fachan spat. "SENT OFF!" he began to cry. John heaved a massive sigh and stroked his own hair with his hand.

"My god— and who are the rest of ye'?" He turned to look. "Martin? Martin Donald is that you? What in heaven's name— why, it is you!" He staggered and waved a finger at one small dirty child. "Why didn't...why didn't yah come to us, boy!" He shouted, causing the poor boy in my grip to cry and struggle more. "Oh- oh! No! You poor child, no! Come here— Come here lad!" He pulled the boy from my hands and knelt, squeezing his shoulders. He paused and looked at the boy with a pair of crystal eyes. "You have the look of a MacTavish, you do! To be certain!" He smiled at the boy, dirty and tear stained. The Colonel finally rose, disrupting several small boys as he did.

"Well! I say!" He dusted himself off. "So our Fairy Thief is no Fairy at all then!" he added as if finally solving some great mystery.

"Heavens no— He. Why he's one of us, he is!" we looked around, the three in my company. Several small faces began to sniffle into tears. The whole of them stammered and chattered.

"I say!" The Colonel put hands to hip. "BUGGERS!" he poked at one nearby. The child knocked him back in the shins causing the Colonel to do a sort of half dance. Shock is all I could say I felt. So swiftly we had gone from a battle with these wee fairies to a presumed rap on the knuckles for them. I began to express the same idea which had been forming since I had awoken- these were not fairies at all. These were children. Wild children, yes. Unwatched children? Sure enough. But children, indeed. I turned to the Fachan again.

"What's to be done with 'em then, John?" I said. MacLeod dropped the club to hang by his knees.

"Why— My god. They must be brought home! Haven't they? Martin!" He turned to this other boy. "Martin, why are you not home minding your dah!" The boy shrugged. "How? How on earth. Alastair you must tell us now. What has been going on. Speak up now, boy!" He took the band from his head, revealing two working eyes.

"TWO EYES!" The Colonel shouted and pointed, again, solving the mystery out loud.

The boy looked sheepish. Hungry even, I'd say. He sniffed.

"Grandah was took off. I— I stayed at home fer…"

"He lives out in the hills. Outside of town. He— He did." John added looking over his shoulder.

"We didn't take much! Just what we needed…I. I told them I was a fairy. I…" he trailed off.

"I'm guessing this band of yours comes and goes then, eh?" I asked, putting the pieces together myself.

"Some. They bring bits of food and we…we. Well. This— I've been living here, and-"

"My, my." I said, a sad feeling now growing inside my gut. John looked around at the gang again and squinted his eyes.

"Who here has family that's been taken off?" Several small hands raised. "Right. And who then has some left at home?" A few more joined, the rest of the group put up their little hands. "Right, well. The game is over, lads. It's time we bring you lot— Home!" He spat the last out. Several small faces grinned.

"I say." The Colonel said and lit his pipe again. "And how!" nodding smartly, he let out a wisp of smoke.

"Oh for god's— Where do you keep that thing!" I shouted. But he ignored me as a small child tugged on his sheepskin. He scooped the little thing up.

"Well then! Not so fierce now, are yee!" He laughed. The child pulled on his moustache. "OUCH!" He proclaimed laughing again.

"Come! Come now!" John grabbed Alastair's hand and the hand of another small fairy boy. He tugged them towards the path we had come from. "Come and let's be off, it's getting dark. Come now boys! Come along!" We all began to march, a new and odd group forming. One giant ferryman, towering over a band of fairies. One chubby and decent townsfolk, a valet and an Acorn. What wild times I have lived to see. The children began to chatter, John leading them out of the fairy world as if some great prophet. And I merely shook my head and rubbed the bruises already forming across my body.

"Right! Forward! FOWARDDDD!" The Colonel began. "Bertie, my stick— there's a lad!" He turned to me as he plopped a fairy on top of his shoulders.

"Why would I have your stick, Colonel? My word. Where have you been!" He stammered something about a 'damn shame' and we walked. I turned to look at MacLeod who began to amble along with us. I shook my head again, a fairy grabbing my hand from below.

"How is it you're here, Mac?" I asked and limped. He smirked for a second and looked at me sideways.

"Welllll shite. Yah didn't think old MacLeod would actually abandon another highlander, did yah?" He winked and I sighed, smiling.

"But— How?" I asked again.

"Well. I had made some good ways before running into John, didn't I? Said he had found his strength after luncheon and decided to head out tah try and find us. He convinced me to turn round, he did. Tha bugger." I laughed at his words.

"Well I am glad you did— God knows we might still be tangled up back in that cursed glen." I went on. "I just can't— I mean. How about this? After everything—it was the clearances that caused this whole capper. My god the rumors have flown as far south as Gloucestershire!" I shook my head.

"Right. Well. These things have become a dark stain on your empire, aye? No surprise rumors have flown, are there?"

"No. I. No I suppose not. What do you think will become of this fairy lot?" he laughed at me.

"They'll be fed up right in Charlottes tonight, is what! And damn if I won't be too— Been running amuck 'round this place for too damn long, I have! I'm owed a decent night and a meal, aren't I!"

"Well." I laughed. "I'm glad you have been, anyways." He thumped my shoulder and gave a roaring laugh.

"You'll have a bit to write back to yah girl then won't yah!"

"Write back?" I asked.

"Ah shite— yeah meant to say. Reason John's come out, it was. Seems a letter has found its way to you here in Uig. Some Abigail Stuart, I think? Do yah know her?" he slyly grinned, the devil!

"A letter from Abigail!" I blushed and stammered. "How? I— how do you know?"

"Cause I've got it here in my pocket, don't I!" he laughed and stuffed the letter into my hands. "Seems our man Archer brought it on his cart— I imagine he's right mad at me fer not bringin' his boat back directly. You lot can explains why." I laughed and eyed the letter as if it were gold.

"Yes, Archer. Right. I suppose I will, won't I?" But I wasn't listening to myself speak, distracted as I was with the events thus unfolding. What a strange and happy ending to this tail, I thought. I stuffed the letter into my pocket and began to whistle. The Colonel, who had a fairy perched on his shoulders and one clung to his leg, recognized my tune and began to sing.

And we strolled along as such, one happy band of Highland folk, all the way back into Uig.

———————

That very evening, back at the Charlotte, I watched the scene unfold from the bar. Children were perched all about, the old plump gals of Uig fussed over them all. They ate, and had their faces cleaned and cleaned again. Many promises were made to return the children to their homes and as the good people of Uig departed for home themselves, one or two fairies were sent along on their charts to be taken to their own small places in the empire. The few who remained were those orphans whose families had been cleared. I watched John speak with them all and plans were made to house and care for the boys; as were promises made to attempt to find their departed family members. The Colonel chorused around the entire show, the hero of the night. He accepted any pint offered to him in thanks for solving their mystery, and I admit I accepted a few of my own. Songs were sung, and many dark pints lifted. We carried on through the night. And as the room thinned, Charlotte squeezed my shoulder in passing, leading a fairy boy to the door. She whispered a thanks, to which I nodded and smiled. Warm as I was.

"WELLLLLL" John said with a thump as he flopped onto a high chair beside me. "The mystery is solved, and the day is saved. We thank yah, lad." He said and nodded his warm face, flushed and red.

"John?" I said. "What will become of our fairy Fachan?" I nodded to one of the only boys left in the place.

"Ahhh yes. The fairy thief. Well he's to be punished, be certain of that!" He winked and leaned into me. He had himself accepted several pints. "He'll be staying with me, he will. I'll put him to work round the place. Tha is, till we can find where his grandah went off to, ah course."

"And what if you don't? Find him I mean."

"Well. Can't say we will truthfully. But he'll be well minded, he will. I promise yah tha! Nooo, no. Well keep him here, with us if we can't. Where the boy belongs, see?" He crumpled his face and leaned back. "Keepin even one more small highlander here on this place? Well. We've got you lot to thank fer that, don't we? And— And If I'm to believe yah— then I think? Perhaps even our Queen is to thank, isn't she?" He tapped my leg and winked.

"Ah. It's Nothing, John. Nothing at all. Just fulfilling our duties at home, is all." I winked back and he smiled letting out a chugging laugh as he did; though I think my words were lost on him.

"And and and, did ya get tha letter then, boy?" he leaned into me again, nearly falling off his chair. I caught the old sod.

"I did! I did, John, thanks!" I tapped my chest where the letter was kept. "Poor old Archer, making the journey from Portree." I turned and looked at the man now sitting with the Colonel and MacLeod, trapped by one of his stories. He rolled his eyes as the Colonel waved his hands with some dramatic flair. I laughed. I had apologized to the man, claiming it was our fault his boat was not returned. He seemed unbothered when I told him, but captured by the Colonel as he was now— I wondered just how angry he might be with me presently. I laughed again.

"Wellllll all's well tha ends well, EH!" John said and slapped his knees. "Im uh— well I'm to find another drink. Drink up yerself boy! Yah've earned it." he winked again and stumbled away. I watched him go, and confident the room was either emptying or occupied I reached for my letter.

The ink was smudged slightly, but it had Abigale Stuart Room 1A, White Swan Hotel, Liverpool, scrolled on it. I sighed at the word hotel, I knew it. The send address was that of MacLeod's home to the south, scratched out and replaced by Portree, scratched out again and hastily replaced with the written word 'UIG' by what I can only assume was Archer's hand. Bless the man. I stroked the envelope and cracked the seal. My heart skipped a beat, like a child's I admit— am I rambling? It read:

> *Captain McGregor,*
>
> *I received your letters! Both of them! I wrote in response after your post from Edinburgh— I'm not surprised the Colonel drug you to Mr. Dillwyn's house! Quite the character isn't he? I suppose my reply never found you as your second arrived from the Isle of Skye days later. I was relieved to see you made it. I do hope this letter finds you however- as I have news you must hear. The man from Sussex was here- he brought a new letter from the Queen. I can't say more I'm afraid. The hand of the Queen of course! His letter will say more. He's arranging a ship, I'm told, and plans to find you on the Isle. He has told me to write to you and to say that this ship shall wait in Portree Harbor for you. I do hope if this letter does not find you that you will at least find him there as you pass through. Fingers crossed! Take care of our Colonel. I am hopeful you both will pass through the Swan before heading out on some new duty. I know the Colonel won't want to wait, as is his way! But I know you'll bring him here, if at all possible. He is eccentric, our Colonel. Is he not? Stay safe— and warm! I look forward to your next knocking upon our door.*
>
> *Fondly,*
>
> *Abigail.*
>
> *(And Fishy-Bob!)*

"WHAT'S THAT NOW!" the Colonel crashed into me. "A LETTER FROM ABIGAIL?" he elbowed me and reached for the note. I battled his dirty hands.

"No— WOULD YOU. Would you just!" I fought him off. He stared at me like a scolded dog. "Yes." I said. "It is a letter from Abigail."

"Wonderful! And what does it say!"

"It— Nothing! It says nothing!" I pursed my lips annoyed.

"BAH! Hardly it does! A letter from a woman that has a Queen's man so befuddled hardly says NOTHING!" He laughed and slapped my leg. I shook my head, the dog.

"Yes, well." I scoffed and gave into his poking and prodding. "It says we've got more work to do is what it says, thanks!"

"More work to do? Why? Whatever do you mean, my boy?" Even drunk, he knew how to pester me. I turned and laughed as he poked at my chest again. "Work to do, eh? And where might that be, then? Eh? EH?" he laughed.

"Oh— Stop it! Stop." I swatted at his hands and grinned. "Apparently there's to be a ship."

"A Ship! How lovely…"

"In Portree." I eyed him slyly, as if the devil.

"In Portree, eh? Well. When are we off?" I turned and looked at him. He matched my gaze, eyebrows bouncing. We shared a grin.

"Finish your pint. We're off in the morning. MacLeod!" I shouted and swept away from the man. From behind, I can't be certain— but I swear I heard a whistle of 'Gods Save the Queen.'

EPILOGUE

Return to the *Hornblower*

A day later MacLeod had dropped us at the top of the road leading into Portree; He had said he wouldn't go near to town lest he were to be swept off into another nightmare adventure. His words, not mine. We had said our goodbyes and thanked the man before allowing him on his way to 'run his bloody ferry after all' —again, his words, not mine. The Colonel was melancholy.

"Oh would you stop that sniffling." I scolded. "Honestly the farewell to Fergus was pathetic enough! You hardly got on with the man the entire time we were with him, did you?" The Colonel batted at me and blew like a trumpet into his handkerchief.

"Please, Bertie! We shared a battlefield with the man!" I rolled my eyes as we trotted on. We had abandoned our local garb, I'm happy to say, and I was pleasantly fixed in a crisp suit once belonging to some husband of Charlottes. I will miss Uig, that much is true. But I was only too happy to have seen our time there complete.

"Such a mess." I said.

"How's that?" The Colonel said wiping his moustache and great nose.

"This whole Charade, Colonel! Fairy in the highlands. Honestly!"

"Come now Bertie, there WAS a Fairy in the highlands!" he scoffed.

"Colonel. And I suppose there was a Ghoul in Brighton as well, wasn't there?" I asked and he winked. I could do nothing but smirk and shake my head.

"Whether or not there was a Ghoul in Brighton, or even a Fairy in the highlands matters not, does it, chap?" The man replied with an air of no concern.

"Does it not?" I stammered.

"Heavens no- old boy! No indeed. Noooo, no. See we've served the Empire haven't we? Got on with the Queen's business- God save her! No no, my boy. It does not matter the task, only that we take to it with speed and due course." He winked.

"Amazing, tha'." I put bluntly.

"How's that?"

"Oh, confound it! Your own ability to switch on and off, so to speak!"

"Switch on and off? I say! I have no idea what you mean at all!" He puffed out his chest and put his arms on his hips, pausing a moment. I could only shake my head and smile.

"You really are the truest and most genuine servant that this Empire has yet known." I marveled, and thought it truly. The man is a savant. A warrior. A great buffoon. An oddity. But so often, and always when it counted, he was as serious as a man in battle. This image would only ever grow for me, but at present, was lost on him, distracted as you now know him to be.

"AH! BERTIE! WHY? LOOK THERE! CAN IT BE? WHY? WHY YES! IT'S THE HORNBLOWER! WHAT LUCK, MY BOY! WHAT LUCK! COME ON! COME ON, DEAR BOY!" I strained down the way to discover in my profound shock, that it was indeed none other than the *Hornblower* sitting in Portree harbor. Curse my luck, I thought and laughed. The Colonel bounced away down the cobbled road ahead, whopping and shouting as he did.

"Hang on Colonel!" I called after my charge and followed smartly.

I caught up with the Colonel as he made a crisp walk around the promenade in town again, swinging his stick at his march. Once more I admired the homes perched along its curved walk. Oh let me stay here, I thought.

"Ah-hah!" Called the Colonel as he plowed up the gangway. "HALLO THERE! HALLO! GOD SAVE THE QUEEN!" He stormed the decks and began shaking hands and thumping the shoulders of the bewildered crew. I strolled behind, looking for someone official.

"Bertie! My GOOD man! To the officer's cabinet, I say! A nip of the King's for a wary soldier!"

"Go on, then." I said. "I'll join you in a moment." But he was already rushing ahead.

"Ahem." A growl from behind. I turned to look. "I suspect you must be Captain Albert McGregor." I turned and found myself facing yet another salt washed face, this one thinner however, and attached a very tough looking sea captain.

"Actually? It's Bertie, Thanks." I shook his hand. "I take it you're our man from Sussex, then?"

"Not quite sir. But he did send me. Captain Robert Bolton, Sir. Her Majesty's Navy. At your service." He saluted. I waved him off.

"Yes. Well. Excellent." I sighed. "And I suppose you have our duties then, Captain?"

"Yes Sir." he smiled, hands behind back.

"And where are we off to this time?"

"West Sir." he smiled and nodded.

"West? How far West?" I asked.

"All the way, Sir."

"I see, my my." I stared blankly, swallowing hard. "God have mercy, then." He smirked.

We got underway. Rule Britannia.